ALSO BY CAROLINE STOWE

Wishing for Christmas

Dreaming of Paris

Dreaming of Paris

CAROLINE STOWE

HARPETH ROAD
PRESS
Nashville

HARPETH ROAD PRESS

Published by Harpeth Road Press (USA)
P.O. Box 158184
Nashville, TN 37215

Paperback: 978-1-963483-51-2
eBook: 978-1-963483-50-5
Library of Congress Control Number: 2026936724

Dreaming of Paris: A Sparkling, Heartwarming Romance

This is a work of fiction. Names, characters, places, and incidents are the product of the author's imagination or were used fictitiously, and any resemblance to actual persons, living or dead, business establishments, events, or locales is entirely coincidental.

Cover Design by Sarah Hansen
Cover Images © Shutterstock, Adobe, Deposit Photos

Harpeth Road Press, April 2026

For my husband and three darling daughters, you are my dream come true

CHAPTER ONE

Jenna

Jenna Westbrook cracked open the window of her office and drew in a long breath of city air. The chill of a late-afternoon wind felt like a disheartening slap on the cheek. She crossed her arms and let out a heavy sigh, observing the bare branches with a scornful glare. She yearned for spring. For a patch of sunlight to emerge from the cool shadows. Instead, the cold that lingered, harsh echoes of the same old season, only served as a cruel reminder of the freeze that had developed in her heart over the past six months.

She pulled the window closed and smoothed out her skirt, preparing to greet some of her favorite clients. She glanced down at her watch and lifted an eyebrow. It wasn't like Paul and Heather Fowler to be late for their monthly counseling sessions. She sat at her desk and sorted through paperwork while she waited.

The door to her office swung open and her secretary, Blair, popped her head inside.

"The Fowlers called," Blair said. "They won't be coming in after all." It looked as if she wanted to say more, but was unsure whether she should.

"They canceled?" Jenna narrowed her eyes and lowered her chin, urging Blair to continue.

"They said they've decided to discontinue their sessions entirely."

Jenna's eyes flew open. "Why?"

Blair softly shook her head. "They didn't say much. Just that they were no longer seeing the progress they had when they first started therapy." She paused, pressing her lips together. "They've decided to split up."

"No." Jenna's hand flew to her mouth. "Why?" she repeated, knowing she wouldn't get an answer, or at least one that would explain anything sufficiently.

Blair only shrugged.

Jenna grabbed the sides of her head and squeezed her eyes shut. She scowled at her desk, shaking her head in disbelief. Not the Fowlers too. They couldn't give up. Not after all the work they'd put into their relationship.

"I'm sorry," Blair said, chewing on a perfectly polished fingernail.

Jenna stared outside, wondering if Blair was thinking the same thing she was. A moment of silence filled the air as Jenna raked her hands through her long waves. Finally, she said what her secretary wouldn't. "It's me."

"No, don't say that," Blair replied immediately, and with a little too much eagerness to sound completely sincere.

"Blair, this is the fifth couple I've lost this month, not to mention countless others over the past six months since, well, you know." She tapped her fingernails against the table.

Blair opened her mouth, then closed it. "It's a coincidence," she said finally.

Jenna bit down on her lip to still the quiver that had formed. If only that were true. If only *everything* hadn't changed the instant she'd heard the words, *I can't marry you anymore.*

If only her own love story hadn't ended in a way that she couldn't make any sense of, despite the work she'd put into it. If only *she* had a therapist, a competent one, to help pull out the reasons she knew were buried somewhere deep in her brain, to uncover the meaning behind it all. A master's degree in psychology, years of experience as a relationship counselor, and one hundred eighty days of constantly analyzing what went wrong, and she still couldn't figure out the missing piece. The one unanswerable question: Why?

Jenna blew out a breath, resigning herself to the awareness that her work week was over, now that the Fowlers—her last appointment of the day—wouldn't be coming in. She felt her chest tighten as she remembered what lay in store for the weekend ahead. She reached into the leather handbag stuffed under her desk and pulled out her phone. She opened her email and held a clenched fist against her chin, squeezing her eyes shut as the pain in her forehead increased. Staring back at her was her flight itinerary, and it felt like another harsh slap in the face.

Paris.

Jenna let out a huff of annoyance and considered faking an illness to get out of the whole thing. She knew her sister hadn't planned a destination wedding in the most romantic city on Earth to spite her. Still, it felt like fate's cruel twist of the knife.

Jenna dropped her phone on her desk. She reached over and grabbed her stapler, squeezing it tight to secure the Fowlers' notes. It instantly jammed. Pulling it open, she tried to dislodge the tiny metal sliver responsible for the disturbance, but it wouldn't budge. She pulled at it, finger-tips slipping around it, her frustration building by the second. She stared at the staple, unable to figure out how something so tiny could completely destroy a plan, even one as simple as attaching two documents to each other.

Jenna's eyes narrowed as she studied the stapler. The brand name, printed elegantly in refined cursive letters, stared back, taunting her. Like the gorgeous calligraphy on a wedding invitation. Before she could stop herself, she'd lifted the stapler over her head and hurled it across the office in a fit of rage. It hit the wall with a sharp click, and a chunk of plaster fell to the ground beside it. In her years of counseling sessions with arguing couples, she'd seen her share of objects thrown in anger. But never by her.

Blair's eyes widened with concern as she stared at the floor and the broken pieces of stapler. She pressed a palm against her cheek in shock.

Jenna played it off with a nervous laugh, hoping she appeared more under control than she felt. "Slipped right out of my hand," she said, hurrying across the office and dropping to her hands and knees to gather up the pieces.

Blair rushed over to help.

Jenna tossed the remains in the trash, then shook out her hands and wiped them against her skirt, erasing any evidence of the messy incident. She gave Blair a nod, brushing it off with a professional grin. Sure, Jenna had been on edge a little more than usual lately, but that was to be expected given the circumstances. Besides, that stapler had it coming. What was she supposed to do when it simply stopped working, with no explanation, and no warning, whatsoever? Everyone had their limits, and she had clearly reached hers. Maybe it wasn't her finest professional moment, but even so, it was only a stapler against a wall. With what she'd been dealing with in her personal life, she'd felt capable of much worse.

She took in a cleansing breath, trying to erase the uncharacteristic anger and replace it with calm professionalism. "Well, that's too bad about the Fowlers," she said in the most tranquil voice she could manage as she sat down. She motioned for Blair to sit in one of the chairs in front of her desk.

Blair Miller, fresh-faced and dependable, had been Jenna's valued secretary for four years, ever since Jenna had opened her practice. She was an expert at organizing Jenna's schedule and always seemed to anticipate her needs with perfect timing. Blair sat down and waited, studying Jenna's expression.

"So, what did they say, exactly?" Jenna pulled out the spiral-bound planner she kept in her desk drawer, the one that held all her appointments. She folded her arms and leaned forward over her desk, waiting for an explanation.

"They said they feel like they've hit a wall." Blair winced. "Sorry, bad choice of words."

Jenna gave her a wry smile. After nearly two years of meeting with them, Jenna knew the Fowlers were both unwavering in their commitment to counseling, and to each other. As a relationship therapist, Jenna adored many of the couples she worked with, and could usually tell right off the bat which ones would ride out the storm, and which would drift apart. The Fowlers fell under the former. They did everything right. They showed up each month, prepared and eager. They always completed the exercises Jenna gave them to work on and never missed an opportunity to read one of her book suggestions. But it was more than that. There was something special about their relationship—something she couldn't quite put into words.

Either way, Jenna had had no doubt they were in it for the long haul. It was simply that, like with so many of her clients, they'd had some challenges thrown in their path over the past couple years—a job loss, a sick parent, a stressful schedule trying to juggle it all. It was only natural the struggles of daily life trickled into their relationships, leaving these committed and loving couples feeling discouraged and, at times, hopeless. For a concept that seemed so ideal on the surface, love was far from perfect. People, and all their emotions, were to blame. Yes, despite the best intentions, life—and love—had a tendency to get messy.

That's where Jenna came in. With a license in clinical counseling, an empathetic ear, and a voice of reason, Jenna's job was to get her clients back on track and help them recover that feeling of hope in their unique love story and, ultimately, turn it into a happy ending.

That was the idea anyway. In reality, she wasn't sure what she was doing anymore. The questions that still plagued her, after months of introspection and countless hours of self-analysis, haunted every session. And she now found herself far from qualified to counsel couples in the one area she was apparently totally ignorant in herself—love.

Jenna rotated her chair and took in the sight outside the window. She rubbed her temples. "They just needed to be patient. Take some more time to work through things. Not let their current feelings decide their entire future."

Jenna didn't trust that emotionally driven kind of love. The kind that was all about butterflies, and feelings, and fleeting moods. No, Jenna's job was to get her clients to move beyond the disillusionment that came when the romance faded and get them to see the value of transitioning into a more mature type of love. One that would endure the hard stuff throughout the years. "Love is not a feeling, it's an action," she would routinely tell her clients. Sure, romantic notions may be fun, but Jenna knew that a mutual commitment to working hard was the only thing that would allow a relationship to survive.

"So are you all set for your trip?" Blair asked, eager to change the subject. She stood from her chair and leaned over Jenna's desk to grab a stack of papers, sifting through them. "It's a long way to go for one weekend. You sure you don't want to stay longer? I could rearrange your schedule for next week if you want me to."

Jenna pretended not to pick up on the subtext behind the offer. Of course Blair could easily rearrange Jenna's schedule when her clients were dropping like flies. If things continued at this rate, Jenna would have to close the private practice she'd worked so hard to build. Her business would be another dream down the tube. Another "L" to add to her increasingly dismal scoreboard of life.

Jenna uncrossed her legs and pulled herself from her chair to begin packing her things for the weekend. "Yes, I'm sure. If I'm forced to attend this ostentatious display of love, at the very least, I want to get out of there as fast as possible." She slung her laptop bag over her shoulder, then gave Blair an apologetic smile. She knew she was being unreasonable and, frankly, acting like a brat.

Her little sister had found her prince and was now savoring her fairytale by getting married in the same city where they'd met during a semester abroad in college. She should be happy for her sister. She *was* happy for her. Still, it didn't help that Jenna's dream had been instantly and cruelly crushed into oblivion without a second's notice. It was just another reminder that she wouldn't be getting the result she worked so hard to provide for her clients. That happy ending that was pulled away from her so suddenly, and so inexplicably, at the last minute.

And it *certainly* didn't help that her mom had been on her case since Luke had left, demanding to know what really happened between them. Sure, her parents had lost some money due to the last-minute cancellation of the two-hundred-guest wedding they had generously offered to help pay for. But with Jenna and Luke having funded the majority, Jenna didn't feel her parents were entitled to more information than she'd already given them. Not that she had any more to give.

She waved a hand over her face as if to reset her attitude. "It'll be fine, Blair. I'll show up for the wedding tomorrow night, be happy for my sister, and then fly back home on Sunday. Quick and easy." She gave a sarcastic smile. "Just in time to be back by Monday to pretend I know how to help people sort out their relationship issues when, really, I don't have a clue what I'm doing anymore." She dropped her chin to her chest and rubbed an eyebrow. "Maybe I'll use the long flights to go over my psychology 101 notes and try to figure out how to be a therapist," she said, only half joking.

Blair tentatively moved in closer, offering a sympathetic grin. "Jenna, this isn't like you. You've always been so confident in your job, so positive about life. So hopeful about your clients. I'm worried about you."

Jenna released a long stream of air. "I know." She shook

out her hands again. "It's this wedding. It all feels like a giant punch in the gut."

"Yeah, I can imagine."

"Do you know how embarrassing it's going to be to show up in front of my entire family and their friends right now? Alone? Me, an expert in counseling couples on how to work on their relationships, couldn't even manage to hold onto my own."

"Jenna, I'm sure they aren't thinking that. I'm sure they know what happened with Luke wasn't your fault."

Jenna let out an aggressive chuckle. "Tell that to my mother. She's been hounding me for answers for months now. She claims she's only worried about me, but I know my mom. Worrying leads to prying, which leads to judgment, which leads to me questioning all my life choices." She glanced down at her phone and opened her text messages. Ironically, but not surprisingly, the most recent one was from her mom.

> Hey honey, we landed in Paris. Call me when you get here and we'll make sure someone meets you at the airport, so you won't be all alone. Look forward to talking more. Love you.

All alone. Jenna pinched her forehead as she realized something she should have much sooner. "I can't do this."

"What?" Blair's eyebrows pulled down in concern.

She looked Blair in the eyes, shaking her head with wide-eyed desperation. "I can't endure everyone's judgment. The poor clueless sap, left at the altar. The incompetent failure of a therapist." Her eyes darted around the room as the problem became more obvious. "No, I have to get my act together, and quick."

"Your act?"

"Yes. I have to act like my life is under control, like I've never been happier, and my practice is a thriving success."

"You are successful," Blair said in a soothing voice, sounding more like the therapist in the room. "And your life *is* under control."

Jenna ignored her, stabbing a finger at the air in front of her. "And so is my love life."

Blair gave her an amused smile. "What?"

"I don't know," Jenna said, eyes squeezed shut as her thoughts swirled around.

Her phone buzzed to deliver another text message. She held her breath as she glanced down, her shoulders relaxing to see that it was only her next-door neighbor, wanting to stop by to grab his mail. She quickly replied to let him know she'd be home soon, then shifted her focus back to the problem at hand.

If only she had a date for the wedding. Better yet, a new boyfriend. One who was crazy about her and would show everyone what an idiot Luke must have been to let her go. How could she organize that now, though? The wedding was tomorrow—on another continent. Her flight left in four hours. Her airfare had cost a fortune, and there was no way she could afford another ticket to Paris, especially last minute. Not to mention the minor detail that she had absolutely nobody who could fill in as said date. She hadn't been out with anyone since Luke.

Another text came in from her neighbor, saying he'd stop by in an hour. She gave it a thumbs up and quickly swiped it away.

All she knew was that the only thing worse than not showing up for her sister's wedding would be showing up alone. It would open the door for questions—ones she didn't want to answer. Ones she still had no idea *how* to answer.

She grabbed her pale-pink trench from the coat rack and draped it over her arm. Then she leaned back against her desk and puckered her lips in thought. Jenna stared down at her phone, hoping a solution would be revealed. Until suddenly, it was. She tapped at the screen and re-opened the message from her neighbor. She studied it, and a glimmer of an idea began to form. A smile crept over her face. Her posture immediately perked up and she pushed herself off the desk.

"Blair, I've gotta run. I have something I need to do before my flight leaves tonight."

"What's that?"

"Get a boyfriend," she said, as she dashed out of the office.

Yes, it was time for her to move on, or at least to convince everyone else that she had. Six months of winter had been long enough. It was time to shake off the frost and pretend spring had arrived.

CHAPTER TWO

Connor

Connor Blake stood on the doorstep of his neighbor's small Cape-Cod style home with a hand in his pocket, fiddling his keys. His stomach was still in knots over the event that had unfolded earlier in the day. He squeezed his eyes shut as he played it over in his mind, still trying to figure out what had happened.

He took a deep breath and stood up straighter, reminding himself that it was over now and everything had turned out fine. He took off his uniform jacket and slung it over his shoulder. The cool night wind drifted against his forearms, bare in his short-sleeved white shirt, with the silver stripes across the shoulders. He quickly decided he looked posed and rushed to put the jacket back on. The brimmed hat perched on top of his head, the final detail that gave him that extra edge of confidence he always had in his pilot uniform—the one that reminded him that he was in control and completely skilled to handle anything. Too bad that confidence didn't always follow him outside the cockpit.

He knocked on the door. He wasn't sure why he felt so uncomfortable being there. He'd lived next door to Jenna for three years, and it had been part of his routine to stop by her house after a trip for almost that whole time. He should have been used to it by now.

Still, knowing that Luke wouldn't be answering the door tonight gave his stomach a queasy feeling he couldn't ignore. Even though it had been six months since Jenna's fiancé left, every time Connor stopped by, he was hit with another awful reminder of the part he'd played in it all.

Jenna opened the door immediately and greeted him with a wide-eyed grin, as if she'd been anxiously awaiting his arrival. An apron was tied around her small frame. "Hey, Connor, come on in." She waved him inside, turning towards the kitchen.

He followed her into the house. A pot of simmering sauce bubbled on the stove, and the scent of fresh basil hung in the air. He closed his eyes and took a long, comforting inhale as his stomach let out a rumble.

Jenna dialed down the burner and gave the pot a quick stir. Her glossy dark-brown hair was pulled back into a loose ponytail, one soft wave falling over her face.

He swallowed. "Thanks for picking up my mail this week."

"Oh, yeah, of course." She tasted the sauce from a wooden spoon then threw a glance towards the counter. "It's over there."

The countertops were covered with papers, but he saw a heap of envelopes under her phone, her passport beside it. He reached over to grab the stack of bills and advertisements. Glancing at the small kitchen table, he noticed it was impeccably set for two.

"Well, thanks again, Jenna," he said, wanting to get out of there before her dinner guest arrived.

"Connor, wait."

He raised his eyebrows.

"So, um, how was your trip?" she asked. She wiped her hands against her apron.

"Oh, uh, nothing exciting," he lied. "Paris and back. Then Amsterdam, and back to Newark. Same old, same old." He gave a nervous chuckle, then cringed at the sound of his voice. *Same old, same old?* Had he suddenly turned into his dad or something?

Jenna gave a soft smile. She turned to pick up the pot from the stove with a pair of oven mitts and moved it to the table, then she hurried to the refrigerator and pulled open one of the doors. "Paris, huh? Do you go there a lot?"

"It's one of my regular routes."

Jenna stared into the refrigerator. "Where to next?"

He stuck his hands in his pockets. "I'm not sure yet. I'm home for the next week or so." He decided not to mention the fact that he *couldn't* go anywhere. At least not until everything had been reviewed by the proper channels on his incident report. It was standard procedure. He knew it would all check out, and he'd be back in the air in no time. He and the captain had done everything by the book, down to the meticulous paperwork. Still, he hoped it wouldn't take too long for the report to clear. He tended to get restless if he spent too much time on the ground.

Jenna's shoulders rolled back, and she inhaled deeply. Her hand made its way to a bottle of white wine and grabbed hold of it. She slowly turned around, her lips puckered as if she was deep in thought. She eyed him with curiosity.

Connor made a discreet wipe of his face to make sure he didn't have anything on it.

She continued to study him as she set the bottle of wine on the counter. "Hey, Connor, when you're not working, do you get to fly for free?"

He nodded, wondering why she was so chatty tonight, when she clearly had a date coming over. "Yeah. I get flight benefits."

"Yes," she whispered, as if to herself, drawing out the word.

"And you're off for the next week, you say?" she said, closing the fridge.

"Mm-hm."

A grin spread across her face and her brown eyes glistened underneath the bright kitchen lighting. Her cheeks glowed, and she looked at him from underneath her long dark lashes. Her head cocked to one side. "Connor, are you hungry?" Her smile deepened.

Connor noticed his face grow warm as an uncomfortable silence hung in the air. He'd never eaten a meal with Jenna before—just the two of them anyway. Wouldn't that be . . . weird? They'd never hung out at all, without Luke, aside from a few polite, neighborly exchanges over the years.

He rolled back his shoulders and cleared his throat, trying to keep it casual. "I could probably eat." He could *definitely* eat. Connor hardly ever said no to a meal, especially a home-cooked one. Being on the road the past week, he'd had his fill of cheap takeout and the airline's bland choices of chicken or beef—always the one the majority of passengers turned down. His stomach growled at the idea of fresh ingredients and the homemade garlicky cream sauce that bubbled beside him.

"Perfect," she purred, as her posture straightened. Her eyes gleamed with excitement as she motioned for him to sit, then she grabbed another wine glass before reconsidering. "Wine or beer?" she asked.

"A beer would be great, thank you." He took off his jacket and hung it along the back of the chair. Was this . . .? No. He couldn't even finish the thought, it being so absurd. So inappropriate. He and Luke had been *friends*. Sure, they only met after Luke began dating Jenna and hanging out next door. But the two men had quickly struck up a friendship, watching the occasional soccer game together or playing poker with the other guys in the neighborhood. He shook the ridiculous idea from his head. Maybe her dinner guest had canceled on her.

She rushed to the refrigerator to pull out a bottle of lager. She compressed her lips, looking as if she were keeping a secret, as she popped the top and carefully poured the drink into a mug. She set it next to his plate, then sat across from him. "Connor, I have a huge favor to ask you." She bit her lip.

He smiled, the relief coursing through him that there was a logical explanation for the impromptu dinner. One that didn't involve something . . . awkward. Jenna may be a good neighbor, but he also knew what they said about good fences. And he certainly wasn't willing to rip down a perfectly good one, just because his neighbor happened to be single now. "Shoot," he said, finally loosening up.

Jenna twisted the cap on the bottle of chardonnay and poured some into her wine glass. She picked up the glass and took a long sip, looking as if she needed a shot of courage to ask him what was coming next.

He nodded with an encouraging smile, urging her on.

"It's pretty big," she warned.

He smirked. "Are you kidding me? You get my mail, turn on my sprinklers, retrieve my packages." He motioned to the plate in front of him. "You even feed me now. As far as neighbors go, you go above and beyond. It's about time I did something for you in return."

"OK." She took in a deep breath and let it out through her tightened lips. "Well, I have to go to my sister's wedding in Paris this weekend. Tonight, actually." She threw a nod towards the carry-on suitcase beside the front door.

He raised his brows. "Oh. You need a ride to the airport?"

"Not exactly." She scooped some pasta primavera from the pot onto his plate and then to hers.

He watched and waited for her to continue. She took another sip of wine, then picked up her fork as if she was going to eat. But instead she set it against the edge of her plate, staring at it.

"It's just a quick trip there and back," she said.

"Ah," he said with a lift of his chin, finally catching on. "I can get you a pass. I know airfares can be expensive, especially last minute." He took a sip of his beer. "Wow, this really *is* last minute." He laughed. "It's no problem, though," he said with the wave of a hand. "Getting my friends a free standby pass every now and then is a perk I've always enjoyed."

"No, I have my plane ticket already."

His eyebrows arched over his glass, waiting for her to continue. "OK. So, what is it then?"

She looked him in the eye, squaring her shoulders. "I need you to come to Paris with me and pretend to be my boyfriend at the wedding."

A dribble of beer escaped his mouth, and he quickly wiped it with a napkin. "What?"

"I know it sounds crazy, but I can't show up to this thing alone after everything that happened with Luke."

He stiffened. "Oh. Yeah, um, I'm really sorry about that, by the way." He swallowed the lump in his throat. He knew that six months was way beyond the acceptable amount of time to pass on his condolences about something like that, but he hadn't known how to bring it up before. Every time he'd seen Jenna over the past few months it had been for a quick hello or a short conversation. In all that time, he couldn't seem to manage to find a way to say *I'm sorry your fiancé dumped you the week before your wedding.*

She waved him off. "It's fine. Really."

He looked at his plate, too afraid to meet her gaze. If only she knew how sorry he was. If only she knew how *responsible* he was. He stabbed a piece of zucchini and popped it into his mouth to cover up the guilty frown that would surely give him away. The refreshing brightness of lemon juice filled his mouth, followed by a tiny kick of heat from red pepper flakes. Connor remembered the dinner parties Jenna and Luke used to host for the neighborhood. He'd always been surprised by the complexity of the flavorful dishes Jenna was able to conjure up, even though she was a vegetarian.

"So will you do it?" she asked, her eyes pleading with him.

He chewed on his food to buy some time, unsure how to respond.

She kept her focus on him, waiting for an answer.

He took in a long breath through his nose. He knew he owed her, more than he could ever explain. But to go all the way to Paris? Tonight? When he'd just gotten home from a long trip—one that involved a heart-racing moment of terror and a plane full of screaming passengers, followed by a ream of paperwork in explanation. All he really wanted to do was catch up on some badly needed sleep.

He considered the idea underneath a skeptical brow. "I'm not sure I understand. Why do you need me to pretend to be your boyfriend, exactly?"

She blinked. "What do you mean?"

"Why?" he repeated simply.

"Why," she muttered in barely a whisper. She let out a frustrated breath, her eyes squinting with annoyance.

He waited for a response.

"I'm so tired of that question, Connor," she snapped at him with an unexpected curtness, her jaw tightening.

His eyes flew open. "I'm sorry, Jenna." He dropped his fork and put up his hands. "I didn't mean to . . ."

She shook her head, and her expression instantly softened. "No, *I'm* sorry," she replied, offering him a grin of apology. "I didn't mean to take my frustration out on you. But it's the one question I can't ever seem to answer." She scoffed, took in a cleansing breath, then tried again. "I'm ready to move on," she said with complete sincerity. "All I want is to finally put that whole Luke chapter behind me for good, something that's been harder to do than you might think. I know it's probably difficult for you to understand."

It wasn't hard for him to understand at all. If only she knew how much he wanted to move on as well—to put the whole awful thing behind him too. He had been torturing himself for six months now.

He looked into her brown eyes, the color of chocolate truffles, and just as sweet. She didn't deserve the sadness that had shone in them lately. He gave her a tight smile. "Of course I'll go with you."

"Really?" Her eyes widened.

He nodded.

"Really?" she repeated, her eyes now dancing with excitement.

"Sure," he said with a casual shrug. "Why not?" After all, what else was he going to do this weekend? Maybe a quick trip to Paris would make the time go faster until the report cleared, and he could get back to flying. If nothing else, it would help take his mind off it. He took another bite of pasta primavera, savoring the first fresh meal he'd had in weeks.

Jenna's face broke into a smile and she balled up her fists and shook them in celebration, then threw back her head. "Thank you, Connor. I owe you big time for this one. You have no idea."

He chewed, instantly feeling guilty for her elaborate show of appreciation. After all, it was the absolute least he could do. It was all his fault that she was in this situation in the first place. Actually, *she* was the one who had no idea.

CHAPTER THREE

Jenna

The two-tone police siren startled Jenna from her sleep. The repetitive high-low cadence served as an immediate reminder that she was no longer in New Jersey. It was funny how even the incessant blare of an emergency vehicle seemed to be more charming in Europe. Well, as charming as a siren could be when it woke you up from a deep sleep.

She peeled open her eyes and was hit with an unexpected blast of sunlight pouring in through the window. She glanced at the alarm clock on the nightstand of her small hotel room to see that it was already midafternoon. An elbow brushed against the sleeping body next to her. Her eyes widened at the sudden awareness that Connor lay beside her on the king-sized bed. Her eyes darted back and forth as she stared at the ceiling, too petrified to move.

"Mm," he murmured, his fully clothed frame rolling over, his shoes hanging off the side of the bed.

The crisp white duvet was perfectly made beneath them, and Jenna immediately let out a breath of relief as she recalled the hazy details of their sleep-deprived arrival. She and Connor had landed in Paris that morning after a sleepless night over the Atlantic, both wedged into their tiny coach seats. As an airline employee, Connor was entitled to a first-class ticket, but since the flight was nearly full, his last-minute addition landed him in the back of the plane with her.

They'd checked in to the hotel that morning to find that only one room was ready for an early arrival. Connor had insisted she take it, and when he helped to bring her suitcase up the steep flight of stairs, they'd decided to each take a small corner of the bed to rest their heads and close their eyes for a quick second—one that apparently turned into several hours.

Jenna sat up and rubbed her eyes. She was there. Paris. The City of Light. Shouldn't she be feeling a *little* more excited? It was her first time there, after all. Sure, the drive from the airport to the hotel had been more of a graffiti-decorated, traffic-laden highway than the magical, charming Parisian streets of her dreams. But what *was* like our dreams, anyway? Nothing in life seemed to materialize the way she pictured it in the deep corners of her imagination. That was the harsh reality. Every counseling session she had with her clients only served as a reminder that, though we may enter a relationship with idyllic expectations, we soon come to find that nothing is quite what it seems. It all eventually shows itself to be less romance and more, well, real life. Paris, clearly, was no different.

Connor stirred beside her. "Coffee?" he managed to say.

She tapped a finger against her lip, then pulled herself up from the bed. "Good idea." She shuffled over to the espresso machine on the counter and filled the chamber with water. Her foot bounced with impatience as she waited for it to heat up.

Connor sat up and rubbed the sleep from his eyes. "I wonder if my room's ready yet."

"It should be. We were asleep for four hours."

"Really?" He took note of his watch as if he couldn't quite believe it. "It feels like we just drifted off. How can that be?"

Jenna pushed the button to release a piping-hot stream of water. The rich aroma of roasted coffee beans, with a hint of caramel, quickly filled the air. She closed her eyes and breathed it in. "You tell me, you're a pilot. You should know how jet lag works."

"Oh, I do, trust me." He quickly shook his head, as if he was trying to shed the extra fatigue. "But, man, I was in a deep sleep."

"Me too," she said. "I had a dream I was back in college. And I was wearing a cow costume to class. What do you think *that* means?"

He snickered. "You tell me, you're a therapist. You should know how our subconscious works."

"Touché." She handed him the steaming cup of coffee, then set up another cup in the machine to make one for herself. "It's true though, you know," she added.

"What's that?" Perched on the edge of the bed, he held the paper cup to his nose and inhaled the steam.

"Being back in school is one of the more common recurring dreams people have. Usually it involves wearing something embarrassing to class—or nothing at all. Or maybe being unprepared for a test or forgetting to complete an assignment entirely."

He lifted his eyebrows over his cup. "Yeah, I've had those."

"One theory is that our minds go back to the time when we first learned how to make sense of the world—when we began to make independent decisions that would affect our future. That some disaster taking place at that time is an indication that our subconscious minds deem ourselves a failure in our current life. That, somehow, we got it all wrong back then, setting into motion what would inevitably become our failed adult life." She turned back to the coffee maker to stop herself from continuing. What had made her say all that out loud? She immediately inspected the floor, regretting the sudden vulnerable reveal of her current mental state.

"That's a lot of analysis for a nonsensical dream," he said.

She shrugged. "You're probably right." Twisting one leg in front of the other as she popped in another pod, she realized she hadn't used the bathroom since they'd landed at the airport. With this tiny room, there was no way she was going to go now, with Connor sitting right there. They may be next-door neighbors, but she didn't know him well enough to be sharing such an intimate space. She bounced her knees, willing the coffee to brew faster. "Well, you never know what your subconscious is going to come up with," she said, turning to him with a nervous laugh.

He gave her a soft smile, then took a sip of his coffee.

"Why don't you go see if your room's ready?" she said, her sights set firmly on the bathroom over his shoulder.

He nodded, rising from the bed. He turned around before reaching the door. "What time's the wedding?"

"Not until six o'clock." She waved him away with a hand. "Go, see the sights or something."

He checked his watch and regarded her with a nod. "I'll text you."

She bounced on her toes and gave him a grateful smile. The door closed behind him, and she let out a breath of relief. She realized how ridiculous this whole thing must seem to Connor. Still, she appreciated him going along with it all, without a single complaint since they'd left Newark last night. She was grateful for his easy-going nature and the levity he brought to the situation—as if it was no big deal, as opposed to the ask of the century that it was.

She recalled the long flight they'd spent sitting beside each other, both trying their hardest to fall asleep. Since they'd checked in for the flight at the same time, the gate agent had put them in adjacent seats. Jenna hadn't known what to talk to Connor about for that long; most of their prior interactions had included Luke. She'd figured sleeping would be the least awkward way to pass the time, but after hours spent tossing and turning in their cramped seats, they'd eventually given up and settled into their own quiet reading. As the cabin lights finally came on, and the flight attendants came around with breakfast, Jenna had realized that sleep, like so many other things you may want in life, didn't always come—no matter how hard you tried.

As pleasant a travel companion as Connor was though, she felt much more comfortable without him in her room. She liked him and all, but finding herself in a bed next to him was a rude awakening she hadn't anticipated on this trip. Sure, it had been an innocent, spontaneous nap, but the last thing she wanted was for Connor to get the wrong idea about why she'd asked him to come. She needed to keep this strictly to the business at hand and get back to New Jersey as soon as possible; to put this whole wedding behind her, with her pride intact.

She dashed into the bathroom, then took a quick shower, thinking more about the dream she'd had as the steam filled her lungs. As a psychology major, Jenna knew what dreams meant—according to the textbooks. They were simply cognitive, sensory, and emotional information from our waking life that carried over to our brains when we were asleep. Sure, they were a lot more nuanced than that, and many different theories existed about how their meanings could be interpreted. But that was it in a nutshell—they were random.

In fact, she *had* spent the seven-hour flight flipping through some of her old books, trying to figure out where she'd been going wrong in her counseling lately. It was no wonder her subconscious felt like a failure when her conscious mind felt equally defeated. How had she lost the ability to reach her clients so suddenly, all because of her own heartbreak? Was it all in her head—the failure of her relationship messing with her confidence? Or had she never *truly* understood love, or relationships at all? If that were the case, she had a lot of reflection to do concerning the future of her career.

She blow-dried her long waves, put on some light makeup, then changed into a clean outfit—a pair of jeans and a tee-shirt. She threw on her light-pink trench coat and stepped into a pair of flats, then grabbed her purse and headed downstairs to explore the city for the few hours she had to kill before the wedding.

As she descended the staircase, she spotted Connor, sitting on a sofa in the center of the hotel lobby, reading a newspaper.

He peeked up at her. "They still don't have a room for me," he said.

Jenna's eyes grew wide with concern. Her room had

been booked well in advance, but they hadn't had time to make a reservation for Connor, crossing their fingers the hotel would have the availability. She desperately hoped they wouldn't have to go hunt for accommodation for him.

He waved it off. "They said they'll have one for me tonight. I'm happy to hang out here, and I can always get changed in the lobby bathroom, so don't worry about me."

Clearly he didn't think he belonged in her room any more than she did, and thank goodness for that.

She smiled softly, her eyes drifting around the lobby. The historic hotel was beautifully decorated with an ideal blend of old European décor mixed with some modern finishes. Soft music played from the speakers above; a raspy-voiced woman singing about "une cigarette." Jenna breathed in a faintly sweet, slightly warm fragrance. Like the scent of toasted marshmallow mixed with a hint of tobacco.

"I was going to take a walk," she said.

He nodded his approval with a grin and licked his fingers to turn the page of the newspaper.

"Do you want to join me?" she asked, to be polite.

He glanced up. "Sure," he said, his posture straightening. He folded the paper and set it down on the side table, then hopped up from the sofa.

They walked through the lobby together, the squeaking of their shoes against the polished marble floors filling the lengthy silence, neither of them knowing how to start the small talk. They stepped outside and were immediately hit by the warmth of the late-afternoon sun. Jenna's eyes grew large as she took in the sight of a perfect Parisian spring day. The temperature was ideal, and the cloudless sky radiated above her with a shimmering brightness. It may still feel like winter back home, but in Paris, spring had clearly arrived.

She gazed around at the gray stone buildings that surrounded them. Flower boxes underlined the windows, spilling over with blossoming petals of pinks and reds. The emerald-colored leaves of a tree blew in the soft breeze that fluttered around her. She let out a sigh of delight at the elegant wrought-iron balconies that decorated every building with that old-world charm.

"Wow," she whispered. The car ride from the airport was instantly forgiven, replaced with the view that unfolded in front of her; a first impression that truly delivered on its promise.

Her eye landed on an awning-covered café across the street, the doorway surrounded by a heaping display of colorful flowers. She clutched a fist to her chest, then slowly released it, feeling her body relax. Jenna took in a long breath. As much as she didn't want to be there, she had to admit, Paris was lovely. The city certainly knew how to make a girl's heart skip a beat.

They walked along the cobblestoned streets as bicycles whirled past and pedestrians strolled about in their glamorous spring ensembles. Picture-perfect postcard images of Paris spread out in all directions. She felt as if she were on one of those walking tours she sometimes took online, to explore new places. Except she was actually, really there. She gave herself a lighthearted pinch and beamed with delight.

They stopped at an adorable pink coffee cart, with a black-and-white striped awning atop. A black chalkboard displayed the offerings in elegant golden writing. She looked up and squinted through the sunlight to catch her first glimpse of the Eiffel Tower off in the distance.

Jenna took a long sip of a Parisian cappuccino, and her eyes closed with pleasure. The fluffy layer of sweet foam evaporated instantly on her lips, leaving a thin layer of milk behind. She dabbed at it with a napkin. The espresso beneath it was rich, bold, and piping hot. Connor walked in step beside her, sipping his coffee, as they made their way down the bustling streets.

"This is delicious," she said.

He nodded in agreement. "Much better than the hotel coffee."

"Paris is incredible. Even more beautiful than I'd imagined," she said, motioning with her cup to everything around them. "Of course, you must be used to all this by now."

His lips turned downward. "Not really. I come here a lot, but most of my time is spent in a hotel room. Either that or at the airport. Sometimes I'll head out for a quick bite, but I'm usually not here long enough to do much else."

"Really? That's a shame. To travel the world, but not get to enjoy it."

"Well, I get to enjoy it in small doses. Just not in the slow, leisurely way you get to when on vacation somewhere. Every now and then I'll get a long layover somewhere, though. That's when I can explore."

"How do you keep yourself on any kind of sleep schedule with your constantly changing time zones?" she asked as they crossed a street. Connor seemed to know which way they should go, and she was happy to simply follow along.

"I don't, really. I just try to sleep when I can and make sure not to sleep when I can't. You know, like when piloting a long flight over an ocean. It's all about managing your fatigue and staying on top of it."

"That sounds tough. Sleep is so important."

He smirked. "I manage to get it in."

"Speaking of sleep, do you ever think about your dreams?" she asked him casually. Her mind was still focused on the dream she'd had back in the room, and what it was trying to communicate about her current mental state. Most likely that her life was a complete failure.

He frowned. "Not really. They're just bits of information your brain collects throughout the day. Then it all blends together to make a movie that doesn't make much sense. You know, neurons, and stuff like that, right?"

She nodded. "Yes, that's true. But a lot of it is influenced by our moods too. Our emotional state." She laughed. "Which explains why they can be so bizarre."

"Makes sense."

She tried to keep the conversation as light as possible. The last thing she needed was to look like an incompetent psychotherapist in front of him. She clutched her coffee cup with one hand and ran the other through her hair as it was ruffled by a gentle wind. She considered an idea: What if dreams weren't influenced by our emotions at all? Think how much more valuable they would be to us. What if, instead, they were rational, lucid, clear-cut directions? Signs of what course to take in life. Warnings of what not to do. Nudges of what we should be paying attention to. What she wouldn't give to get some practical advice from her subconscious—advice that could actually help her, instead of wasting her brain power on a ridiculous dream of her in a cow costume.

"Do you think our dreams can tell us things we need to know?" she asked.

He seemed thoughtful. "No," he said firmly. "Do you?"

She was quiet beside him and raised a shoulder to her ear. "No. Some things will always remain a mystery," she said. "We can't have the answers to everything, as much as we wish we could." Wasn't that the truth. The one question that haunted her popped up again: Why?

"I suppose you're right," he said.

Jenna peered off in the distance to see the River Seine sparkling in the light of the afternoon sun. The shine reflected off the stillness of the river, making it look like a jeweled belt, winding through the city. Her eyes widened and she sped up. They walked towards the river, Jenna feeling drawn in by the real-life beauty of the gentle, flowing body of water that had, up until then, only lived in her imagination. The banks of the river were joined by a series of charming bridges, pedestrians strolling over them and boats passing underneath. As they got closer, she noticed a slight hop in her gait, her arms swinging with enthusiasm. She was in Paris!

They took the stone steps down from the street level so they could stroll along the riverfront. People sat in the sun along the walls, picnicking on cheese and wine. Jenna took in a deep inhale of the unmistakable scent of Paris and let it out through her nose as she sipped on her perfect cappuccino. She pulled out her phone and snapped a few shots of the flawless scenery around her. The wind blew gently across the top of the Seine, filling her with a stir of tranquility that took her by surprise. With all this talk of dreams, she couldn't help but feel she was in one.

"So, what's the plan for the wedding tonight?" Connor asked.

It instantly woke her up to reality as they continued to walk. She felt a dull pain in the side of her neck from the flight, and rubbed it. "I don't know. I haven't really been involved in the planning. I kind of took myself out of it since, you know . . ."

His eyes drifted to the ground.

She bit down on her lower lip to stop the slight quiver that had unexpectedly formed. "Connor?"

"Yeah?"

"Thank you again for doing this for me. I know it's hard to understand why I feel the need to put on this act in front of my family, but maybe when you meet my mom you'll understand. I love her, but she worries a lot. I want to get this over with, without all that." She didn't tell him the rest—that her fragile mental state couldn't handle everyone's judgmental pity right now. That she was still struggling with it all more than anyone knew. That she felt an intense desperation to deflect the attention away from her failed relationship and—not unrelated—her failing career. No, she couldn't admit any of that to him.

"I understand," he said. "And, really, it's no big deal. If I weren't here, I'd be at home, doing boring chores around the house."

She smiled with quiet appreciation.

He cleared his throat. "So how have you been doing?" He swallowed and ran a hand through his hair. "Since . . . um . . ." He didn't finish.

She dropped her chin to her chest. Since being dumped a week before her wedding? Since spending years of her life, the best years of her life, with a man she thought would be by her side forever, only to have him change his mind at the eleventh hour? Since realizing that love and commitment are just as fickle as everything else about the human condition?

"I'm fine," she lied.

He gave her a tight grin.

"I just wish I knew *why*," she added with complete honesty. She cringed, realizing it was a humiliating thing to admit, given her profession. "I mean, I know *why*," she quickly clarified. "He got a job offer of a lifetime in Seattle and couldn't possibly turn it down. But you know, still." She bit the inside of her cheek, refusing to say more. She would not say out loud all the questions that burned through her mind daily for months now. Why hadn't Luke even given her the option to come with him? Why had he been so sure that ending the relationship was the only choice? Why did he wait until the week before their wedding to spring it all on her, the decision having already been made?

Above all, *why*, with her education and experience, hadn't she seen any of it coming?

Connor nodded. "That question again."

"Yeah." She scoffed. "I guess it doesn't matter now. All that matters is that he didn't want to marry me after all." She tucked her phone back in her purse, then let her hand fall limply by her side. She clamped her lips together.

Connor stopped and turned to her. The sound of a boat horn sounded in the distance. A light breeze blew the top of his neatly groomed sandy-brown hair. "Jenna . . ."

She looked up at him, his tall frame looming over her.

"I need to—"

"Wow," she said, gazing at the view over his shoulder. She drew in a breath, surprised by the massive stone structure behind him. She stared at Notre-Dame Cathedral and pointed to it. With its grand spires and Gothic architecture, it brought on a feeling of awe she wasn't expecting.

He turned and followed her gaze. "Yeah, it's beautiful, isn't it?" He turned back towards her. "Jenna, I should tell you something."

"OK," she said, her eyes unblinking, still focused on the cathedral as they resumed a slow walk in its direction.

The whistle of the wind and the sound of Connor's footsteps against the stone filled the silence as she waited for him to speak. Her thoughts were fixed on Notre-Dame as they shuffled along. She thought about the fire she knew had damaged it several years ago. She considered the intricate stonework, the beautiful stained-glass windows. She remembered reading that they'd thought the fire was caused by an electrical short circuit, but it wasn't known for sure. Some thought it may have been a cigarette left on the scaffolding by one of the workers renovating it. Either way, it was amazing how something so simple could destroy so many years of history. Of fortitude.

She thought about her clients. All it took was a tiny spark to ignite a relationship, but that same force also had the power to be destructive. Sometimes one life stressor, one misunderstanding, one rough patch, could have a devastating effect on the framework of something that had stood solidly for many years. It was Jenna's job to help repair the damage. To rebuild the framework. To restore the beauty. She let out a puff of air, knowing that with the cause of her own relationship fire still unknown, it was impossible to feel confident that she could help others find their cause and rebuild.

She shook the thought from her head. "I'm sorry, Connor, what were you saying?" she asked.

"Just that . . ." He turned his attention in the direction of Notre-Dame as well and seemed to lose his train of thought.

"Yes?"

He cleared his throat. "That I hope you have a good time at this wedding tonight. You deserve it, especially after everything you've been through. I'll try to be a fun date, despite the jet lag."

She took a long pull from her coffee. "Thanks." If only she *could* enjoy it. If only she really *did* have a boyfriend, a successful new relationship. If only this wasn't all a farce. If only she could have for herself what she'd been trying so hard to give her clients for years.

She gazed again at Notre-Dame and couldn't help but smile at its overwhelming beauty. Completely restored. Well, maybe a restoration was still possible for her too. Someday. She wouldn't rule it out anyway. After all, if there was anywhere in the world to fall into the idea of a romantic dream it was here, in Paris. She tilted back her head and let the sun warm her face and the wind blow her hair, surprised by the sudden optimism of her thoughts. She chalked it up to the perfect springtime weather. She smiled at Connor and gave him a playful nudge. His blue eyes sparkled in the shine of the afternoon sun, the creases around them deepening.

"Thanks, Connor," she said, her stomach growing warm with gratitude that he'd come with her. She watched a soft ripple of wind sweep over the surface of the river and took a deep breath. Despite the resentment she'd held over being forced to come here with a broken heart, she had to admit the city was already beginning to shine a little bit more.

She beheld the view in front of her, noticing a cherry blossom tree in full bloom. She ran toward it, eager to see it up close. A fluffy white petal gently floated down and landed on the grass in front of her feet. Alive for decades, yet only blooming for days out of each year, she always appreciated the cherry blossom for its symbolism. Here today, gone tomorrow. Appearing for a short time, then gracefully falling away. The ephemeral beauty. The transient nature of life. A reminder that nothing lasts forever.

They continued a slow walk in silence. She forced herself to temper her emotions, unwilling to get too carried away by the charm of the city. Just like in relationships, things were never perfect, or at least they would never be for long. She took a sip of her cappuccino and noticed it had cooled. Making a face, she threw it in the nearest trash can. Yes, hot coffee would always grow tepid before she was finished. The cherry blossoms would wilt away before she was ready. The sunshine would fade to darkness far too early. The perfect moments of pleasure always had to come to an end.

CHAPTER FOUR

Connor

"Mom, Dad . . . this is Connor." Jenna paused. "My boyfriend."

Connor stood beside Jenna, his arm wrapped loosely around her shoulder. A polite smile was plastered on his face while he struggled to remind himself why he'd agreed to this charade. The whole thing seemed unnecessary. Luke breaking up with Jenna wasn't anything she could have controlled; he wasn't sure why she felt the need to act as if she'd moved on, and so quickly. He let go of a tiny shrug, supposing the reason wasn't that important after all. He was doing her a favor, and that was all that mattered.

Connor couldn't help but roll his eyes when he heard the words *my boyfriend*. Still, as ridiculous as it sounded, he had to admit it would be a title he'd be proud to have, for tonight anyway. Jenna looked incredible in a black dress that fit her in a way that made it impossible for *any* red-blooded man to avoid looking. Her hair was pulled back in the front, soft dark waves falling down her back. Sure, she was attractive—in the most obvious ways—with her gentle brown eyes, a smile that glowed, and hair that cascaded perfectly over her tanned shoulders. Even so, as unavoidable as her good looks were, Connor wasn't going to allow himself to dwell on them.

The early evening wedding ceremony had been held in a small, intimate garden among thousands of blooming flowers. They arrived just as the fading sun quickly gave way to a fully moonlit evening with the sweet smell of roses hanging in the air.

As darkness had fallen, Connor could feel his circadian rhythm swirling with confusion. His body was used to it by now, often sleeping during daylight hours, or catching his rest when and where he could. And yet, tonight, he was full of energy. It wasn't just because of the long nap they'd taken, or that it was only midafternoon back home—there was also an unmistakable energy in the air. Maybe it was the excitement of the lie, or perhaps it was the thrill of the performance, of an act only he and Jenna knew about. Either way, he was hit with a rush of adrenaline that he knew wouldn't allow him to fall asleep anytime soon, no matter how hard he tried.

The ceremony over, Connor and Jenna stood side by side at the reception. It was the first opportunity of the evening for him to finally do what he came there to do— meet her family. The small restaurant that had been rented out for the occasion was simple and elegant, with ivory tablecloths and bright string lights hung throughout the space. Thick bunches of bright-pink roses sat on each table, surrounded by the soft glow of dancing candlelight.

Connor breathed in deeply. The air was thick with the

musk of women's perfume, combined with the velvety sweetness of French wine. He held a glass of champagne and lifted it to his lips. His third of the evening. Or was it his fourth? The bubbles sent a tingle through his mouth as he let the creamy citrus notes fall over his tongue.

Jenna's mom, Deena, let out a squeal of delight. She leaned in for a hug and squeezed Connor so tightly, he almost dropped his glass. "Oh, Connor, it's so nice to meet you. Jenna, why didn't you tell me you were dating someone new?"

A loud sizzle sounded from behind him, and Connor turned to see a chef in a pristine white apron in front of an open cooktop. His stomach rumbled as he took in the buttery scent of scallops and escargots being sautéed in garlic. He was ready to get this whole charade behind them so they could go eat.

"Oh, well," Jenna said with a flippant wave of the hand. "Things have been so busy for me lately. With the practice, you know. I'm having to turn away new clients daily. Business has just been booming."

Deena clasped her hands together with enthusiasm. Next to her, Jenna's dad, Joe, smiled.

French instrumental music, heavy on accordion and piano, played softly in the background. Connor heard the opening notes of "La Vie en Rose" and felt his shoulders lighten and his eyelids soften. He rarely got to enjoy Paris like this. The whole evening was a nice departure from the mundaneness of the Marriott Hotel and the Charles de Gaulle airport.

Jenna continued with a conversation he'd only been half listening to. "And then Connor, here. He's certainly been keeping me busy." She let out an awkward giggle and eyed him with a flirtatious flutter of her lashes.

He offered up a laugh as well and pulled her in tighter. "I sure have," he said with a mischievous smile. *Wait, why did that sound creepy?* He probably needed to tone it down, be a little more believable. His acting skills were certainly nothing to write home about, but he *had* taken a theater class in college. He could do this.

"Well, how'd you two meet?" her mom asked.

Connor grimaced. They hadn't discussed how they'd handle that part of the story. He didn't think it would sound very good to say he had been a friend of Luke's. After all, it was weird. More than weird. It was wrong. If Connor and Jenna *were* actually in a relationship, it'd be entirely inappropriate, and there was no way to spin that. He squinted at the floor, trying to think of how to respond.

Jenna spoke first. "Connor's my neighbor," she said truthfully.

He let out a breath of relief, then looked up with an enthusiastic nod. "But we recently realized we're crazy about each other," he said. He moved closer and gave her a nudge to remind her to reciprocate the enthusiasm.

She leaned her head against his arm, barely reaching the shoulder of his six-foot-two-inch-tall frame. He pulled her in closer and bobbed his head with a toothy grin.

Deena tilted her head to the side and shook it, placing a hand over her heart. "That's wonderful. I'm so happy to hear this." She lowered her voice to a whisper and cupped a hand around her mouth in secrecy as she leaned closer to Jenna. "I'd been so worried about you lately," she said, as if Connor couldn't hear.

He noticed Jenna's eyebrows rise and her mouth tighten. "Don't be. I'm doing great." Jenna swallowed nervously and shot him a worried look.

Joe stuck out his palm and offered Connor a handshake.

"It's nice to meet you, Connor. So, what do you do over there in Newark?"

"I'm a doctor," Connor said. "Brain surgeon, actually." He clamped his lips together to suppress a smile and avoided Jenna's gaze.

Joe quirked an eyebrow and stuck his hands back in his pocket. "Wow. Impressive."

"Lauren, come here!" her mom screamed to Jenna's sister, the bride, who was talking with someone nearby.

"Brain surgeon?" Jenna asked Connor under her breath.

He shrugged. "Well, if we're acting . . . may as well make it good, right?"

Jenna let out a laugh.

Sure, he was having some fun, playing the part of her imaginary boyfriend. But the truth was, he simply didn't feel like talking about flying tonight.

His thoughts returned to the incident from the other day. The plane had only lost a few thousand feet in altitude, not a catastrophic event when they were at 35,000 feet, and no injuries had occurred. Still, the uncontrollable dive had taken the pilots by surprise in a moment of confusion and near panic. Connor knew things didn't simply fall out of the sky like that. Especially a commercial airliner. *Something* had caused it to happen. A physical force. A human intervention. It didn't happen on its own. As was the case with Jenna's breakup, there was always an explanation. A missing piece involved. He pinched his forehead. He only hoped that unlike that case, it wasn't *him* that had been at fault with the plane.

Jenna's sister bounded up to the group with a beaming smile. She looked like a junior version of her sister, with brown eyes and long wavy hair to match. She wore a simple white dress, with lace covering the sleeves. She gave Jenna a hug, then pulled back and glanced at Connor with a smirk.

"And who's this?" she asked. "I noticed at the ceremony that you had a date, but I haven't had a chance to meet him yet," she said, looking Connor up and down.

"Lauren, this is my boyfriend, Connor."

Connor put on his perfect-boyfriend grin again, wrapping his arm around Jenna in a flawless display of loyalty.

Lauren's eyebrows raised and she exchanged a look with her mom. "Oh, my. Did you know about this?"

Deena shook her head, her eyes wild with excitement.

"This is a beautiful wedding," Connor said, motioning around them. "This restaurant is really nice."

"Have you seen the view from the terrace yet?" Lauren asked.

"Not yet."

"Well, you two should go check it out." She turned to Jenna with a wink, then waved at someone she'd spotted across the room. She hurried off, meeting her new husband with a long kiss.

Connor noticed Jenna watching the two of them embrace, and he couldn't blame her for the cynical glare she threw in their direction. It had to be hard for her to watch it all, thinking about the plans she'd made, imagining herself in a white dress. He closed his eyes and felt the dull pain of guilt deep inside his chest.

"When are you two heading back to Jersey?" her mom asked when it was the four of them again.

"Tomorrow," Jenna said.

"So soon?"

"Work," she answered in simple explanation. "I could hardly get away," she added, a high-pitched note of deceit detectable in her voice.

"Oh?"

"I've been so busy, with all my clients," Jenna said, as if she hadn't made that point clear already.

"It's great your practice is doing so well, sweetie. It seems like things are starting to look up for you. Well, you two have fun tonight." She bounced her eyebrows at Jenna then threw a nod towards Connor. "Who knows, maybe we *will* have one of these for you one day after all."

Ouch. Connor noticed Jenna wince and he also couldn't help but cringe at the dig. After meeting the Westbrooks, he could understand Jenna's rationale for this whole fake relationship thing. There did seem to be a lot of pressure on her, more than she deserved.

Deena, unaware of any insensitivity, grabbed her husband's hand and led him away. "We'll see you two around; we're going to get some food."

The comment had clearly stung Jenna, and Connor could certainly understand why. It may have rubbed him the wrong way too—if he were actually her boyfriend. But since he wasn't, he only chuckled at the ridiculousness, urging her to as well. After all, if that was the worst comment she'd have to endure then it looked as if he'd successfully done his job. He teased her with a small nudge of his elbow, but the tight-lipped smile on her face indicated she wasn't amused. She stared into the distance, her thoughts appearing to be a million miles away.

"Well, that wasn't so bad," he said, lowering his face to study her expression.

She shook her head. "No, it was perfect. It was exactly what I needed to happen. That conversation"—she motioned with a circling index finger—"and the questions that went along with it would be going on all night if you weren't here. I'd be hearing all about the mistakes I must have made, the money that was wasted, the fears that I screwed up my only chance at marriage, and—above all—the questions on how I could have been so oblivious to it coming in the first place." She clapped a hand over her mouth, as if she hadn't meant to say all that out loud.

He pinched his eyebrows together, surprised her mother could be so cruel. "Really?"

She twisted her wrists and let out a stream of air. "I know deep down she wants me to be happy. She means well."

"But what about us?"

Her eyes flew open. "Us?"

"I mean, at some point she'll ask what happened to our relationship, right?"

Jenna fixed her gaze on him as if she hadn't considered the idea until now. "Oh, well. I'll worry about that later," she finally said with a toss of her hand. "For now, let's get some more champagne."

He grinned, and his shoulders relaxed at the sight of her eyes staring back at him with mischief. He was glad he'd come. Not only to help her out in a pinch, but also because he was having fun with her. Weddings weren't usually his favorite way to spend a Saturday, especially at the age of thirty-five when it seemed all his friends were already married, making it increasingly apparent with each one that he was still single.

In the past five years alone, he'd attended enough weddings to last a lifetime, most of them with a different date. He'd never felt the pressure Jenna seemed to be under, but still, he wondered if everyone assumed he was single by choice, that he enjoyed playing the field. Was it by choice? Even he wasn't sure. Maybe it was simply that his lifestyle made a long-term relationship too hard to maintain. A life on the go; no predictable schedule. Not everyone was willing to go along with the flow like that when it came to a boyfriend, let alone a husband.

Or maybe that was the excuse he told himself to feel better about having never settled down.

All he did know was that he was enjoying being at the wedding that evening, and he was happy to be in Paris and not working.

He led Jenna to the bar, where they were each handed a fresh glass of champagne. He held up his. "To an unforgettable evening. Although this is all a front, and I don't see any Academy Awards in my future, it's still been kind of fun. We'll always have Paris."

She laughed and clinked her glass against his, then they headed to the French doors that led out to the terrace. Connor held the door open, offering his arm to steady her on the brick tiles as she walked through before him. When he caught sight of what was ahead, he inhaled a sharp breath of surprise.

"Wow."

There, right in front of them, was the Eiffel Tower, ablaze with hundreds of thousands of white lights. It was sparkling; as if it were covered in tiny specks of gold, each gleaming with the brilliance of shimmering candlelight.

Jenna took in a breath as well. "Oh, my goodness."

"Yeah," he said, his eyes unblinking. He'd seen the Eiffel Tower plenty of times before, he'd even seen it lit up at night like this. But there was something different about it tonight, something almost magical. It felt as if he were dreaming; none of it seemed real. He supposed none of it *was*; the entire night was a spectacle.

He and Jenna made their way to the edge of the balcony, where they continued to stare at the view. He glanced at her and could tell she was as enchanted as he was; her mouth slightly open and her eyes twinkling in the effervescence, full of wonder. She turned and met his eye. He smiled at her. She held his gaze and beamed back at him, and his stomach flipped. An electric jolt made his heart beat rapidly, and his entire body tingled with a shiver of excitement. It was all so breathtaking. The night air was beautiful, with the perfect addition of a crisp breeze. *She* was beautiful, her soft cheeks radiating in the glow of the scenery around them.

Jenna seemed happy, happier than he'd ever seen her before. His eyes landed on her lips before he could stop them. They were pink and full; delicate, like a freshly bloomed rose picked from the garden ceremony they had just watched. They puckered slightly and seemed to turn up at him in an invitation he wanted to accept—something he never would have thought of, if it weren't for the magic of the moment they found themselves in.

He leaned in closer as if he were being drawn by some magnetism, not thinking about anything other than the spine-tingling romance of the current slice in time. None of it was real, he reminded himself. It was all just for one night. One illusory night. After all, in Paris, our lives are one masked ball.

He reached for her, touching her gently on the shoulder as his face moved closer to hers. She lifted her chin and closed her eyes. The sweet scent of champagne blew through the air. He leaned in, tilting his head, seeking her lips with his. He felt the spark before he even reached her. No, he saw the spark—

A bright flash of light popped in Connor's face.

He pulled back, startled. The click of a shutter sounded, followed by another flash of light. He squinted, trying to see

Jenna's face, but could only see the haze that came with being blinded by a burst of light from out of the blue. A photographer angled his way around them, clicking away at the tower behind them.

Disoriented, Connor rapidly blinked his eyes. "Do you mind?" he asked the man.

The photographer pointed to the table beside them, indicating that he'd been trying to get a picture of the cake, with the tower behind it.

Jenna looked up at Connor, her eyes wide and her expression unreadable. The wind blew a piece of her hair in front of her face. She swept it aside, then blinked a few times before scooting over. Connor stepped aside as well, letting the photographer in to get his shot, exhaling a huge sigh of relief that *he* had completely missed his. A shot he should have never taken. A shot that would have been a huge mistake. He gave Jenna a look of apology, as if he couldn't quite believe what had happened. Or almost happened.

She nodded at him with a tight smile and quickly turned around to head back inside.

CHAPTER FIVE

Jenna

"Hello, everyone," Jenna began, holding tightly to the microphone. "For those of you on Ben's side of the family that don't know me, I'm Lauren's older sister, Jenna." She stood in the middle of the dance floor, gazing at all the smiling faces staring back at her. She tightened her grip on the microphone and spotted Connor in the crowd.

He gave her a nod of encouragement.

"You know," she began, "I was supposed to get married before my little sister." She hadn't meant to begin things so bluntly, but the wide eyes—and one clear gasp—from the crowd indicated she may not have been off to the smoothest start.

Connor raised his eyebrows, as if he was curious to see where she was going to take things.

She pushed through the discomfort and continued with her point. "In fact, as most of you know, I was supposed to get married six months ago." She paused for effect, watching as the encouraging grins from the audience turned into nervous chuckles as they all probably wondered if she was about to talk at length about her own breakup. "But I didn't," she continued. "No, life had other plans for me, and thank goodness for that." She threw Connor a theatrical wink and tapped her heart with her palm.

He gave her an awkward smile in return and blew her an over-the-top kiss. Wow, he really was a terrible actor.

She forced herself to loosen her limbs and put a soft smile on her face. "Which brings me to the point of my speech—fate." Jenna glanced at her sister, who gave her a closed-mouth smile, her head cocked to the side as she listened intently. Jenna continued. "My sister knew that Ben was the man she was going to marry from the first moment she met him, right here in Paris."

There were sentimental sighs from the crowd.

Jenna licked her lips and pressed them into a fine line. "Now, I know some skeptics out there may wonder how she could possibly have known in an instant. How could she have gotten *so* lucky, that the love of her life simply appeared out of the blue like that?" She snapped her fingers and then raised a guilty hand, her elbow close to her body. "I may have been one of them."

A few people laughed.

"After all, I've never believed in love at first sight."

It was true; Lauren had claimed to know the second she met Ben that she was going to marry him. It was written in the stars, she'd said. As if love worked that way. Jenna had been around couples far too long to believe in something that simple, that serendipitous. *Just wait, little sis. It'll get real in a few years.*

She shook off the uncharitable thought, rolling back her

shoulders as she eased into the speech. "Now, in addition to being Lauren's big sister who gives amazing life advice"—more chuckles from the crowd—"I'm also a relationship therapist, so I think I'm qualified to give a pointer or two in that department." She glanced at the floor, saying a quick prayer of gratitude for Connor, imagining the humiliation this moment would have brought if not for him.

"I see a lot of couples go through a lot of things." She stood still, looking with a serious gaze at her sister alongside her new husband. "But the one thing I've learned in my line of work is that it isn't about luck at all. No, for a relationship to last a lifetime, there's a lot more that must go into it. There are many mistakes that must be forgiven. There are many problems that must be worked through. And there are many years of learning how to become a better partner that must be endured. So I'm sorry to tell you, my dear sister, that your *destiny* is in your hands. It always was, it still is, and it always will be."

She threw another check at Connor, who nodded along in agreement.

"When we find something as special as *the one*," she said with air quotes, "it is up to us to decide whether we let it slip through our fingers, or if we are going to work for it—fight for it."

Jenna's mind instantly hopped to the Fowlers. She wondered if anyone had given them a speech like this on their wedding day. They must have been so blissfully happy, thinking they had found the key to their happiness, unaware of the hardship that was in store for them. She thought about all the wedding-day toasts that talked about soul mates found and dreams fulfilled. How many people had someone to tell it to them straight like this?

She thought about Luke and bit her lower lip. She

stifled the quiver of her voice as her eyes prickled at the reminder. If there was anyone who knew how to fight for a relationship, it was her. And look at where that got her. *I did everything right.*

She forced her thoughts away from her failure and back to her sister. She looked Lauren in the eye and placed a hand to her heart, a genuine smile on her face. "So whether it was coincidence that brought you together, or something else, the most important thing, and the reason why we're all here today, is that you two have chosen to endure the hard work together. And that is a choice you two will continue to make for many years to come." She lifted her glass. "Here's to Lauren and Ben, and to a lifetime of choosing each other, and working for each other, every day."

Everyone clapped, and Jenna let out a breath of relief. The music started back up and she scurried off the dance floor, relieved to have that behind her.

Connor approached her with a casual high five. "Great speech. I imagine that was hard for you to do."

"You have no idea." She thought about the part of her speech that went unspoken, her innermost thoughts that were surely in the forefront of everyone's mind. As she stood in front of them all, with the authority of an expert, lecturing them on the hard truths of love, she was sure they'd all been thinking the same thing. Despite everything she knew, and everything she had just told them, why hadn't *she* worked for her relationship? Why hadn't Luke? How could she have let him slip away without even realizing it was happening?

Connor and Jenna stood next to each other, a generous space between them, as they watched the happy couple share their first dance as husband and wife. Jenna was silent. Connor crossed his arms.

The moment on the terrace still hung in the back of her mind. Should she mention it? Surely not. Thank goodness they'd been interrupted before he had actually kissed her. The last thing she needed right now was confusion. Sure, Connor was handsome, with his tall, muscular frame and gorgeous blue eyes. He was sweet, and fun to be around. But getting any romantic ideas on this trip was a recipe for disaster, especially in her current state of mind. If moving on from Luke was her goal, then getting involved with one of his friends was the worst idea imaginable.

Clearly, he'd come to the same conclusion, as made evident by the avoidance of anything that could be considered intimate ever since that near miss on the balcony. Now, as they were invited to join the couple on the dance floor, she felt as if she were at a Catholic-school dance, swaying uncomfortably with plenty of room between them for the Holy Ghost. She cupped his shoulder awkwardly as they danced, her right hand clasping his as loosely as possible. He avoided her gaze.

Why *had* he been about to kiss her anyway? Too much to drink, probably. After they'd been interrupted by the photographer, they had hurried inside, both desperate to get something to eat. No doubt, the champagne had certainly gone to their heads, but the food quickly put a stop to that, thankfully. That must have been all it was, right?

Connor's fingertips were stiff upon her waist. Neither of them spoke, and she was relieved about that. She hoped she hadn't been sending him mixed signals. Maybe she needed to say something to make her intentions clear. She peeked up at him and he quickly looked away. No, he understood. A momentary lapse in judgment was all it was.

After the song had finished, they returned to their table as waiters poured coffees. Jenna took a sip—strong and steaming. It sent a surge of comforting warmth throughout her entire body.

Jenna and Connor watched, along with the other guests, as Lauren and her new husband cut into their ivory-frosted, four-layer cake and fed each other a small piece. Jenna drew in a long breath and studied the two of them. Lauren and Ben. Her chest expanded at the sight of them, in this intimate act. She felt a familiar flutter in her stomach that she hadn't felt in a long time, or perhaps ever. She wasn't even entirely sure what it was. Maybe it was the romance of it all, hitting her unexpectedly. Perhaps it was the tradition, the meaning behind it. Sure, it was customary for the bride and groom to feed each other cake. But tonight, in this room, it seemed to be so much bigger than tradition. It was special to *them*. To this moment. Just the two of them, in a mutual display of pure affection. Providing for each other. Sharing with each other. Beginning a life together.

Jenna felt a mist form in her eyes at the romanticism behind the gesture. She quickly mocked herself, thinking how much like her mother she was already becoming, at the mere age of thirty-four. Her mother adored traditions and rituals—especially wedding ones. Jenna remembered when she and Luke had first announced their engagement. Her mom had shown up at her house the very next day and planted a tree in Jenna's backyard, without even asking. She'd told them it was tradition for a couple to plant a tree to symbolize a new life taking root. Unfortunately, that tree had died, just as the relationship had. Perhaps they'd forgotten the part about caring for it to make sure it grew.

No, she and Luke had never had what Lauren and Ben did. It was glaringly obvious by the way they gazed at each other now. How could one look communicate *so* much? Was it possible her sister had been right? Could love at first sight actually exist? Could it tell you everything you needed to know in a heartbeat? Your future. Your happiness. All handed to you in a literal instant.

As she observed Lauren and Ben, something awakened inside her. It felt like reality hitting her with a forceful jolt. She sat straighter in her seat as if the glow of truth had lit up inside her brain. Perhaps it *did* exist. Maybe Lauren and Ben had something pushing them together that she and Luke had never had—fate. If it *was* true, well . . . maybe her happy ending was still out there after all.

Jenna could never be mistaken for a hopeless romantic. Everything in her relationship with Luke, and even in those she'd had before him, had always been so measured. Practical. Sensible. Tonight she felt something drastically change, as if for this one night she was someone else entirely. For one night in Paris, it was kind of fun to lose herself in the romance of it all.

No, she was too level-headed for all of this. She forced herself to return to reality. These romantic ideas and talk of fate may appeal to her sister, but Jenna was different. She required concrete evidence. Proof. Actions, not feelings.

The wedding was beginning to wind down as she drained the last drops of her coffee. The dance floor grew increasingly empty, with only a few stragglers remaining. Jenna knew they should probably head back and try to get some decent sleep before their flight the next day. Even so, part of her didn't want the night to end. It felt as if there was a certain kind of magic in the air. Everything seemed to shimmer with an extra layer of dazzling light.

Connor held out his hand; an offer to dance again. She took it, relieved the night's performance didn't have to end just yet. She beamed softly and let him lead her to the dance floor. They began a slow sway. He held her closer this time. She thought again about that moment on the terrace. She still couldn't believe she had been about to let him kiss her. That she had *wanted* him to. It was just another example of getting swept up by her feelings. It was another stapler flying across her office. Blair had been right; it wasn't like her to be this emotional.

"Hey, you two."

Jenna heard her mom's thick New Jersey accent cut through the peacefulness of the moment. Startled, Jenna pulled back from Connor.

Her mom had a clutch tucked underneath her arm, while holding a Saran-wrapped paper plate. "We're heading back to the hotel now. We'll be here in Paris for another week though. I'll see you back at home?"

Jenna leaned in for a quick hug. "You guys have fun. We're on the noon flight out tomorrow." She threw a glance at the plate. "Whatcha got there?"

"Leftover wedding cake." She held it out and urged Jenna to take it. "Here."

Jenna shook her head. "We already had cake."

"I know. But this is to take back to the room with you." Her eyes grew big with excitement. "Sleep with it under your pillow tonight." She gave an encouraging nod, still holding out the plate, practically underneath Jenna's nose.

Jenna narrowed her eyes. "What?"

"You know that tradition, don't you? If you put a piece of wedding cake under your pillow, you'll dream of the man you're going to marry someday."

Jenna scoffed, then realized her mom wasn't joking. "Nope, never heard of it," she said.

She thought again about her mom and her love for traditions. Every year at Christmas, she used to fill Jenna and Lauren's stockings with a heavy orange, instead of candy.

"It's an old tradition," she used to say proudly. She would tell them how receiving a piece of fresh fruit in the winter used to signify luxury. Abundance. Jenna and her sister would roll their eyes, not understanding why tradition had to involve receiving health food for Christmas instead of the sticky, sweet treats they really wanted.

"Don't you want to dream of your future husband?" her mom asked now with a lift of one brow. She leaned over to Connor. "Maybe some divine intervention is what she's been needing this whole time," she said in the loudest stage whisper imaginable, before throwing back her head in laughter.

Jenna closed her eyes in frustration. *Here we go again.* Was it necessary to keep reminding Jenna of her failure in the whole finding-a-husband department? Couldn't her mom simply enjoy this night, when *one* of her daughters had gotten married? How greedy could she get?

"It sounds made up," Jenna said with a frown.

"Of course it's not. It's an old wives' tale that's been around for hundreds of years," her mom argued.

"Well, it sounds like a messy one," Jenna said with an annoyed roll of the eyes. She fixed her gaze past her mother, hoping to get out of the conversation. She caught her sister's eye and gave her a pleading look. Lauren only waved back then pointed to her bouquet to indicate she was going to toss it soon. Jenna shook her head violently, her eyes bulging with panic.

Deena ignored it all with a wave of her hand and leaned in to kiss Connor on the cheek. "I'm so happy for you two," she said to him, as if she hadn't just shamed her daughter for not being married right in front of him. Then she leaned over to Jenna and let out a long wine-scented breath. "Don't mess this one up too." She pulled her in for a close hug.

Jenna gritted her teeth while her stomach dropped to the ground in shame. Those final words, the nail in the coffin, solidifying everything she feared her mother thought of her.

And maybe she was right.

Jenna resigned herself to accepting the piece of cake. "OK, Mom. I'll try it," she lied as she grabbed the plate.

"Great!" Her mom gave them an excited wave goodbye with both hands.

Connor peered at Jenna when they were alone again on the dance floor. "Are you OK?" he asked.

She nodded.

"That was harsh."

She waved it away. "I'm used to it by now."

He gave her an amused grin.

"What's so funny, Doctor?"

He shrugged. "Tonight was fun."

"Yeah, it was," she agreed.

It was true; there was something about Paris. She grinned from ear to ear, unable to stop. The energy was almost intoxicating, as if it took over all other senses. Clearly.

WHEN JENNA GOT BACK to her room, she kicked off her shoes, threw her purse onto the bed, and set the plate with the slice of wrapped-up cake on top of the nightstand. It had been a long day, and she was physically exhausted, though her mind was racing. She still felt the lingering buzz of champagne and a swirl of excitement from the romance of the entire evening. She was happy for her sister. Truly, genuinely happy. The feeling somewhat surprised her after carrying around six months of bitterness in her heart.

She changed out of her dress and into her pajamas, then entered the bathroom. As she washed off her makeup and brushed her teeth, she thought again about that moment when she first walked out onto the terrace. Nothing could have prepared her for that instance of seeing the Eiffel Tower, all lit up and sparkling. They had been so close, it felt as if she could have reached out and touched it. And that if she had, it would have made her entire body tingle with joy. It was all so purely beautiful. So electrifying.

She walked over to the bed and pulled back the covers. She thought about Lauren and Ben. And the sweet blessings of fate.

Tomorrow, she would go back to reality. To New Jersey, her dwindling client base, and her constant heartache. Tonight, though, felt as if she had been in a dream, and it felt good to be in a dream. It was much better than real life, anyway. She wanted to savor the feeling before she went to bed and it was all over for good.

Before her ethereal state was over, she decided to do one final dreamlike thing. She grabbed the plate from the nightstand. She squeezed her eyes shut in disbelief at what she was about to do, before she slipped the slice of wedding cake underneath her pillow. Then she lay down and drifted off to sleep.

CHAPTER SIX

Jenna

Jenna awoke with a start, her heart pounding with excitement. She quickly sat up, her eyes wide, and her brain trying to catch up with her current situation. Her mind reeled from the intense dream she'd had, her brain still in a transcendent cloud of intense pleasure. She tipped her head back and closed her eyes. Her cheeks felt flushed, and a cold sweat covered her forehead.

She took a few breaths to calm the hyper-aroused state of her body as she adjusted back to reality. She was in her hotel room. In Paris. Her sister's wedding was over, and she had survived it all. Her ruse with Connor had worked and—She gasped and cupped her hand over her mouth. Connor had almost *kissed* her.

She shook the reminder from her head. They'd both had too much champagne.

That dream though. What was *that*?

Darkness covered the room. She glanced at the night-stand and saw it was just after 3 a.m. She flipped on the tableside lamp and popped out of bed, full of energy despite the hour and the short stint of sleep. She hurried over to the dresser and stole a glance in the mirror. Despite her lack of rest over the past twenty-four hours, she instantly noticed the brightness in her eyes. A smile covered her face that she couldn't seem to wipe off, and her pupils sparkled in the reflection of the lamp light with an intensity that matched her enthusiasm.

She let out a long, contented sigh and thought about the dream she'd just lived through. Her body was still shaking from the thrill. She hated that it was over already, that it *had* only been a dream. Even so, the euphoria seemed to linger as she reviewed the details. It had felt so real.

JENNA HAD STOOD in front of the Eiffel Tower, wearing a beautiful dress. It was a star-filled night. The soft grass brushed against the sides of her high-heeled feet. As she wandered towards the tower, her shoes melted away slowly with every stride until she was completely barefoot. She strolled through a patch of flowers, the delicate petals cushioning each step she took. She gazed up to find a cherry blossom tree in full bloom. Even in the darkened night, she could see the flowering white flora waving softly in the breeze. So *fragile*, so fleeting. Like a dream.

She continued to walk towards the tower, drawn in by something she couldn't explain, something she had been longing for her entire life but could never quite catch. She came closer to the structure, and looked up, her eyes filling with amazement. There, in front of the Eiffel Tower, stood a handsome stranger. He had been waiting for her. He had jet-black hair, green eyes, and a tiny dimple in the center of his chin. When he smiled at her, his left eyebrow dropped a bit lower than his right. For someone she'd never seen before, she could remember every detail of his face, and knew she'd never forget them.

She'd felt the thrill of intense excitement all the way down in the pit of her stomach, even in her sleep. The feeling was oddly comforting, but also something she'd never experienced before. It felt as if all her dreams were about to come true, as if there was something wonderful out there for her to look forward to. It was a feeling she thought had left her for good when Luke had changed his mind.

She walked closer to the green-eyed man, drawn in like a lovesick moth to a radiant flame she had no power to resist. The next thing she knew, he was down on his knee—proposing to her!

SHE HAD WOKEN up at that point, the romantic scene cruelly cut off far too soon. She stared now in the dark, processing the innermost giddiness of her subconscious brain.

Who *was* that man? She'd never seen him before. He didn't even resemble anyone she knew.

Although his gorgeous face was engrained in her mind, what stuck out to her most was the way she'd felt when she saw him. It was as if all her wildest fantasies had finally come true at that one moment. As if she'd finally found the man of *her* dreams. Just like her sister had. The Jenna in the dream had no doubt in her mind that serendipity was real.

It had fallen out of the sky and straight into her path—her happily ever after.

Her eyes popped open as she recalled the words he had said to her in a breathy voice, right before she woke up.

"The cake."

The cake! She had nearly forgotten about the piece of wedding cake she had slipped underneath her pillow.

She ran over to the bed and lifted the pillow to check if it was there, to verify that she had actually done something so impulsive, so romantic, so uncharacteristic for her. There, squished underneath the pillow, was the small plate, now holding a flattened piece of white cake, covered in a layer of frosted plastic wrap. She picked it up and examined it. She lifted the plastic, and gave it a sniff, although she wasn't sure why. It smelled of buttercream and sugar, and she breathed it in as if she could analyze the meaning behind this piece of messy leftover cake, as if it were one of her patients. She snickered. Was she crazy? No, just a little too emotional.

As far as traditions went, this was certainly a sweet one. But could placing a piece of wedding cake under your pillow really make you dream of your future husband? Of course not. But could it have a ridiculous effect on your state of mind and make you desire things you don't even believe in?

She shook the complicated thoughts from her head. No. It was only a dream. A random firing of neurons.

She scrubbed her hands over her face and exhaled, forcing her mind back to the present. She frowned, awake now. Unfortunately, as was always the case, reality had to rear its ugly head. Of course it had all been a dream, a figment of her imagination. Her conscious, awake mind didn't believe in any of that nonsense anyway. Did it? She chuckled to herself once more and felt embarrassed for the momentary lapse of judgment. Obviously the romance of the night had affected her more than she'd realized.

She supposed it made sense. After watching her sister marry the man of her dreams, it was only natural that Jenna's subconscious brain imagined it all happening to her. It was probably that underlying desire to please her mother, the one she had lost any hope of achieving over the past six months. Even so, the emotions swirling inside her were intense. It was too bad her subconscious got to have all the fun.

It would be time to get up soon. Back to New Jersey. Back to her broken heart and a long week ahead, full of arguing couples and increasing doubts about her ability to help them. She reluctantly turned to the bed, stopping for a moment to glance out the window. The city streets were dark and deserted. The lights from the Eiffel Tower that had affected her so much earlier were nowhere to be seen. It was as if the sparkle of Paris had been turned off entirely. The power was out. The party, truly, was over.

But that dream. It was probably a hangover from the state she had been in before going to sleep. Even so, she couldn't ignore that the idea behind it had given her some weird flutter of excitement she didn't fully understand. A question mark where there had only been a period before. She climbed into bed and fell back asleep with a tiny, glimmering smile of hope on her face.

CHAPTER SEVEN

Jenna

Connor appeared bright-eyed and clear-headed when Jenna met him in the lobby later that morning, with no visible sign of the excessive amounts of champagne that had clearly been responsible for him nearly kissing her.

"You ready for another long flight?" she asked.

"I always am," he said, stuffing a sweatshirt into his carry-on. He wore a pair of khaki pants with a button-down shirt and an olive-green quarter-zip sweater pulled over.

She motioned to the sleeveless lavender cotton dress she had packed for the day, wanting to make good use of her spray tan before it wore off. "Is this dressy enough?" she asked. She knew Connor had to follow a certain dress code to fly as an airline employee. As a ticketed passenger, she didn't have the same requirement, but she felt she should follow suit.

"You look great," he said. He paused and looked up, meeting her eye. "I mean, that's fine."

She bit her lip, knowing she needed to address the elephant in the room. "So about last night . . . I really appreciate everything you did for me. But Connor—"

"I may have had too much to drink," he quickly supplied with a nervous chuckle.

She bobbed her head in agreement. "Me too," she said, and left it at that. After all, that's exactly what it had been. She broke eye contact, not wanting him to say anything else. What could he say anyway? She knew it hadn't meant anything. She blamed the enchanting sparkle of the Eiffel Tower, and the accompanying champagne, for a momentary blunder. A slight misstep. She hoped they could simply move on as if it had never happened.

The car they'd ordered pulled up in front of the hotel with perfect timing. Jenna let out a breath of relief through the side of her mouth. She took one last look around the lobby, avoiding Connor's eyes, doing a mental checklist of all her belongings. Anything to shed the reminder of the almost kiss.

As they drove to the airport, Jenna's attention was focused on the scenes outside the window. She watched people casually strolling along the city streets on the gorgeous Sunday morning—couples walked hand in hand, tourists slowly shuffled about, and locals strode with purpose. People sat at outdoor cafés, sipping on drinks, enjoying pastries, and leisurely reading newspapers or having conversations. Shopkeepers and bistro owners stood outside their charming businesses along narrow alleyways, encouraging guests to come inside. She smiled as she took in her last glances of a Parisian morning, feeling a moment of regret for not staying longer. Maybe she'd come back someday—when she was in a better place in her life and could fully enjoy it.

The car stopped at a red light. Connor was silent beside her, looking down at his phone to check the flight information. As she stared outside, her eyes landed on a man sitting alone at a tiny table at an outdoor café. He wore a gray sport coat and a pair of jeans that fit him tightly, in the European fashion, with a pair of expensive-looking leather shoes. She watched, drawn to him for some reason, as he slowly stood to leave. He pushed in his chair and grabbed his to-go cup of coffee, then picked up a black bag from the ground beside him. He threw the bag over his shoulder and made his way out to the sidewalk. She continued to watch as he headed to the corner and waited for the light to turn at the crosswalk. She couldn't seem to take her eyes off him. There was something familiar about this man. Where had she seen this guy before? Maybe he was a celebrity or something.

He crossed the street, hurrying his steps along the way. Now on the other side of the street, he stopped and tipped back his head, finishing the remains of his coffee. He threw the cup into a trash can, then looked up and glanced in her direction. Her heart skipped a beat, and her eyes flew open. She felt a jolt deep in her stomach, as if it were forcing her brain to pay attention. She blinked a few times, clearing her vision. Yes, this man certainly was familiar.

His jet-black hair was neatly gelled and styled, and she swore she could detect the faint sparkle of green eyes in the morning sun . . .

Her mouth fell open. She could not possibly have seen that kind of detail from so far away. She narrowed her eyes and studied his face. No, it couldn't be.

But it *was*.

She knew where she'd seen him before. This man was

more than familiar: this was the face she would never forget. She instantly drew back her head, her eyes wide and unblinking with disbelief. He was real.

The light turned green, and the car started to move again.

"Stop!" she screamed.

The driver slammed on his brakes, throwing Jenna and Connor back against their seats.

"Madame?" the driver asked.

Connor gaped out the window, trying to identify the dangerous situation that had obviously resulted in her sudden outburst. Finding none, he surveyed her under knitted eyebrows, waiting for an answer.

Saying nothing, she pulled open the door and jumped out of the car. She quickly crossed the street, dodging traffic and ignoring the honks of several annoyed vehicles. The crowd grew thicker. Jenna weaved in and out, leaving Connor and the car behind, keeping her eyes fixed on the back of the man's gray jacket and his tall head of dark hair as he scurried down the busy sidewalk. She darted around people, desperate to keep up with the man who was quickly disappearing before her eyes.

Eventually her view of him was cut off by a large group of tourists huddled over a map. She stopped and bit her lip, turning in a tight circle, like a cat chasing its tail, frantically scanning the crowd. Closing her eyes, she said a quick prayer for guidance, for direction, before scrambling through the crowd again, not even sure which direction she was moving anymore.

Suddenly, she landed with a hard thud against someone. She hit them so hard that her breath rushed out of her. The man dropped his bag to the ground with a grunt, and she watched in mortification as his things spilled out of it.

"Excusez-moi!" he cried in French.

"I'm sorry," she replied, dropping to her hands and knees to help collect his things. "Pardon." She looked past him, desperate not to lose the man she was trying to find.

He continued to mutter things at her, all in French. She couldn't understand a word. She peered around him, taking one last look for the gray jacket. It was gone. She finally turned her gaze to the man in front of her, shaking her head with a humiliated look of apology. She stared at him, directly into his green eyes, and her mouth fell open in disbelief. It was *him*. It was the same face from her dream, and just as handsome. He looked exactly as he had in her imagination, only hours ago. His chin even had that same tiny dimple in the center.

She let out a gasp. There was absolutely no doubt in her mind that this was the man she had dreamed about last night. In those green eyes, she was looking at her entire future.

She wanted to say something, but no words would escape. She stared at him, her mouth hanging open, her eyes wide like a doe, her muscles rigid. This couldn't be happening, could it? Surely, she was imagining the whole thing. Was she dreaming again?

He seemed to notice her sudden inability to speak, and his expression immediately softened. He smiled at her, his left eyebrow drooping slightly as he did. She felt as she had in the dream when she'd gazed upon that face—that something wonderful was on the horizon, and that maybe a happily ever after could really begin with just one look.

She stared at him, still feeling as if she were frozen in some kind of trance. "I'm sorry," she repeated, the only thing she could come up with.

"It's OK," he said in English. Before she realized it, he'd

scooped his things into his bag. He stopped and stared into her eyes. "The cake," he said in a breathy voice, just as he had in her dream.

Jenna inhaled sharply, her hand flying to her mouth.

Then he quickly stood up and turned away. He departed in a hurry, leaving her to stare after him with paralyzed bewilderment.

"Wait!" she finally called, popping up too late to catch him. She pushed her way through the crowd, running after him. "Wait."

She flew around people again and sped up, her eyes darting in every direction. Running as fast as she could, she scrambled from one side of the sidewalk to the other. She had completely lost him. Her lungs burned, and she breathed in shallow gasps as her heart raced with panic.

Someone grabbed ahold of her arm, bringing her to an abrupt stop. She pulled at it, trying to get loose. As she turned around, she landed face first against a man's chest. She focused her vision. Connor.

"What are you doing?" he asked, panting. His eyes were wide with concern. "What was that all about?"

She smiled at him, shaking with exhilaration. "I think I just met my future husband."

CHAPTER EIGHT

Connor

"Slow down." Connor pulled Jenna gently by the arm. "What do you mean, your future husband?" He held her by both shoulders, looking into her eyes and trying to force her to stand still on the busy city street. To focus. To explain what was going on. He threw a nod in the direction of the man who had disappeared. "Who was that? Do you know that guy?"

Jenna shook her head, a confused look of panic on her face. "No."

"So you saw a stranger on the street, and decided you're going to marry him?" He studied her expression.

She bit her lip, her eyes darting frantically around the busy street. She was silent, scanning the crowds.

He waited for an explanation, but didn't get any. "So it was love at first sight or something?" he asked with a throaty laugh to show how ridiculous the idea was.

"Something like that," she whispered, her eyes unblinking.

"Seriously? I thought you didn't believe in the idea. Didn't you say something to that effect in your speech last night?"

"I don't. I mean, I didn't. But . . ." Her eyebrows were drawn together, slowly releasing as the corners of her mouth rose into a gradual smile. "The cake."

Connor threw a frustrated hand in the air. "The cake." He rubbed his temple, trying to make sense of what she was telling him. Jenna seemed to be in a fog of disorientation. "Well, the car is waiting for us." He looked at his watch. "We've got a flight to make." He put an arm around her and turned her gently. "Come on, it looks like he's gone, anyway."

He tried to lead her back towards the car, but she didn't budge. "Maybe next time," he added, beginning to worry a little about her mental state. Sure, he'd known she'd been under some stress lately with this wedding, and the shots she'd taken from her mom at the reception had seemed particularly unfair. But it seemed as if Jenna was beginning to crack under the pressure of her failed relationship with Luke.

Jenna shook her head, staring in the direction the man had disappeared. "I think that was it."

"What?"

She looked at him in apparent disbelief. "What I'm destined for."

Connor scoffed. "Well, you're also destined to be on a flight that leaves in an hour and a half. So I suggest we don't get sidetracked by an irrelevant fate at this particular moment."

She turned away from him, continuing to observe the

sidewalks with a frantic look of desperation. He stood waiting, unsure what to do except follow her aimless gaze.

She let out a gasp. "There he is!" Jenna took off running again.

"Hold on. Jenna, wait." Connor turned back to the car that was taking them to the airport and watched as it slowly drove off in the opposite direction, leaving them to fend for themselves. "Our luggage is in there!" he yelled.

She ignored him, continuing to move through the crowds.

He followed behind, shaking his head in frustration. "Jenna, this is crazy." He moved faster to keep up with her as she pushed past people. "What are you doing?"

Her eyes were glued to someone up ahead. Connor's concern began to grow. Was she feeling OK? Why was she suddenly chasing a strange man through the streets of Paris? Most importantly, why was *he* following along?

She stopped at the corner in front of a café, and Connor managed to catch up.

"That's him," she said, pointing to a man who had just sat down at an outdoor table, his back to them. He wore a gray jacket and had thick dark hair.

They watched as a waiter approached the man and turned over his coffee mug then started to fill it. Jenna immediately ran over to grab the nearest empty table, with Connor following. He sat down beside her, his eyes still wide with shock. Jenna angled her chair to try to get a better look at the stranger in the gray jacket. She strained her neck and narrowed her eyes for a better view, but couldn't seem to get one from where they sat. The man's face was turned downward, buried in his phone, his back towards them. He picked up his coffee and took a sip without lifting his gaze.

"This guy must love his caffeine," she said.

"Why do you say that?" Connor asked.

"When I first spotted him he was finishing a cup of coffee. He's already sitting down for another." She inhaled sharply. "I wonder who he is."

Connor let out a long breath and shook his head with annoyance. Leaning back in his chair, he crossed one leg over the other and pulled out his phone, turning his attention to the rideshare app and trying to track down the car that still held their luggage.

Jenna, apparently now indifferent to whether they even made their flight or not, took out a compact from her purse and applied some lipstick. She smoothed down her hair.

Connor rolled his eyes. He glanced at the nearby table, nodding his head in that direction. "Well, there he is, your future husband." He pinched his forehead and looked down at his watch. "Can you go say hello already, so we can get to the airport." He turned his focus back to his phone.

She squeezed her lips together and gave a nervous nod. "OK. I guess I need to do this." She took in a long breath through her nose, then let it out slowly through her mouth, tucking a stray hair behind her ear. "OK, here goes nothing." She stood up and smoothed down her dress. "I'll just . . . see what happens," she whispered to herself, then turned in the direction of the man's table and took a few timid steps.

Approaching from behind, she tapped the man on the shoulder with a shaky index finger. Connor peered up from his phone and watched with interest. The man raised his head and turned around to look at Jenna.

Her face fell. "Oh. I'm sorry, I thought you were someone else," she said. She squeezed her eyes shut and returned to the table with a grimace.

Connor forced himself to give her a sincere look of

sympathy. "Not as good-looking as you'd thought? He does seem a little old for you, if you ask me."

She shook her head. "That wasn't him." She sat down, folded her arms on the table, and lay her head on them.

Connor watched her back rise and fall a few times as she took several deep breaths. He rested his chin on his fist, waiting what he thought would be an appropriate amount of time to let her grieve losing some guy she didn't know. After a few seconds, he cleared his throat. "So can we go now? If we hurry, we can still meet the car. It's only a few blocks away."

She lifted her head and shot him a look, running a hand through her hair. Furrowing her brow, she stared at the table as if she were pondering something. Perhaps her own sanity. He waited for an answer.

"No," she said firmly.

"What?"

"That wasn't him." She gestured to the man at the next table. "But the guy I spotted on the street *was* him. It was definitely him. He's here, Connor."

"Who's here?" he asked, his fists clenched in frustration and his patience wearing thin.

"I can't leave Paris, yet," she replied, not answering the question. "Not without finding that man and, at the very least, meeting him first."

Connor let out a huff and threw his hands in the air. "I don't understand you, Jenna. I thought you didn't believe in that sort of fall-out-of-the-sky kind of love. I thought you didn't believe in love at first sight, or destined soul mates, or any of that stuff. You gave a whole room full of people a speech about it last night." He narrowed his eyes. "What is this really about?"

She stared at him, as if she wanted to say more, but didn't know where to begin.

He exhaled and softened his expression. "Was it all those comments from your mom? Because I know they were hard, but you said it yourself, she just wants you to be happy. Jenna, don't read too much into it and try to conjure up a boyfriend like this. This isn't the way to do it. You'll find someone, trust me."

She leaned forward in her seat, her folded arms resting on the table, looking at him underneath a raised, intense brow. "OK, I'm going to tell you something that's going to sound impossible."

He raised his eyebrows.

"Remember when my mom gave me that piece of wedding cake and told me about the tradition, the one where you put it under your pillow to dream of the man you're going to marry?"

"Yeah," he replied cautiously, already unable to believe where this conversation was headed.

"Well, I did it." An intense laugh burst from her lips, as if she was shocked at her actions. "And I had a dream. A dream unlike any other. It seemed so real. And that man"—she motioned out to the street—"was in it."

Connor rolled his eyes and crossed his arms in front of him. "Oh, come on."

"It's true," she continued. "Now, here he is in real life—in the flesh—the very next day. Do you really think that can be a coincidence?"

He blinked. "Yes. That's exactly what it is."

She shook her head.

"This is ridiculous, Jenna. A dream can't tell you who you're going to marry."

She gave him a pointed look and sat back in her chair.

Her foot bounced while she fidgeted with her bracelet. "Then how would you explain it?"

"I don't know. I guess you had a dream about a guy last night, a guy that happened to be good-looking, and now you see someone who looks similar, and you think you've found the one. Jenna, you of all people—a psychotherapist—should understand this better than anyone. It's all in your mind."

She shook her head slowly, her eyes still wide. "I know. That's what makes this so unbelievable." She let out a slight groan, appearing to struggle internally with whatever analysis was going on in her brain. "Maybe I wanted this to happen so badly, either for myself or for my mother, that I brought it into existence."

He nodded. "So you manifested him."

"In my dream, or in reality?"

"Both, I guess."

She puckered her lips. "Like, maybe I'm subconsciously satisfying my unfulfilled desires with this random guy?"

"Exactly," he said with a firm nod. "That sounds like the most likely explanation."

She shook her head. "No. I didn't imagine him."

His expression softened. "I'm not saying that you did. I'm simply saying that your dream was all a confusing mash up of details from last night: your sister's love-at-first-sight story; the pressure from your mom; that silly wedding-cake tradition. It all merged together and then this happened."

"Don't you think I've considered that? But how do you explain *that man?*" She motioned to the sidewalk again. "That strange man, whom I've never seen before in my life, was *exactly* the guy in my dream. There is absolutely no doubt about that. And then I see him in real life only hours later? No, my subconscious didn't create him only to have him materialize into my reality the very next moment. I think there's something bigger going on here."

"Fate?"

"What else could it be?"

He pinched his lips together, realizing that even *he* didn't have an answer for that. "I mean, if you really believe this—"

"Something awakened in me last night, Connor. The dream wasn't only about that man," she continued. "It was also about the way I felt when I saw him in it. It was like the key to my happiness was right there for the taking. Suddenly Luke leaving me was justified. No, it was more than justified. It was all part of a greater plan."

His eyes widened at the mention of Luke. "Really? You believe that?"

"Connor, this dream felt providential. It was as if all the mistakes I'd ever made in a relationship were justified, because it was all leading me to that man, at that moment."

He sat up straighter in his chair, his interest piqued. *All the mistakes would be justified.*

"This dream man has come to life and is here in Paris. And *I'm* in Paris. And I can't just leave without finding him first. I owe it to myself to check it out, even if nothing comes from it. I'd always wonder what could have happened if I don't."

"And our flight?"

She tapped her fingers on the table, then took a breath. "I'm going to miss it." She glanced at her watch. "You should probably get going, though."

"So you're going to stay here and wander the streets of Paris, by yourself, until you find this guy?"

She gave a tight-lipped nod, as if she didn't have any

other choice. "I have to. I'll call my secretary to reschedule my upcoming appointments for the week."

"You can't do that."

"Why not?"

"Because it's crazy."

She gnawed on her lower lip, probably realizing he was right.

"And what if this handsome stranger turns out to be a serial killer or something?" Connor said.

She crossed her arms and raised a shoulder to her ear. "I have to at least meet him and find out who he is."

"And then what?"

She scratched the back of her neck and turned up a corner of her mouth. "I don't know. Fate will take over after that, I suppose."

He let out a long breath. "My, how your tune has changed overnight."

"I know." Her face grew serious, and she leaned forward once more. "That's just it. Look, Connor, I know you can't understand this. But there was something transformative about this dream. It was more than a premonition. It was a message. My happy ending *is* out there for the taking. I can't let that go without trying. I need to fight for it, to work for it. I need to *choose* it, like I said in my speech yesterday, right?"

He blew out a puff of air, realizing this was not an argument he was going to win. He tilted back his head and directed his eyes skyward. Then he looked at her with an amused grin. "So it just fell out of the sky then?" he asked.

She shrugged with an innocent smile.

He looked away with a shake of his head and stared at his phone. A new email had appeared in his inbox. It was from his fleet captain at the airline. His stomach knotted and his muscles tightened.

First Officer Blake,

Based on the findings in your report, the airline has decided to launch a full investigation into the incident in question. You will be grounded with pay until further notice.

Connor closed his phone, intent on turning the focus away from his problems and back to Jenna. He looked into her eyes. "OK. I'm going to stay and help you then."

Her eyebrows flew up. "What? No, Connor, I've asked enough of you already. You don't need to do that."

He was silent, chewing on the inside of his cheek as he tried to figure out what to say next. He couldn't imagine leaving her to pursue this man alone. After everything he'd done, he had a responsibility to look after her, especially when this dream man proved to be who he most likely was —just a random guy on the street. Jenna shouldn't be left alone in this state of mind. Connor needed to do what he knew was right.

"Although," she added with a sly smile. "It *would* be nice to have someone who knows the city." She viewed him from underneath her dark lashes, tilting her head to the side just as she had when she'd asked him to come to Paris with her.

Letting out a slight laugh, he said, "I'm not going to let you do this alone. This is just crazy enough for me to worry about you."

She pressed her lips together and drew her head back with a smile. She clapped her hands together in front of her face in excitement.

He needed a distraction anyway. Something to take his mind off the investigation. There was nothing he could do about it at this point, so it was best he didn't waste time worrying. Though he could justify it in his brain in every way he could think of, Connor knew the truth. The real reason he wanted to help Jenna find this guy was a lot more complicated. And something he could never tell her.

Sure, he was skeptical of this whole dream thing. But on the off chance that there was something to it—if this was *really* the man who would make her happy—then he owed it to her to help her find him. After all, she'd said it herself: What had happened with Luke would be entirely justified if she ended up with this guy instead. And then Connor would be off the hook. What he'd done, the role he'd played in her heartbreak, wouldn't matter anymore. It was the only way he could foresee getting the absolution he'd been wanting so badly over the past six months.

Jenna leaned in and grabbed his arm with both hands, her eyes glowing with excitement. "So, really, you'll stay and help me find him?"

He analyzed her, and for a second he recognized a familiar gleam in her eye. She beamed with happiness, her face shining in the sunlight. It was the same expression he'd seen on her last night, standing on the balcony in front of the tower. He couldn't recall another time he'd seen her look like that since her breakup.

If he was the one responsible for causing that light to go out in her, well, he supposed he had the responsibility to help her get it back. He smiled softly. "Sure, why not?"

CHAPTER NINE

Jenna

Jenna sat at an outdoor table in front of the café with her legs crossed, one over the other. She stared at her white platform tennis shoe, bobbing up and down with nervous excitement. She hunched over the small notebook she'd tucked away in her crossbody purse. Thank goodness she'd had that on her before leaving the car. Connor was off trying to track down their ride to find the rest of their luggage. She drummed her fingernails against the white porcelain cup beside her then glanced down at her phone to check the time. Connor had been gone for a while, and the afternoon sun was now blazing high above her. Their flight was long gone—on its way to Newark without them. She began to worry that Connor had reconsidered the idea and gone with it. She sent him a quick text to see what was taking him so long to find the car.

She tapped the pencil against her chin and took a sip

from her tiny mug. The coffee that rolled over her tongue was strong and robust. Exactly what she needed—something to wake her up, to give her the energy to see this thing through now that she'd committed herself to this outlandish scheme. Surely, *something* would come of it, right? She only hoped it wouldn't make her look like a bigger fool than she already felt.

She wrote down every detail she could remember about her mystery man. The words he had spoken—though most had been in French—the clothes he wore, the things he had with him. She racked her brain for any recollection of the pile of items she'd watched spill out of his bag onto the concrete. She'd been so distracted by his face at the time that she hadn't paid attention to potential clues that had fallen directly at her feet.

What was taking Connor so long? It had been nearly two hours since he'd left. She checked her phone for any messages then looked up to see him approaching—empty-handed. She bit her lip and held her breath for the bad news.

He wore a proud grin. "Well, I tracked down the car."

"Great!"

"I grabbed our luggage, brought it back to the hotel, and re-checked us in to two new rooms."

"Really?" She let out a breath of relief, shaking her head with an impressed smile. "What would I do without you?"

"I'm a little afraid to know."

She laughed. "OK, so here's what I've come up with so far." She motioned for Connor to sit down and showed him what she'd written in her notebook.

He sat next to her, ran a hand through his hair, and settled in, ready to focus on her notes. He stared at them. "That's it? That's all we have to go on?"

She covered the notebook with her hands, wincing at his obvious questions. OK, so he was right. It wasn't a lot, but still. "Hey. It's all I could come up with. But at least we know he was at that café down there initially." She pointed down the street in the direction she had first spotted him.

"Well, we're going to need more than that." He pulled the notebook in front of him and took the pencil from her hand. He drew out a sloppy map of the part of the city they were in. "OK, he was heading east toward Rue de Grenelle when you first spotted him, right?" He pointed.

Jenna nodded, her eyes staring blankly at the map. "Yeah. Rue de . . . that sounds right."

"He wore a suit. A gray suit, right?"

Jenna's thoughts were too scattered to focus. "Yeah, I think so. Or maybe it was only a gray jacket. I didn't see the pants." She shook her head. "Wait, I did. Khakis. Or jeans. I can't remember now."

She wondered if Connor was thinking the same thing she was. If she couldn't remember the outfit this man had worn only a couple of hours ago, what were the odds that she had unmistakably identified his face from a *dream* that had happened longer ago than that? Even so, she pushed the doubt from her mind. This was no time to question things, especially out loud. She was too far invested now.

"And he had a black bag, right?" Connor asked.

She scratched the back of her neck. "Right."

"Like a shopping bag? Did it have anything written on it?"

"No, it was more like a camera bag."

"So the kind plenty of tourists walk around with?"

She stared at her hands, willing her brain to remember more. Anything that would help them find this man.

Connor rubbed his chin, then threw up his hands.

"How are we supposed to figure out who he is based on that?" He narrowed his eyes as he examined something she'd written. "What do these words say?"

"Those are his mutterings, all in French. You don't speak French, do you?"

"No," he said, squinting at the paper. "But at least they're clues. OK, so we know he's French, so it's likely he's local. If that's the case, maybe this is his regular neighborhood." He leaned back in his chair to gaze down the street. "We know he had coffee at the café down there. So maybe it's his daily routine."

"Maybe," she said, realizing it was weak, as far as detective work went. She was disappointed they didn't have a more solid plan, even after hours sitting there racking her brain. She was ready to get moving, to search the city streets. But with no direction, and some very foggy clues, she didn't know where to begin. "So you think we should go back to that café tomorrow morning, and see if we catch him?" She gave a timid raise of a brow. "*Hope* that it's his morning routine?"

"Hope is never a good plan. That's one of the first things they teach you in pilot training." Connor shrugged and lifted a corner of his mouth. "But it's the best I can come up with on the little information we have. It's a long shot though."

She sat back in her chair and sipped her drink. Simply waiting around for an entire day felt like a waste of time, time she didn't exactly have. Surely there was something else they could do to move the process along.

The waiter stopped by to take Connor's order and offered Jenna another coffee. She held up her pinched fingers. "Just a splash, please."

She grabbed the notebook and held it out. "Excusez-moi? Any chance you could translate these words into English for me?" she asked, having no idea if he even spoke English.

The waiter scrutinized her list, his eyes narrowing as he tried to identify the words she had written out phonetically. He shook his head in confusion. Then he stifled a laugh.

"What is it?" she asked.

"Well, I could translate one or two of these, madame, but I'd rather not. There may be children around."

"Oh."

Connor let out an ardent laugh and threw back his head. "So Mr. Wonderful has a potty mouth, huh?"

Jenna smiled behind her mug. She gave him a playful kick underneath the table. *Who says things like "potty mouth," anyway?*

Connor ordered an espresso and a chocolate croissant to go along with it.

"Oh, make that *two* chocolate croissants," Jenna said. "Oh, wait!" she glanced at the menu. "We'll take that too, please," she said, pointing to the first thing she saw. She wasn't entirely sure what a *mixed plate* was, but she assumed it would be delicious. Everything she'd eaten in Paris had been so far, after all.

Connor nodded in enthusiastic agreement.

"Oh, and that too!" she said, adding on an order of pommes frites, her mouth watering.

The waiter smiled and sauntered off.

She glanced at Connor in explanation for her overzealous order. "All I've had today is coffee. Not that I'm complaining. But I'm hungry."

"Me too. You don't have to twist my arm to eat. Especially here." He fixed his amused gaze on Jenna and gave her a playful wink.

She giggled back at him, and her heart sped up a notch. It must be the excitement of the city, the thrill of the chase. She could barely stifle the exhilaration that threatened to bubble over. She probably needed to temper her enthusiasm, prepare herself for the possibility of a gigantic let down, a fruitless search.

On the other hand, patience and persistence usually paid off. And if fate was on her side, she couldn't imagine how her plan—as weak as it may be—could possibly fail.

Her eye drifted along the Parisian scenery that enveloped her. Lazy, lovely, and beautiful—like a handwritten poem on an elegant piece of stationery. She let out a contented sigh. If she was forced to spend more time in Paris, she may as well soak it up. Besides, the weather was perfect. The sun bathed her skin in warmth as the light breeze of a lazy afternoon blew past. The fragrance of Paris hung in the air. It was a scent she could probably never accurately describe to someone, but one she was growing increasingly fond of. A musky aroma of antiquity, mixed with a kick of coffee, and a hint of freshly baked bread. The streets in front of her bustled with afternoon activity, and she took in a relaxing breath as she watched the people go by.

She settled in her chair, sipped her espresso, and gazed at each man as he walked by, hoping that serendipity could make things easy for her, just this once. Every time she saw a tall man with dark hair—more common than she'd ever realized—she felt her heart quicken and her breathing come to a halt. Each time it was a false alarm. She supposed having him walk into her path once was enough of a stretch, even for this crazy situation. Still, if this was truly preordained, surely it would happen twice. Right?

The waiter delivered their croissants, and Jenna immediately picked up hers to rip off a bite with her teeth. The buttery flakes melted in her mouth, and the chocolate oozed out in a pool of rich sweetness.

"Connor, this is delicious," she said, her mouth full of croissant.

He nodded in agreement, his chin collecting a drip of chocolate as he bit into his. She burst into laughter and reached over to wipe it off with a napkin without even thinking. He threw her another wink in appreciation, and she wondered why her heart raced whenever he did that. She averted her gaze and sipped her drink, picking slowly at her croissant. She loved the way she could spend hours at a café here and never feel the pressure to leave. Unhurried, free to enjoy the weather, the food, and the drink at a leisurely pace. She could certainly get used to this type of lifestyle. Her eyelids grew heavy, and she tilted her head to absorb the sun.

"Is that him?" Connor asked.

Jenna's eyes flew open. Connor also appeared to be scanning the hordes of people that walked by. He pointed to the busy street. Jenna's gaze followed, landing on a man in a gray jacket. She narrowed her eyes. He was buying a bottle of water at a newsstand. His hair was much longer than her mystery man's though, and he wasn't nearly as tall.

"Not him." She closed her eyes in frustration. She set her elbows on the table and placed her forehead in her hands, realizing how common gray jackets were in Paris. Everyone wore such muted colors, compared to back home. It certainly wasn't going to make the search any easier.

She appreciated Connor's focus, but wondered if he thought she was nuts for doing this, and for pulling him along with her. Maybe she *was* in some sort of disturbed state of mind. Clearly the stress of being dumped, combined with her floundering practice, and her sister's wedding, was making her rethink everything in her life. What if her mind was betraying her in some sort of self-preservation mechanism after everything she'd been through? Maybe this whole thing *had* been stirred up by her imagination. Was that possible?

What if they waited around all day, came back to the first café tomorrow morning, and he never showed up at all? What then? She couldn't stay in Paris indefinitely, hoping to randomly run into someone in one of the biggest cities in the world, could she? At what point would she put an end to this ridiculous dream and return to reality? She didn't know. She took another small bite of the croissant and closed her eyes in pleasure. Well, not yet anyway.

Connor's phone rang and he hopped up from his seat to answer it. "Excuse me," he said, holding up a finger. He left to take the call, moving away from the table and towards the street.

Jenna watched intently and noticed a bright smile appear on his face immediately. His mouth opened with surprise, and he ran a hand through his hair. By the look on his face, she figured he must be talking to a woman.

"I'm in Paris," she heard him say with enthusiasm.

She pursed her lips and squinted, trying to listen in. She pulled out her phone, pretending to be engrossed in something while she leaned in his direction, straining to identify who he was talking to over the street noise. She didn't want to be nosy, but her curiosity was getting the better of her. She could only faintly make out a few words: Paris, meet up, would love to. He threw his head back and laughed. The reminder of their near kiss on the balcony popped into her head and she narrowed her eyes as she watched him. Champagne or not, it was no excuse, especially if he was dating someone. Yes, he had definitely lost his senses that night. She shook her head, annoyed with men and their ever-changing proclivities.

Connor returned to the table, a relaxed smile still covering his face.

Jenna opened her mouth to ask him who he'd been talking to, but stopped herself. Sure, she wanted all the details, but she didn't feel it would be right to ask. After all, he had chosen to take the call away from the table, and she should probably respect the boundaries on his personal life.

Besides, even with everything that had happened with Luke, Connor had never once asked her for details. He was one of the few people she could have a conversation with over the past six months who didn't go straight for that burning question: What happened? It was something she appreciated about him, and she supposed she owed his privacy the same respect.

The waiter brought them the rest of their food, and Jenna's eyes grew wide. He set down a large platter full of savory snacks—an array of assorted cheeses, crackers, mixed greens, and some thinly sliced meats.

"You take the meats, and I'll take care of the rest," she told Connor with a grin.

A basket brimming with fresh baguette, cut into perfect slices, was set beside it. She breathed in the smell of fresh yeast and rich butter. Her mouth watered.

"Can we eat all this?" Connor asked.

She snickered. "We won't know if we don't try." She picked up a slice of bread and spread some creamy brie over it before popping a bit in her mouth. Her eyes closed with contentment. The food here tasted so pure; so flavorful. She felt as if she could eat an entire basket of bread and never feel full.

Jenna scanned the streets again, her eye landing on a young couple holding hands. They looked so happy, so in love. She wondered if they had fallen in love at first sight. It was funny how something so outlandish in her everyday life now seemed possible in this city. She imagined this couple's love story and wondered if they ever went to therapy to work on it. Had the romance faded for them yet, and the work begun? Or were they still in that blissful initial state when all that mattered was the way they felt? She thought about the clients she'd lost over the past few months. How she'd committed her career to getting these couples to focus on what *really* mattered. Why hadn't it worked?

She watched as the couple kissed and then separated from each other, going different ways. When they parted, her gaze shifted to a man coming up from behind. Her eyes popped. His gray jacket. His dark hair. The black bag slung over his shoulder.

She gasped. "Connor, that's him." She grabbed his arm and pointed. "That's absolutely him. I mean it this time." She squeezed him tighter. "I have to go."

She jumped up from her seat, mind racing. It had happened. He had fallen out of the sky. Again. Jenna's eyes were huge, and her heart hammered in her chest. What were the odds of it happening twice? Nearly impossible. Miraculous. There was no way to explain it that made any logical sense.

There was no longer any doubt in Jenna's mind, as she moved into a frantic run. Her pulse raced and her breathing quickened. This was it. *He* was it. Meeting this man was absolutely, positively her destiny.

CHAPTER TEN

Jenna

Jenna followed closely behind her mystery man as he moved along the streets, much slower than he had been earlier. He took his time, gazing down at his phone every now and then, as he sauntered down an alleyway.

Once she'd caught up with him, she slowed her steps. What would this guy think if the same woman who had bumped into him earlier appeared again, hours later? She forced herself to back off a bit so it didn't look like she was following him, and imagined how she would approach him when the moment was right. What would she say to him? She needed to do it casually. Organically. As if their paths had simply randomly crossed. Well, hadn't they?

Bumping into someone on the street may make for an adorable meeting in the movies, but she needed a do-over. She needed more than a *cute* meeting at this point. She needed a *clear* one. One where he wouldn't turn on his heel and run away. One where he couldn't help but want to get to know her. A witty one-liner would effortlessly flow from her mouth, initiating a long, stimulating conversation. The rest would be history.

Better yet, maybe he would notice *her* first. Yes, that would be better. She needed an undeniable sign that she was doing the right thing. If he noticed and approached *her* first, it would only solidify their relationship. She imagined him scanning the crowds, his eyes drifting aimlessly before suddenly landing on her. This time he wouldn't be distracted by his things spilling everywhere. Perhaps it would hit him like a lightning bolt, and his face would light up instantly. He would have no choice but to approach her and start up a flirty conversation. Like a lovesick moth to a radiant flame.

She shook the daydream from her head, noticing right away how uncharacteristic these thoughts were for her. What was going on with her lately? It was almost as if she'd fallen victim to some romantic spell. She thought again about that moment with Connor on the terrace. Maybe she'd been under it since being in Paris. She resolved to get her head screwed back on straight as soon as she returned home. For now, though, she was too involved to give up. She needed to, at the very least, give this man the opportunity to notice her.

She continued to slowly follow him down a narrow street until it met with a bustling intersection. The man stepped up the curb, headed towards a flower market on the corner. She discreetly trailed behind.

He approached the market and stopped to smell the roses, literally. The tiny indoor space had its accordion-style glass doors folded open, giving way to a massive display of colorful flowers spilling out in all directions. Rows of wooden baskets held bundles of roses, tulips, daffodils, freesias . . . more flowers than Jenna could even name. The wind swept by, and the sweet smell of stargazer lilies floated in the air. Each bouquet was wrapped neatly in pretty wax paper and a thick ribbon. Tiny black chalkboards stuck out from each basket with the type of flower written in elegant white cursive.

Jenna ducked in quickly behind the gray-jacketed man and hid behind a row of lavender, watching to see what he would do next. She moved along casually, as if she were shopping. She breathed in the light honeysuckle scent that brushed against her face, keeping one eye fixed on the tall, dark head of hair. Her dress blew gently in the wind, and she had the sudden sensation that she was in a country garden, or an open meadow of flowers, right there in the middle of the city. So delicate. So sweet. It made her think of the dream, when her bare feet had touched the soft flowers. As if something beautiful was growing beneath her. New life. Her eyes closed in relaxation as she remembered it all.

She picked up a bouquet of tulips and held it to her nose, breathing in the scent. She frowned and immediately put it back, unable to ignore the sick feeling that overcame her. It reminded her of the flowers she'd chosen for her wedding. She wiped her hands against her dress, vowing to stop getting caught up in the beauty of everything around her. Sure, it could lure you in, but it could also kick you in the stomach just as quickly.

Jenna weaved her way in and out of the rows of flowers, following close behind the man as he moved leisurely through the market. Why did the people here move so slowly, anyway? How quickly her mindset had shifted about this unhurried pace of life, now that she had her goal in sight. She wished he would pick some flowers already, so he would look up—so he would notice her. Talk to her. In New Jersey, where everyone moved with purpose, the flowers would've been decided on and paid for by now. Maybe she needed to hurry things along a little. She moved closer to him, pretending to inspect the flowers across from him, putting herself directly in his line of sight.

He didn't look up. He continued to meander along, then stopped and bent down to smell another bouquet of roses. He picked it up and turned it around in his hand, looking at it from all sides. She wondered what he was shopping for that required such care. Jenna was struck with a thought. *Who* was he shopping for? A girlfriend? Worse, a wife? A man didn't usually buy a bouquet of flowers for himself, did he?

For the first time Jenna considered a question that unbelievably hadn't struck her brain in all the time since she had first laid eyes on him: What if her dream man was already taken? She shook the thought from her head. Of course not, that's not how fate worked. She smirked, then closed her eyes. And yet wouldn't it be just her luck for fate to toy with her like that?

She glanced out the doors to see Connor jogging in her direction, winded and bewildered. She bit her lip. The last thing she needed was for her mystery man to see her with another guy and get the wrong idea. She casually made her way over to Connor, who stepped up the curb.

"Look like you're not with me," she muttered under her breath, keeping a safe distance from him in case the man looked over.

"Don't worry," he said. "I'll stay over here."

"Who do you suppose he's buying those flowers for,

anyway?" she whispered to him, her eyes firmly fixed on the handsome stranger.

Connor scoffed. "I don't know," he said, running a hand through his sweaty hair.

"You don't think he's married, do you? I can't tell if he has a ring on from here. Can you?"

He shrugged.

"Well, why don't you go talk to him?"

"What?" His eyes popped open.

"Yeah." She nodded rapidly, realizing it was a perfect plan.

He held up his hands. "No way. I'm just here for moral support. I draw the line at getting involved." He folded his arms across his chest.

"Please? Strike up a casual conversation. Find out if he's single, before I go humiliate myself by flirting with a taken man."

He let out a breath of annoyance. "Seriously? You're really making me do this?"

She stuck out her lower lip, holding her hands together in prayer.

He rolled his eyes and dropped his hands to his sides, his head falling forward.

Jenna watched Connor as he slowly made his way over to the man. She ducked lower and peeked around a large bundle of flowers, her gaze focused on the interaction that was about to occur.

She watched as Connor casually approached the Frenchman with a polite smile. She couldn't make out Connor's opening line, but whatever it was it must have been good because the guy let out a laugh right away. He had a nice smile. His straight white teeth gleamed, and that drooping eyebrow she had already fallen in love with made its trademark appearance. He chatted with Connor breezily, while still focusing his attention on the flowers in front of him. He nodded along and listened to Connor with a haphazard focus. Finally, he seemed to settle on an arrangement—a beautiful one! Were those pink peonies? Her eyes gaped and her heart sped up. What were the odds that he was buying her absolute favorite flower?

He took out his phone and held it up to a QR code that was posted to pay. He grabbed the bouquet, adjusted the black bag slung over his shoulder, then shook hands with Connor.

It must not be true what they said about the French. The guy seemed to be affable and friendly. Maybe even funny. He seemed perfect. Handsome *and* friendly. Great taste in flowers too. Definitely a plus in a boyfriend.

But of course he was perfect. He was plucked right out of the sky, just for her.

She was certain Connor was getting some good information for her. She fluttered her eyelashes in anticipation of their first meeting, now imminent.

Suddenly, Connor looked towards her and pointed. The man followed Connor's index finger and stared Jenna straight in the eye. Her breathing paused, and her cheeks grew warm. She felt heat in her stomach, and she crossed her arms in front of it, forcing herself to remain upright. She tilted her cheek to her shoulder and grinned.

He gave her a slight smile. Did he remember her from the street earlier? Hopefully he'd forgotten all about it—that she was the one responsible for dropping all his stuff only hours ago. She smiled back, the corners of her mouth spreading out into a straight line. *Jenna, stop looking awkward. Look relaxed. Attractive.* She forced herself to soften her face and gave him the most genuine smile she could muster.

He grinned in response, that dreamy eyebrow drooping. Then a car horn honked, and he quickly turned away as it approached the intersection. He gave Connor a quick, casual wave, then her dream man opened the car door and hopped into the backseat before she even realized what had happened.

Before she could do anything about it, he was gone.

Her eyes widened in terror. No. What happened to leisurely strolling, to taking his time? What was the rush all about, anyway?

Connor jogged over to her, looking proud of himself for a successful mission.

She put an angry hand on her hip. "Why'd you let him go?" she asked.

"He left before I could finish the conversation. I was about to mention you. I had just pointed you out, but before I could say anything else, he jumped in the car."

She squeezed her eyes tight with frustration. "Well, what'd you learn?" she asked.

"His name is Marcel. He lives here in Paris." He started ticking things off on his fingers, looking upward so as not to forget any of the details he'd unearthed over the past few minutes. "He's not married. No girlfriend. He was buying flowers for a client."

She let out a breath of relief, feeling her limbs loosen. "How did you get all that?"

He shrugged. "I guess my acting skills are really shaping up."

She lifted an eyebrow.

"I pretended I work here. A temporary job for an American studying floral design in Paris."

"Surely, that's not a thing."

"I offered to help him select the perfect bouquet. Of course, to do that, I needed some information—who he was buying for, what the occasion was, that kind of thing."

"Oh, that was smart."

"So he's bringing the flowers to his clients tonight."

"And he picked pink peonies!" She squealed with excitement.

"At the advice of *moi*, thank you very much."

"*You* picked those flowers?"

He shrugged again. "I thought they were the nicest ones."

She rolled her eyes. "Well, where is he headed now?" she asked.

He shook his head. "No idea."

"Connor." She clenched her jaw and placed a frustrated palm on her forehead.

He let go of a smile. "But I do know he'll be at the Ritz at eight thirty tonight."

Her mouth fell open. "The Ritz? Really?" she said. "Well then, so will I." She closed her eyes and placed her hands over her heart. "Marcel," she whispered with a dreamy sigh.

CHAPTER ELEVEN

Connor

Connor shook out the blanket and spread it over the grass, setting the picnic basket on top. He and Jenna had popped into a tiny cheese shop, planning to grab a couple of sandwiches before heading back to the hotel—since they never had the chance to eat the food they'd ordered at the café. With an afternoon to kill before venturing to the Ritz later, they'd been talked into buying a ready-to-go picnic lunch by the charismatic shop owner. After all, it's *un jour de printemps parfait*, he had told them. A perfect spring day.

Connor sat on the blanket and let out a slight groan as he relieved the pressure on his feet. He was exhausted from running all over the city. First chasing down the car to get their luggage. Then heading back to the hotel to check them in again. And, finally, following Jenna around the city from cafés to flower markets, and now to this grassy park overlooking the Eiffel Tower. He hadn't had much rest since he'd been in Paris either. He hadn't slept much the night before, the high from the wedding keeping him jittery until the early hours. It wasn't only that, though. He'd also tossed and turned over the secret he was keeping from Jenna. The one that reminded him of what he was *really* doing there. The one that truly explained why he was so intent on helping her find this dream guy.

Connor rested back on his elbows, his legs stretched out. He closed his eyes and soaked in the warm afternoon sun, while someone played a slow tune on an accordion nearby. Jenna sat next to him; her knees tucked beside her. She opened the basket and peered inside before she pulled out a bottle of chilled white wine and poured them each a little.

Connor shifted to a seated position and pulled off his sweater, rolling up the sleeves of his button-down shirt. He held up the plastic glass Jenna handed him. "To finding the man of your dreams."

"I'll drink to that," Jenna said, clinking hers against it.

He took a sip and felt the bright, buttery softness glide over his tongue like satin. It reminded him of the wedding last night and the intoxicating effects of the entire evening. He wouldn't ever choose to drink wine at home. It was usually too sweet for him and gave him a headache. But there must be something different about French wine. Here, it seemed to fill him with zestful ease. But he reminded himself to take it easy this time.

A light wind blew Jenna's hair behind her, and a tranquil smile covered her face as she appeared to survey the peaceful scene around them. She helped Connor unpack the basket, setting it all out in a perfect display of culinary riches. She popped a berry into her mouth and smoothed out her dress.

"So tell me the truth," she said. "Do you think this is all a fantasy I'm chasing?"

Connor was thoughtful. He supposed it was reasonable that she'd have a moment of reflection, now she'd had a chance to slow down and think more deeply about everything. On the other hand, he needed to be considerate of her feelings and remember how important it seemed to be for her.

He was careful with his answer. "Well, maybe," he began, "but I guess you won't know if you don't try, right?"

"Exactly," she said with an enthusiastic nod.

"And even I have to admit that it's pretty wild that you keep running into him," he continued. "What are the odds that he's walked directly in your path *twice* now?"

"Right?"

He gave a hesitant smile. "But what I still don't understand is how your stance on love at first sight could have changed so drastically. All from one dream."

She twisted her mouth. "I wish I knew."

He waited for her to say more.

She let out a breath. "I guess I never did believe in the idea." She studied her lap. "It certainly wasn't love at first sight for me and Luke."

"Really?" he asked, surprised by the admission.

She tore off a piece of bread and stared at it. "Yeah. It took a while for me to fall in love with him. But that's typical. Relationships take time, despite what the movies will lead you to believe. Trust me, I would know in my line of work."

"OK, so then what's changed your thinking?"

She sat up straighter, her gaze focused on the Eiffel Tower in front of them. "It's hard to explain, but it's as if that dream was an awakening, or something."

"An awakening?"

"Yeah, almost as if it was shaking me by the shoulders, telling me to pay attention."

"To what?"

"New possibilities, a change in perspective . . . I don't know. Look, nobody is more confused by this than I am. But it's almost as if the romance swirling around last night seeped into my brain, absorbing into my psyche. Causing me to reconsider everything I ever thought to be true."

He nodded, encouraging her to continue.

"And then when Marcel showed up in real life . . . well, it couldn't possibly be a coincidence, could it?"

"My mom always told me coincidences are simply God's way of staying anonymous."

"I think she borrowed that from Einstein." She smiled softly. "But can fate really work like that? Can it take something as complex as love and boil it down into something so simple? So effortless? Can it really be as simple as stumbling upon that *right* person? It seems I've built an entire career on a mindset that is betraying me at the moment."

She shook out her hands. "I don't know. Maybe I missed all the signs with Luke because I was asleep at the wheel. I mean, I still don't know how I could have been so out of it with him. So blind to everything that was actually going on between us. Or wasn't going on."

Connor stared down at the wedge of waxy cheese in front of him. "Well, Jenna," he said, realizing it was time to finally set something straight. "About Luke . . ." He cleared his throat. "There's something—"

A grape flew at his face, hitting him square in the nose.

His gaze flew up. "What was that for?"

She broke into a wide grin. "No more talking about Luke."

"What?" he said, laughing. "You started it."

She picked up the wine bottle and topped off her glass, then poured some more into his. "And feel free to throw something at me if I do it again." She took a long sip. "If I'm about to meet my future husband, it's far time I stopped talking about Luke—" She covered her mouth with her hand.

He reached over to pick a grape off the bunch and immediately pelted it at her. It hit her in the shoulder, then landed in her glass with a plop, sending wine spilling over the side and onto her lap. Her mouth opened wide in disbelief, then she threw her head back in laughter. She fished the grape out and popped it in her mouth.

"Delicious. Thanks for that," she teased.

He peered at her, squinting in the brightness, a hand held over his forehead to block the sun. Smiling, he watched as she wiped her hands on a napkin and dabbed at the wine on her dress. He unwrapped his sandwich and took a bite. The airy bread melted in his mouth. He stared at the Eiffel Tower as the slow accordion music transitioned into the jazzy notes of a clarinet.

"I should probably do some shopping later," she said. "I only packed for one day. And I certainly don't want to meet Marcel in wine-stained clothes."

He nodded and gave her an amused smile, before picking up a dark-chocolate-covered strawberry that was starting to melt.

Although picnicking wasn't usually one of his favorite activities, Connor couldn't help but feel relieved to have some time to slow down. He cast a glance around the picturesque park and enjoyed the moment. He scratched his head, thinking about how he had ended up *there*, as opposed to flying back to New Jersey as planned. Life was funny like that, throwing a surprise at you and changing the trajectory of your best-laid plans. Like with flying, who could know what life would throw at you on any given day?

"You may need to do some shopping too," Jenna said, pointing to the spot of chocolate that had dribbled onto his white shirt.

He looked down and studied it with a smirk. "Well maybe if people weren't throwing food at me."

"No, that you did all on your own." She laughed.

He eyed her with a playful grin and brushed crumbs from his pants. "If shopping is on the agenda this afternoon, I know just where to go."

"Oh, yeah?"

"Best place in Paris," he said with a knowing grin.

"OK." She smiled. "But not yet." She pulled in a long breath and closed her eyes softly as she let it out. "I think this Parisian lifestyle is starting to wear off on me already." She took a slow drink of her wine and set down the glass, then ran a hand through her hair and shifted her focus to the musicians as they played an upbeat French tune. Her smile deepened.

Connor picked up another strawberry and took a nibble. He licked his lips and they relaxed into a lazy smile. "I couldn't agree more."

THE CHAMPS-ÉLYSÉES WAS MORE than a street. It was a sight to behold. Laid out in front of them like an elegant tree-lined carpet leading straight to the Arc de Triomphe. Luxury stores and high-end restaurants lined the expansive boulevard.

Jenna drew in a breath and placed her hands on her

chest. "It's gorgeous." She gazed around at all the iconic brands that surrounded her. "A fashion utopia," she said.

"Funny you should say that," Connor said, looking down at his phone. "Champs-Élysées translates in English to Elysian Fields—the methodical Greek paradise. A place of perfect bliss or delight."

She eyed him with suspicion. "How do you know so many things?"

"I pick up tidbits here and there." He held up his phone with a grin. "Also, I googled it."

She let out an amused huff. They began strolling along the sidewalk. Jenna looked like a kid in a very expensive candy store. As they walked the avenue, her eyes grew large with wonder at the luxurious grandeur that surrounded them while the sounds of the busy city street filled the air. A couple walked past, holding hands and smiling at each other, engaged in a breezy conversation. They spoke in fast-flowing French, like a fountain of verbal elegance.

"Wow. French is so beautiful," Jenna said. "Each word sounds more romantic than the last."

"Oui," Connor agreed.

She chuckled. "Bonjour, monsieur," she said, nudging him with her elbow as they strolled.

He raised his eyebrows. "Bonjour to you," he replied.

"Parlez-vous français?" She looked at him from underneath her lashes, her chin against her shoulder.

He gave her an amused shake of the head. "What are you doing?"

She moved a stray hair out of her face. "I'm trying to converse in *français*. I know Marcel speaks English, but I should probably work on learning the basics. Don't you think? Parlez-vous français?" she repeated.

"Oh. Uh, oui," he said, playing along.

"Très bien. Moi . . ." She twisted her mouth. "Deux?"

He peered at her over his sunglasses, confused at her translation.

"Où sont les toilettes?" she tried instead.

He let out a laugh. "That one's important to know. But I think we still have some work to do before your first date."

"I think you're right," she said with a chuckle. "OK, maybe I need to work on my accent first." She puckered her lips and tilted her head as they drifted down the sidewalk. "Marcel, mon amour, it is love at first sight. No?" she said in an over-the-top French accent. She looked at Connor with eager eyes. "How did that sound?"

He let out a snicker at the sound of her slight New Jersey accent seeping into the French language. "Like a Mid-Atlantic Pepé Le Pew," he said.

Jenna let out a peal of laughter, leaning into him as they walked. Her eyes teared up, and her body shook as she gasped for breath. He met her eye, and he dissolved into hysterics along with her.

"I think we're delirious from a lack of sleep," she said, wiping the moisture from her eyes.

"Probably," he agreed, doubled over, unable to stop laughing.

Jenna came to a sudden halt in front of a store and grabbed his arm. "Sacrebleu!" she exclaimed.

He lifted an eyebrow. "I don't think anyone actually says that here."

"No, really. Look at that." She pointed and gazed at a dress displayed on a mannequin in the front window. "It's beautiful," she whispered, dragging a slow hand down her neck.

Connor watched while she stared at the dress. Her eyes were wide, lips slightly parted. She placed a finger against the window and gently swept it down the length of the dress, as if trying to feel the rose-colored satin fabric through the glass. He let go of a smile he couldn't suppress.

"Try it on," he said.

"Oh, no." She shook her head. "I don't have a need for anything that extravagant. And I'm sure it costs a fortune." Even so, she continued to look at it with longing, tilting her head as she inspected it. "But it has that . . . je ne sais quoi about it," she said with her hand held up, her thumb touching her fingers. She looked at Connor with a wiggle of her eyebrows. "That French phrase has always been my favorite."

"That *is* a good one."

"Although I don't exactly know what it means. Do you?"

"It means something that is hard to put into words, but has that little something extra. I think it translates directly to *I don't know what.*"

"Doesn't that describe Paris perfectly?" she asked with a playful wink.

It describes you perfectly. The thought popped into Connor's head before he could stop it. It was true though; he couldn't quite figure out what he thought about Jenna. There was *something* about her he couldn't quite explain. She was complicated. Rational. Analytical and insightful. But a dreamer at heart, clearly. Her name was even right there, embedded in the beautifully flowing syllables—*je ne sais quoi.* Her rosy cheeks shined in the sunlight. She tossed back her hair with a casual motion, the dark waves falling against her back as her brown eyes sparkled in awe at the dress in front of her.

He broke his gaze from her, looking at his watch. "Well, we better focus on finding some clothes to buy before it's time to meet up with Monsieur Right. Eight thirty will be here before we know it."

"I guess so," she said, slowly tearing herself away from the window. She let out a long sigh. "We've lollygagged enough today." She rolled back her shoulders and lifted her chin. "I suppose it's about time to move things along."

CHAPTER TWELVE

Connor

Connor stepped out of the car and cast a gaze at the pre-twilight scene, the late Paris sun still not fully set. They were surrounded by the bewitching charm of Parisian architecture at dusk. Cobblestone covered every square inch of the ground beneath them, and black iron streetlamps cast a glow of shadows from each perfectly polished street corner. A row of sleek sedans with heavily tinted windows lined the street outside the hotel entrance, which was covered by an elegant white awning and adorned with the French flag. A doorman in a traditional bellhop suit opened the massive double doors, which were covered in iron detailing.

Connor and Jenna walked along a red carpet that led to the lobby, where a marble crest glistened beneath their feet, welcoming visitors to the Ritz Paris. He watched Jenna take a breath, her mouth falling slightly open as she pulled out her phone and snapped a picture. He immediately felt out of place amid the formality, still in his basic khakis and chocolate-stained shirt—thankfully covered by a sweater. Jenna had changed into one of her new purchases, a simple black dress, but Connor hadn't planned to join her there. He was all set to go back to their hotel alone—giving Jenna privacy for her date with destiny—until she had made a timid last-minute request for another round of "moral support." He understood why she was nervous about all this. Still, he needed to make sure he wouldn't get in the way. The last thing he wanted was to be a third wheel in this bizarre situation.

An enormous vase of fresh flowers sat atop a round glass table, greeting them as they walked further into the lobby. The air was thick with the aroma of amber and jasmine, with a hint of leather—like an extremely expensive cologne. Connor smoothed out his pants and made some quick adjustments to his hair. He had never seen a hotel so luxurious before. Most of the places he stayed while on his work trips were different versions of the same hotel, no matter what city he was in. This one, though, was undeniably Parisian in every way. The character, the glamour, the elegance. It almost felt as if all the charm of the metropolis had been gathered up and put on display in one luxurious city block.

Jenna's awe quickly shifted to focus as she scanned the lobby for any sign of Marcel. She eyed the people bustling about, biting at her lip. They sauntered past the security guards—dressed in black suits with coiled wires in their ears—offering a nervous smile as they did so. The men gave a slight nod of acknowledgment in return, probably used to curious tourists snooping about the famous hotel. Jenna stopped to take another photo.

They followed a corridor that led further into the hotel.

The polished marble floors gleamed under the radiance of warm light that dripped from the crystal fixtures hanging from above. They rounded a corner and came upon a lounge that looked as if it belonged in the Palace of Versailles, framed by high archways adorned with heavy velvet curtains of blue and gold. Sconces lit the room, adding a refined glow to every corner of the space.

"Wow," Jenna said. She lit up from within as she stared at the shelves of leather-bound books encased in glass cabinets lining every wall.

Connor stopped suddenly, narrowing his eyes as his gaze followed a man in a gray jacket walking down the hallway in front of them. Jenna instantly noticed him too. It was Marcel, holding the bouquet of flowers he'd bought earlier, heading towards the back of the hotel.

"Go," Connor said. "I'll stay back." If Marcel spotted Connor again, he'd surely suspect he was being followed.

Jenna nodded and hurried her steps, following closely behind, but not too close as to draw attention. She scurried down the hallway, obviously trying to act casual.

Connor slowly trailed at a safe distance, to keep an eye on things. He placed himself out of view and peered around the corner. He watched as Marcel entered one of the hotel ballrooms. Jenna snuck up close behind and tried to discreetly follow him inside. A security guard stopped her, preventing her from going any further.

"Madame?" he heard the man say in a French accent. "Your invitation?"

"I'm just going in there," Jenna told him, pointing to the door that had just closed behind Marcel.

The security guard glared down at her with flared nostrils and gave a shake of his head. "This is a private event. Invited guests only," he said.

"I just have to pop in and say hello to a friend who's in there," Jenna said. "I won't be long, I promise."

"I'm sorry, madame. If you don't have an invitation, I cannot let you in." He pointed at the sign displayed outside the door: Pierre/Dubois Wedding.

Jenna turned away, lowered her head, and leaned against a wall. She sagged against it, her hands falling loosely by her sides, seemingly drained by the endless chase.

Connor came out of hiding and carefully approached her, shaking his head. "Now what?"

She pressed her lips together as she thought. "Well, we'll just have to wait until he comes out."

"It's a wedding reception. He could be in there for hours," he said.

"Then we better find a comfortable place to wait."

"Are you serious?" he said with a chuckle.

She grinned at him with that entreating look that was becoming a bit familiar.

He rolled his eyes, lazily following her back to the main lobby. They sat down on a fancy sofa beside the front desk in exhausted silence.

Connor checked his watch then glanced over at the security guards, noticing they were watching them out of the corner of their eyes. Jenna yawned, her eyelids growing droopy. She leaned her head against the arm of the sofa, just as one of the guards started towards them. Maybe Connor was being paranoid, but this was the Ritz. This was not the kind of place people could simply lie down on the lobby furniture and go to sleep.

Connor nudged Jenna and pointed towards a small, darkened corner where they would be less noticeable. "Come on," he said, pulling her up from the sofa. They shuffled over and sat on a tiny loveseat, barely big enough to hold the two of them. He pointed. "We can keep watch on the lobby from here for as long as we need to."

She nodded with a sleepy smile, her body squeezed tightly against him. "Good idea." She yawned again.

He was tired too. This jet lag was no joke, and they certainly hadn't adjusted to Paris time yet. Still, he knew someone needed to keep an eye out in case Marcel left the wedding early. He could walk through that lobby at any time. Or many hours from now. They had no way of knowing.

"I'll stay up and keep guard. You can rest," he told her.

"Are you sure?"

"Go ahead, I'm not that tired," he lied.

Jenna rubbed her eyes and rested her head on the back of the loveseat, her feet on the ottoman in front of them. Connor propped his head up with a fist, his elbow firmly on the armrest—weary, but determined to stay awake. He glanced at Jenna beside him. Her head swung over and leaned against his shoulder. He watched as her eyelids grew heavier, eventually closing completely. Soon he heard the rhythmic breathing sounds of her having fallen asleep. Her hair brushed against his face, and he let out a breath. He detected the soft smell of lavender, and couldn't resist breathing it in, his body softening as he did.

His eyelids began to grow heavy as well and he shook his head to wake himself up, slapping his palms against his cheeks. He would watch for Marcel. After all, this was his responsibility. He owed it to her.

To keep his mind awake, he scrolled on his phone, reading the news while also glancing up every time he heard anyone walk through the lobby. He cleaned up his email inbox, listened to a podcast, and reviewed his flying manuals. At some point, well after midnight, he grew bored and switched off his phone. He began to ponder the day, considering how it hadn't been anything he could have ever imagined. That didn't happen very often in his daily existence. His life revolved around schedules and routines. That was the way he liked things. It made him feel he had some control.

But flying was a lot like life. So much of it was within your control, but there was always a part that was not. Those unpredictable, uncontrollable elements. His thoughts returned to the investigation and what it would uncover. Had he gotten enough rest the night before? He still wasn't sure. The funny thing about sleep was that it could creep up and grab ahold of you when you least expected it. You could fight it all you wanted, but in the end, it could be more powerful than your own will sometimes. He remembered the incredible, unexplainable pull he felt to kiss Jenna at the wedding. It was clear some impulses were stronger than he realized.

Maybe fate was a similar concept. Maybe there *were* forces out there that were stronger than our plans. He closed his eyes for only a moment to consider the thought. Just for a second. Without even realizing it, Connor surrendered to sleep.

CHAPTER THIRTEEN

Jenna

Jenna awoke to the soft whir of a vacuum cleaner. She peeled open her eyes and blinked a few times to clear the sleep out of them, then took a minute to remember where she was.

Connor's sweater was draped over her, the soft wool brushing against the bottom of her chin. She turned her head to look at him, sound asleep beside her, his chest rising and falling as his head lay on the armrest of the sofa. She sat up straight and her eyes widened in alarm. She placed her feet firmly on the ground and pulled her phone from her purse to check the time. It was morning. She stood up and looked out the window at the pre-dawn darkness of the streets outside the hotel. Her eyes darted frantically around the lobby. She woke Connor with an abrupt shake of his shoulder.

"Connor!"

He lifted his head and lazily rubbed the sleep from his eyes. He ran a hand through his hair then stopped halfway through, his eyes flying open. "No."

They stared at each other, holding their breath. Connor leaped up from the sofa and Jenna grabbed his arm, pulling him down the hall towards the back of the hotel where they'd last seen Marcel. When they got there, the unattended door was open, and they hurried inside.

Empty tables sat lonely and deserted in the elegant ballroom. The chairs had been stacked in the corner and linens had been stripped, rolled up into a ball of ivory upon each table. The air was stale with the telltale signs of a late-night party. Jenna cast a slow glance around the room. There was no sign of anyone. Some partially empty wine glasses, a few dirty leftover plates, and some wilting flowers were the only signs there had been a wedding at all.

"We missed him," she said, her mouth falling open and her eyes unblinking. "I don't believe it."

Connor lowered his head, placing a hand against his stomach. "Jenna, I'm so sorry. I must have closed my eyes for a second."

She wrapped her arms around herself. "No, it's OK. It's not your fault. I'm the one who fell asleep for nearly . . ." She shook her head in disbelief. "How many hours?" She placed her palms over her eyes, a slight pain forming in her jaw. How could she have possibly slept an entire night on a hotel lobby's loveseat? She let out a defeated breath.

Connor took one last backward glance at the ballroom, as if he couldn't quite believe it had happened either. "Leave it to me to fall asleep just when Marcel finally decided to leave. Timing has never been my strong suit." He stared at the floor. "How did we not wake up in the commotion of guests leaving a wedding?"

"I don't know," she said. "Maybe there was another exit." They began to walk towards the lobby in resignation. "Come on, let's go back to our hotel," she said. "I could sure use a shower."

Connor followed along. "Jenna, really, I'm so sorry. I said I'd look out for him, and I let you down."

She stopped and raised her chin, looking into his blue eyes gazing at her with remorse. She didn't say anything, only gave him a soft smile of understanding as they headed for the door. Of course it wasn't his fault. He was doing more for her than she could have ever imagined. She felt her heart expand at the thought of Connor having stuck by her side through the entire crazy day.

They stepped outside and entered the cobblestone courtyard. The gray quiet of the pre-dawn city was eerily breathtaking. Jenna took in a long inhale of the crisp air and shivered. Connor draped his sweater over her shoulders, just as he must have last night when she'd been asleep. The large, olive-green wool wrapped around her perfectly, like a small blanket. He placed his strong hands over her arms, sending a surge of warmth through her body. She smiled and her eyelids softened as she breathed in the now-familiar scent of his clothing. It was a comforting smell, like clean cotton and fresh soap. It reminded her of freshly laundered linen hanging in the New Jersey summer sun. She recalled breathing it in as she slept soundly beside him all night.

They began a slow walk back to their hotel as the sparkle of the night sky subtly grew softer. She beheld the faint darkness that was in front of her and pulled Connor's sweater tighter around her. She had no idea where they were, or where they were headed. But she trusted that he did. She followed, the changing colors of the sky a telltale sign of the approaching dawn.

"I'm really sorry I fell asleep," he said again.

She waved him off. "I couldn't stay awake either." She took in a deep breath. "Connor, what do you think about all of this?" She stopped walking and turned to him with a focused stare. "Really, do you think it's pointless?" She bit her lip, nervously waiting for his reply. She had finally had a solid sleep—the first one since being in Paris—and now she was ready to think logically, without the distraction of her emotions getting in the way. Maybe it was time to accept this thing for the feeling-driven, ludicrous idea that it was. "Is it time to give up on this ridiculous search? Is it even possible that the dream meant anything at all?"

He let a heavy breath escape. "I don't know. Anything's possible, I guess. You understand so much more about this stuff than I do, about whether your subconscious can tell you things or not." He rubbed his forehead. "The only thing I understand right now is the feeling of sleep deprivation, which I most definitely have. So I'll defer to your judgment on this one."

She gave him a wry smile. "You must be exhausted. Let's get back to the hotel so you can get some decent rest. Thanks for trying."

They continued to walk in silence.

"We should probably head back home today," she finally said. "I'll call the airline."

His jaw firmed. "So you're done then?"

She shrugged. "It's Monday already. I should have been back by now." She ignored the prickle that was forming behind her eyes. "My clients are expecting me. And I'm sure you need to get back to prepare for your next trip."

He lifted a shoulder. "I can't fly right now anyway."

She gave him a questioning look.

"There was an incident on my flight the other day," he said. "I have to remain grounded until it's been investigated. It's nothing," he added quickly. "Things like this happen all the time. I'm just ready to get back in the air." He cocked his head and stared into her eyes. "But, Jenna, are you sure you want to give up on this?"

Her chin quivered and she quickly wiped the beginning of a tear that had formed. She blew a long stream of air through her mouth. "I know this whole thing is absurd. And it was probably a long shot anyway. Yeah, it's probably time to give it a rest."

"Are you OK?" he asked.

She let out a shaky breath. "I thought this was it," she said, tossing a hand in the air. "My chance to finally get the happily ever after I've been waiting for, you know. As much as I hate to admit it, I do sort of believe in all that romantic stuff. At least, I want to believe in it."

He slowly nodded, looking into her eyes with empathy.

"It's just that I see the other side of it every day. I see what happens after the passion fades, when we begin to question our life choices and all our decisions come back to haunt us." She blew out a puff of air. "Sometimes I wonder if my career has affected my ability to do all this properly."

"Do what?"

"To fall in love, in the right way."

He nodded, seeming to understand her perfectly.

"I know this whole thing must sound ridiculous to you, but I guess I felt this was fate's way of stepping in and making the tough decision for me. Like, after everything I messed up with Luke, I couldn't possibly screw up destiny's plan, right?"

He shook his head. "It doesn't sound ridiculous at all."

"Really?"

"I think everyone ultimately wants that. To feel like they made the right choice. Ended up with the right person. Isn't that what we're all seeking—validation—in one way or another?"

She shrugged.

"And everyone wants that romantic happily ever after too."

Her eyebrows raised. "Do *you*?" Her thoughts jumped to the woman he'd been on the phone with at the café the day before.

"Of course." His eyes remained glued to his feet as they walked.

She chewed on a fingernail. "You know, I've been thinking a lot lately about why I even became a relationship therapist in the first place."

He raised his head with interest.

"Growing up, my mom always put a lot of pressure on me, or at least that's how I felt." She scoffed. "I guess I still do. Anyway, it led to some arguments between us, especially during the teenage years."

They turned a corner, and Connor led her down a quiet road. The first hints of daylight glistened against the ground. The city streets were quiet as the morning sun started to creep up, bathing everything in a faint, shimmering glow. Café employees began their daily opening rituals, hosing down the sidewalks and setting out chairs. Patisseries, fromageries, and bistros slowly came to life.

Jenna continued. "There was this one time we had a huge disagreement about something that was important to me." She rolled her eyes. "I don't even remember what it was now."

Connor nodded, encouraging her to continue.

"So after a lot of yelling from both of us—having assumed she simply didn't care about my happiness—I finally decided to sit her down and have an adult conversation with her. For the first time in my life, I listened to her. I got her perspective. I learned things about my mom that day that I'd never realized before. I uncovered the reasons behind our differing opinions. The *why*. She was a product of her upbringing, her personal experiences, her beliefs—like we all are. We are all made up of our own framework, our personal foundation."

The idea made her think again about Notre-Dame Cathedral and the destruction from the fire. All due, possibly, to a cigarette left behind on the scaffolding during renovations. She thought about the idea of scaffolding, in terms of how it was used in psychology: A temporary support structure one gradually reduced their reliance on until it was no longer needed at all. Wasn't that what parenthood was, really?

"Anyways," she continued, "I learned then that when we share a life with someone who has a completely different world view than we do, it takes a shift in perspective to learn how to communicate with them. *That* is at the heart of working through any issue with someone you love."

She thought about her current relationship with her mom. It seemed lately they had again forgotten how to communicate. Or perhaps Jenna had simply stopped taking the time to sit down with Deena, to understand where she was coming from. She rubbed the wool of Connor's sweater between her fingers.

"I know what you mean," he said. "My parents split up when I was young. I wonder what would have happened if they'd had someone like you to help them through it, to listen to their problems, to help each other understand the other's perspective." He shrugged. "Guess we'll never know."

"I'm sorry," she said. "I didn't know that about your parents."

"It's OK. It's part of *my* framework. Sometimes I wonder if it's why I became a pilot."

"What do you mean?"

"Well, I didn't have the most stable home life. We moved around a lot when I was younger, before they split. My dad was always dabbling in something new, always trying his hand at some promising business venture. I hated it at the time, although eventually I think I became drawn to a life of being on the go, never settling down with one person or putting down roots in a relationship. It's probably why I'm still single." He scoffed. "Although, my sister became a pilot too. And she's happily married. So I'm sure the job isn't to blame." He stared at the ground. "I guess it's me."

"Really? You and your sister are both pilots? That's cool."

"Yeah. Maybe we were both drawn to the same things. A safe, solid, stable career at a major airline—unlike what our father had. But at the same time, there was something about his spirit that appealed to us. Taking risks, not playing it safe, going out on a limb. Piloting a plane certainly gives you that. Either way, we were both enamored with flying ever since we were little, and I tended to follow in my older sister's footsteps on most things."

Jenna smiled. "That's nice. I'm sure it's great to have an older sibling to look up to. My little sister probably looks at me with pity."

"I'm sure that's not true." He paused, looking at her

with a tilt of his head. "And I don't think your mom does either."

"What do you mean?"

"Well, maybe she's not judging you as harshly as you think. As harshly as you're judging yourself. Maybe your mom simply wants the best for you, and getting involved is her way of showing you how much she cares."

Jenna considered his words. She felt her shoulders relax at the tiny admission to herself that, deep down, she knew he was right.

They descended stone steps that led to the river just as the sun lifted from the horizon. A bright layer of shimmering light reflected off the water. The gray sky was completely painted over with the dazzling coral brushstrokes of a spectacular, jaw-dropping sunrise.

Jenna inhaled sharply. "Connor, look!" She grabbed his arm without thinking, wrapping her hands around it and leaning her head into it. She breathed in the cool air and raised her chin to look up at him.

"Yeah," he said, his eyes wide with wonder, staring at the sky. "It's gorgeous."

She turned her gaze back to the glowing colors in front of them, her soul enveloped by a state of ecstasy. "Wow," she said, feeling as if she were being carried away in the air. She wondered if it was similar to how Connor felt when he soared above the clouds. "I think I have just experienced a perfect moment," she said without thinking, not even knowing what it meant, only that it was true.

He closed his eyes and pulled in a deep breath. "Yeah," he agreed in a light whisper.

She relished in the feeling of reassurance, of promise. It was as if all the mistakes of the previous day were behind her, the sun having set on them. Having set on Luke. As if her entire heart had simply emptied itself of everything, and was open to a fresh start. Today was a new day, full of endless possibilities. It was a sign that she was ready to move forward. That there was something beautiful out on the horizon, waiting for her. Like this spectacular sunrise.

"Connor?"

"Yeah?"

"I don't want to give up on finding Marcel, just yet."

He didn't say anything, but he drew in a long, slow breath and relaxed his shoulders. He smiled at her. They continued with their walk, neither saying anything, both under the spell of the surreal experience that had unfolded before their eyes—as if in a daze of enchantment.

They reached the entrance to a metro station and walked down the concrete stairs, descending into the cold, damp darkness. She didn't know where they were going, but it didn't matter. She was safe. Somehow, she had an assurance that everything was going to work out. For them both. One thing she knew was that the sun would always rise again, with each new day. And she also knew that she was glad to have Connor to lead her around this confusing city, to lead her around this confusing time.

"Connor?" she said, as they waited for the train.

He looked at her.

"You're going to find your happily ever after too."

He gave her a faint smile, then surveyed the ground. He weaved his fingers through his hair. "Jenna?"

"Yeah?"

He raised his head and looked her in the eye. He swallowed as he held her gaze, then he tightened his jaw. "We're going to find this guy for you. I promise," he said.

She was taken off guard by his sudden resolve. She wasn't sure why he'd promised to do something she knew he couldn't deliver on. But something behind his eyes made her believe him. Something must have stirred inside him as well as he'd watched that sunrise and experienced the emotions that came with it. The excitement of taking a risk. The thrill of the unknown. That unmistakable feeling of hope.

CHAPTER FOURTEEN

Connor

After a steaming shower and a long nap in his sprawling king-sized hotel bed, Connor woke up feeling refreshed. Even so, he needed a moment to get his bearings. It was Monday afternoon, although it felt like an early morning. His schedule was all out of whack. Not uncommon for him, although this was more than usual.

He grabbed his phone to quickly check his email. No updates on the investigation. He gritted his teeth, wondering what could possibly be taking so long. Of course, an actual accident investigation could go on for months, if not years. But this hadn't been an accident, only an *incident*. As concerning as it may have been, it simply needed a definite cause identified—or as was most often the case, a chain of contributing causes, so that it could be prevented from happening again. Anytime something occurred in a flight that could potentially affect the safety of the aircraft, every move the pilots had made up to that point, even before they'd entered the cockpit, was put under a microscope. The flying public remained blissfully unaware of minor occurrences that happened regularly and which ended in a paperwork trail that resulted in changes to policy and procedure to make commercial air travel as safe as it was.

He pushed it all from his thoughts, determined to focus instead on what he *could* control: being cleared of the incident that had resulted in Jenna's broken heart. He sent her a text to let her know he was up and ready to start the day; to resume the search.

He still couldn't believe he'd fallen asleep while keeping watch at the Ritz. It must have only been for a split second, or at least that's how it had felt. He'd always had such a firm handle on his sleep habits and ability to stay awake when he needed to. He had to catch rest when he could, sometimes on off-kilter schedules. But falling asleep mid-flight was never an option. He'd been trained to recognize his fatigue and take appropriate action so that it would never jeopardize the safety of a flight. How had it taken him by surprise like that in the lobby of the hotel?

It must have been the wine's fault, again. Sure, it may taste amazing here in Paris, but it was taking its toll on his judgment, in more ways than one. He made a quick resolution to avoid the intoxicating beverage from now on. In fact, he needed to stop getting pulled in by the sparkle of Paris in general, not only its cocktails. It was just another city. A destination on his typical route. He'd been there dozens of times, and this was not the occasion to get sidetracked by its charms. He had to remember he had a mission here, and the sooner he accomplished it, the sooner he could shed his guilt and move on. He simply needed to stay focused on the task at hand.

"So, what's the plan now?" he asked Jenna as soon as they met in the lobby.

She wore a white blouse, along with a perfectly fitted pair of jeans and her pink jacket slung over her arm.

"I think we should visit the same area we did yesterday," she said. "After all, we saw him *twice*, over the span of several hours. If those are his usual haunts, surely we'll see him again." She tapped her fingers against the strap of her purse. "I realize it was a lot earlier in the day when we saw him, but what else can we do?"

He scrunched his nose, wishing they had something more concrete.

Jenna pulled out her phone and glanced at the map. "We'll start at the café on the corner, the one with the best view of things," she said, a finger gliding across the screen. "And then we can spread out from there. Maybe we can talk to some of the waiters, or the shop owners in that area. See if we can figure out his routine to anticipate where he'll be next?" She peeked up at him with an insecure half smile.

He rubbed his chin. "OK, sounds like a plan."

They stepped outside the hotel and began the walk to the café where the entire thing had begun. The streets bustled with the activity of a gorgeous springtime afternoon. The weather was flawless, without a cloud in the sky.

They stopped, and Jenna caught sight of the branches above them, brimming with cherry blossoms, and let out a delighted squeal.

"I love these," she said, taking a deep, satisfied breath. "I've been seeing cherry blossoms all over the city, and they make me think of everything spring signifies. Beauty, growth, new life." She held out her arms wide and threw back her head, her eyes closing in delight as the warm, breezy air drifted through her cascading hair. "Spring is here," she sang, a soft ray of sunshine reflecting off her cheeks.

Connor watched her, standing with his thumbs in the front pockets of his jeans. He loved the sight of cherry blossoms too, though he'd never quite realized why until that moment. They were lovely, sure, but there was something more to appreciate than their beauty. He thought about the many times he'd visited Japan over the years, where cherry blossoms are considered the national flower and viewed as a metaphor for life. Precious, but also fleeting. Impermanent. Delicate. Like his growing friendship with Jenna, they had a short lifespan.

Yes, it was spring. But nothing lasted forever. He observed Jenna and wished he could freeze this perfect moment in time. A beautiful spring day in the Parisian sun. If only the darkness weighing him down—the truth—didn't linger somewhere in the shadows.

WHEN JENNA and Connor arrived at the café, they found a street-facing table and took a seat. The quintessential French waiter, complete with a handlebar mustache, came by and they ordered their drinks.

"Un café, s'il vous plaît," Connor said. He liked these fancy European café drinks and all, but he was craving some basic, American-style black coffee.

"I'll have a café au lait," Jenna said, with one of her cute mispronunciations, putting the emphasis on the t. "Only a splash, though," she instructed, holding up her pinched fingers.

Connor clamped his lips together. The waiter nodded and left, and Connor let out a laugh. "Why do you always order 'a splash'? You always end up getting refills. Why don't you order an entire cup?"

"So it doesn't get cold," she said, as if it were the most obvious thing in the world. "I like to sip my coffee slowly, and if there's too much, it gets cold too quickly and goes to waste."

He raised his eyebrows. "I guess that makes sense. I've just never seen anyone order it that way."

She shrugged. "Yeah, well. We all have our quirks. I'm sure the waiters here are used to eccentric Americans and our strange habits."

He cocked his head. "I think that's only a *you* habit," he teased.

She gave him a playful kick underneath the table.

Connor pretended to wipe his mouth with a napkin to hide his giddy smile. He let out a breath of relaxation, taking in the scenery. For a moment it felt as if they were on a vacation, as opposed to the ridiculous situation they were actually in. The idea gave his stomach a light flutter, and he had to resist the urge to tell Jenna how nice she looked. Her dark hair fell over one shoulder; her brown eyes glistened in the sun's rays; her rose-colored lips held a relaxed smile as she leaned against the charming green-and-ivory checkered, woven chair in an idyllic Parisian café. Like a garden in bloom.

The waiter came to deliver their drinks. Jenna's mug was perfectly underfilled, while Connor's black coffee was deliciously bitter and wonderfully strong.

"Excusez-moi," Jenna said to the waiter in her unmistakable American accent. She paused, waiting for a response with an eager ear.

Connor could tell she was doing that thing that was becoming common for them—saying something in French, then waiting a beat to see if the waiter offered to return the conversation in English. Nearly everyone did, but one could never assume.

"Yes? What is it?" the waiter asked in perfect English with a French accent.

Connor was always impressed with the ability of French waiters to converse with them in English. He made a mental note to learn more of the native languages when he found himself in these foreign cities. It only seemed right that he made an effort to communicate in their language when he was in their country, as opposed to relying on them to know his.

"Do you happen to know a guy named Marcel?" Jenna asked the waiter.

The waiter gave her a pointed look. "I'm sure."

"Really?" Jenna asked, her eyes lighting up. "How often do you see him here? Will he come in today?"

Connor chuckled. "Do you know how many Marcels must live around here?" This whole thing was beginning to feel more impossible the longer he went along with it. This was Paris—one of the largest cities in the world—and all they had to go on was a first name, and a pretty common one at that. Did she really think they were going to track him down this way?

"Well, do you know one with black hair and green eyes?" Jenna clarified, undeterred.

"I suppose I do." The waiter frowned. "Order food?" he asked with a sudden curtness, the typical Parisian attitude beginning to surface.

The French may not be known for their outward friendliness, but there was something Connor appreciated about it. They weren't rude, exactly—although some may call them that. It was more like they were authentic. Real. Over the years he'd found that once he got involved in a conversation, they ended up being somewhat friendly, and incredibly kind. They simply didn't have it hanging on the surface all the time. They didn't tend to smile at strangers a lot or make unnecessary small talk. He supposed the same could be said about the people of New Jersey—especially compared to folks that lived in the southern states. It was simply that different cultures had different customs, and in all his travels Connor had learned to appreciate every single one of them by now.

"What time does this Marcel usually come in?" Jenna asked.

The waiter shook his head. "It depends. If he has a job, it doesn't seem to be a steady one. I see him here at all hours."

If he has a job? Connor caught sight of Jenna, and it seemed she'd picked up on the same, concerning words. Although he had been buying flowers for a "client", that still left a lot of room for interpretation. She wasn't chasing after some deadbeat, with no prospects and no ambition, was she? He wondered what would happen if, after all this, she realized this guy wasn't so great. Would her serendipitous dream trump her judgment? Or was she already so convinced this guy was her destiny that she'd be willing to overlook any shortcomings? Those questions caused his jaw to tighten and his head to ache. He placed his forehead into his hand, his elbow propped on the table, and rubbed it.

They slowly sipped their drinks. He cast an eye around the café, appreciating another leisurely moment in Paris. As often as he came here, his time was usually spent running from one end of the city to the other, getting to his hotel, to the airport, and doing it all over again. Most of his meals came from room service or the airport's fast-food restaurants. He was certainly enjoying himself now, though. He was glad he had stayed. Despite his reservations about how this whole thing would turn out, he was happy to be there at that moment.

After they finished their drinks, they continued to stroll aimlessly, afraid to stray too far from the area they knew Marcel frequented, but also wanting to cast a wider net. It was so unlikely they'd find him. And yet he *had* already walked into their path more than once. It wasn't impossible.

"Which way now?" Jenna asked.

"Your guess is as good as mine."

"You pick," she said.

Connor took in a steely breath, then chose an alley at random. They made their way down it, scanning the crowded sidewalks for any signs of Marcel. The narrow street was full of charm and filled with quaint shops and restaurants. Connor inhaled the scent of freshly baked bread and the rich aroma of cheese melting in a fondue pot.

Jenna's steps suddenly stopped, and she inhaled sharply. Connor followed her gaze, his eye landing on the entrance to a shop that appeared straight out of a fairytale. It looked like a perfectly polished dollhouse version of a French bakery. The soft-mint-green storefront was surrounded with heavy swags of pink flowers, and elegant gold lettering spelled out a French name with upscale sophistication. The enormous display windows were filled with confections that resembled priceless pieces of art more than edible desserts. Tiny, round macarons were showcased in neat arrangements, formed into elegant towers, all covered in a beautiful sheen of opulence.

"Wow," Jenna said, staring in the windows.

"You say that word a lot," he said.

"Only here in Paris." She gave him a wink. "Maybe I should start saying 'Ooh, la la' instead," she said with a shimmy of her shoulders.

He chuckled. "Some expressions should be left to the French."

She gave him a playful shove. "Come on." She grabbed his arm and led him through the door.

They entered the shop and Connor's eyes grew large. The air was thick with the scents of sugar and butter, with a hint of caramel and nuts. The walls were lined with shelves full of pastel-green, pink, and lavender boxes, all tied up with white ribbons. Everything was so pretty. So feminine and delicate. It reminded him of the cherry blossoms Jenna loved so much.

Small bistro tables were dotted throughout the café, and Connor headed over to one while Jenna went to check out the offerings. He sat down and took in a long inhale of sweetness. The soft colors shimmered throughout the light-filled space, the crystal chandeliers casting an elegant frost over everything. Like a layer of fresh morning dew spread out over a vibrant garden. It made him think of Jenna's sister's wedding ceremony. He took in another cleansing breath. It felt like spring.

He thought about being a kid at Easter, when his family would get dressed up in their best for church. He'd be forced to wear a seersucker suit with a bowtie, or something similarly ridiculous, his boyishness standing out among the dresses and bows his mom and sister wore. He remembered how they would decorate Easter eggs, blowing out the yokes, before dipping the fragile shells into the soft colors of spring. The same colors that surrounded him now.

Spring had always been his favorite season as a child. He remembered how he and his sister would fly their kites in the early April wind, imagining they were up there too, soaring through the clouds. Look at them now. Both flying, as they'd always imagined. Some dreams did come true, he supposed. He only hoped his wasn't in jeopardy.

Jenna came to the table carrying a pistachio-colored box tied up with a ribbon.

He gave her a look of amusement. "I thought we were here on business."

"I couldn't resist. Plus, we deserve a little break."

He let out a slight cackle. "A break from sipping coffee in cafés, and leisurely strolling the streets of Paris?"

Her face shined with a smile. "It's hard work. We need our fuel."

"Well, if by fuel you mean sugar, count me in."

She sat down and untied the ribbon with delicate precision as if she were unwrapping a very special present, one she knew would undoubtedly delight her. Her eyes widened as she opened the box of macarons.

"What kind did you get?" he asked.

"An assortment."

She held out the box to him, and he picked up one, careful not to ruin the perfection of everything. She set the box in front of her and carefully chose one for herself. Her eyes lit up.

"I love the pink ones." She turned over the tiny, round pastry in her hand. It looked like a doll-sized sandwich, oozing with meringue.

"Are you sure we're supposed to eat these?" he asked.

She nodded, her cheeks glowing. She pinched the pale-pink macaron between her fingers and held it to her lips. She took a careful nibble. Her eyes closed, and she smiled.

Connor popped his into his mouth in one quick motion. It was a bite-sized treat after all. He chewed it twice. The sugary wafer melted in his mouth and was gone in an instant. "Well, that was underwhelming."

"What do you mean?" she asked, her eyes bulging wide.

"Well, they don't taste like much, do they? With all this fanfare and elaborate display"—he motioned around the café—"I was expecting something richer, more flavorful. Like most French desserts. Like crème brûlée or chocolate mousse."

She stared at him, her mouth open in disbelief.

He shrugged. "The flavor is definitely lacking."

"Lacking? What are you talking about?" she craned her neck forward, then straightened up in her chair. "The flavor is perfection. The thing that makes a macaron so special *is* the subtlety. It doesn't have to jump in your face. In fact, it's not supposed to. You're supposed to eat it slowly and savor it, then let the flavor come out and find its way to you. Here, try another one." She held up a finger. "But take your time, don't just pop it in your mouth. In fact . . ." She stood up and grabbed the white cloth napkin from the table in front of her. She shook it out and folded it lengthwise several times. "We're going to do this the right way."

Jenna came up from behind him and wrapped the napkin over his eyes, tying it behind his head to make a blindfold. Her arms wrapped around his shoulders and he felt a flutter of nerves in his core. She leaned over him. He felt her breath against his neck as the soft waves of her hair fell onto his shoulders, and the faint smell of lavender made his heart speed up.

She pulled the napkin tight, then checked for any openings. "OK?"

He nodded, swallowing the lump in his throat.

He heard her return to her chair, then she gently took his hand and placed a macaron into it. Her soft fingers lingered underneath his. "Now, try to identify this one," she said in a soothing voice.

The feel of her hand against his skin made his cheeks grow warm. He carefully pressed the macaron between his fingers and raised the pastry to his mouth for a small nibble. He felt the wafer dissolve against his lips. The sounds and smells from the café disappeared as he focused only on the sweet tang of fresh fruit that radiated over his tongue. Strawberry? No, raspberry, maybe. Maybe, it wasn't a berry at all. It seemed less tart. Sweet, but also complex. He took his time before answering, knowing that patience and attention could uncover the truth.

It reminded him of an exercise he had to complete in pilot training, where he was blindfolded and forced to rely on his instincts to find his way out of a difficult situation—by feel alone. It was a way to make sure he could fly the plane in case of smoke in the cockpit or other visual obstruction. But the way it made him tune into his other senses gave him an entirely different perspective on how to navigate his instruments. It made him more aware of everything that was crucial to the moment, while blocking out the distractions that were not.

"Mango," he finally said with a confident grin as he pulled the napkin from his eyes.

"See?" she cried with excitement. "OK, one more." She clapped her hands with enthusiasm, then motioned for him to put his blindfold back on.

He dutifully did, but then the napkin slipped down.

Jenna got up and walked around behind him again. She pulled it tighter. He felt her body against his back. The smell of her shampoo. The feel of her fingers against his neck. The warmth of her skin against his. He forced himself to direct his attention to the task at hand.

She returned to her chair and placed another macaron in his outstretched hand. He took a tiny bite and let the wafer dissolve on his tongue as before. He narrowed his eyes. The flavor was less sweet but more intense than the last one. He held it to his nose and breathed in the strong, nutty aroma. He took another bite and let the crispy outer layer dissolve against his teeth. His mind instantly went back to the café where they'd sat together in the sun; already feeling nostalgic over something that had happened only moments ago. He felt a warm comfort in his stomach and a kick of excitement in his heart.

"Espresso." He knew that flavor well. The smell would always remind him of Paris. It would always remind him of Jenna.

"Yes!" She stood up and came around behind him, pulling the napkin down from his eyes.

He turned around in his chair to face her and looked up. They held each other's gaze. She blinked, her dark lashes fluttering as he stared into her brown eyes, like the soothing richness of café au lait. His heart hammered against his chest.

Finally, she broke the silence. "Well, we should probably get out there. Keep looking around for Marcel."

He cleared his throat. "Of course."

She closed the box, grabbed her purse, and pushed in her chair.

The buzz of the moment was over before he knew it, and Connor let out a breath of relief. He needed to stop allowing the allure of Paris, and Jenna's attractiveness, to cloud his judgment. As thrilling as those tiny moments were, like smoke in a cockpit, he needed to extinguish the heat and return everything to a safe situation.

He closed his eyes shut and forced his breathing to slow, to steady his lightheadedness. Then he followed Jenna out of the shop so they could continue their ongoing quest for her future husband.

CHAPTER FIFTEEN

Connor

Connor strolled the alleyway beside Jenna, their eyes darting from one side of the street to the other, observing every man who walked past. Jenna stopped in front of a small, cream-colored store with sweet-smelling notes of vanilla drifting out of it and black block lettering that read, *parfumerie.* She wanted to pop in for a minute, and Connor just wanted to stop. His feet were hurting, and he was starving for a decent meal. It seemed as if they'd been surviving for days on only bread, sugar, and caffeine. He scanned the street, searching for a place to grab a hearty bite before ducking into the tiny shop behind Jenna.

Inside, she picked up a perfume bottle and sprayed it onto her wrist, holding up her arm for Connor to smell. He breathed in the floral notes of the fragrance against her skin then immediately turned away, nervously shifting his attention to something else. Backing away from her, he bumped against a table and sent several bottles toppling.

"May I help you?"

Connor knocked over another bottle in a fluster, as if he'd been caught trying to pocket it. He looked up to see a store employee, a woman with platinum-blonde hair swept up in a tight bun, glaring at them.

He cleared his throat. "Um, we were just looking around," he said, unsuccessfully trying to put the bottles back in their proper positions, before bumping over a few more. He forced his pounding heart to settle down. "I mean, um, can you suggest a place for dinner around here?" he asked her.

"Oui." She pointed. "There's a lovely brasserie just down the street. They have an excellent beef bourguignon."

"Any vegetarian options?" he asked, quickly remembering that Jenna didn't eat meat.

"Oui," she said again. "Plenty."

He glanced at Jenna, his eyebrows raised. "What do you say?"

She hesitated. "Dinner?"

"Yeah. Let's get a meal and regroup. We know we're in the right neighborhood. And you never know where he'll pop up."

She tapped her fingernails against the glass table. "OK, I suppose it wouldn't hurt." She set down the bottle of perfume and followed him out of the store.

They continued with their walk further down the alley, this time with a focused destination. "What is a brasserie anyway?" she asked.

He shrugged. "A restaurant?"

"So, what's the difference between a brasserie, a café, a bistro, and a restaurant? They all seem the same to me."

Connor frowned. "Good question. My understanding is that brasserie translates to brewery, although they serve simple, hearty food in addition to beer." The thought of hearty food made his mouth water. "A café is usually for coffees and cocktails, although they also serve food. A bistro is casual dining, and a restaurant is more of a fancy meal."

"So basically, they all serve food and drinks?"

He was thoughtful. "Yes."

"Well then, I'm on board with all of them."

He chuckled. "My thoughts exactly." He placed a hand over his stomach, thinking about what he was going to order. It rumbled in anticipation.

They approached a burgundy-awning-covered entrance and walked into the darkened restaurant. The place was bathed in candlelight, and the scent of black pepper hung in the air. The maître d' led them to a corner where a small table sat in front of one cushioned bench to share. A waitress approached the table, and Jenna ordered an Aperol spritz. Connor did the same.

"It's not a European vacation without one, right?" she said.

"Definitely," he agreed, relieved they wouldn't find themselves alone, at the most romantic table in the restaurant, with another bottle of wine.

He leaned back against the cushioned bench. The warm glow of the candle in the center of the table swayed softly against the burgundy tablecloth. It didn't matter what heading the establishment fell under, every eatery in Paris was full of unique charm. This one felt more formal, with a touch of glamour; there were no open windows leading to the outside patio, like most of the places they'd been to, instead everything was cozy and enclosed. Intimate. Romantic.

He shook the thought from his head, reminding himself to remain in control. He looked around the restaurant, his eye landing on a man sitting alone at a nearby table. It took him a second to place the familiar face, his brain having transitioned into relaxation mode. It quickly switched back, and his eyes flew open.

Jenna gasped beside him as she recognized the man at the same instant. "Connor, it's him!"

Connor squeezed his eyes shut and rubbed them, then opened them again to take another look. Was it *really*? Was it possible they were both imagining him? A mirage, of sorts? He squinted through the darkness, not quite able to believe what he saw.

Jenna's mouth hung open. She also closed her eyes and then took a slow, shaky breath. She shook her head as if she simply couldn't believe it. "Connor, this is incredible. There can be absolutely no doubt about it now. Of all the restaurants, of all times!?" She balled up her fists and jiggled them next to her face. "Fate is leading me to him. I can feel it."

Even Connor couldn't argue with that. It did seem extremely unlikely that this was all a mere coincidence at this point. He bit his lip. "Jenna, I'm beginning to think you're right."

She quickly ran her hands through her hair and adjusted her waves so they fell in front of her shoulders. She held her lips together and wiggled them against each other. She glanced over at Marcel, sitting alone with his meal, completely unaware he was being watched.

"This is it." She shook out her hands. "I'm finally going to meet him," she squealed.

Connor smiled and nodded, relieved they had finally found Marcel again. He let out a long breath of gratitude that he hadn't ruined everything by falling asleep at the

Ritz. He never would have forgiven himself if she'd given up because of that. And if he felt this vindicated now, he could only imagine how he'd feel when Jenna and Marcel actually ended up together. Falling asleep at the Ritz paled in comparison to what he really needed to be let off the hook for.

Jenna stood and quickly pulled off her jacket. She smoothed out the white blouse underneath, then made one last adjustment to her hair. She took a few steps toward Marcel's table, then stopped and looked back at Connor. He gave her a nod of encouragement. She bit her lip and continued. Connor watched, elbows on the table, his chin resting on the back of his hands. His jaw firmed, and he held his breath.

"Jenna!" a loud voice boomed through the quiet restaurant, forcing them to whip their heads around.

Jenna inhaled sharply. "Mom?"

CHAPTER SIXTEEN

Jenna

Deena's arms wrapped around Jenna and pulled her tightly into her chest. Jenna's eyes, full of shock and confusion, remained unblinking, pressed against her mother's neck. She glanced over to where Marcel sat at his table, her presence still completely unnoticed by him.

"I thought you two had left already," her mom said, pulling back to look at her. Deena wiggled the fingers of one hand in greeting at Connor, who sat watching, bewildered, from their corner table.

Jenna let out a nervous laugh through her teeth. "Yeah, well, we ended up deciding to stay a little longer, after all."

"I don't blame you," her mom squealed. "Paris has a way of pulling you in, doesn't it?"

Jenna stared at her parents in complete disbelief over the unfortunate timing. She felt her stomach grow queasy, and she placed a hand over it. "Hi, Dad," she said, having no idea how to proceed. Her future husband was within feet of her on one side, while her fake boyfriend was on the other. Her meddling mother, in true fashion, was in the middle of it all. Jenna's lips clamped together, and her breathing quickened. She needed to get them out of there. But how?

Deena clapped her hands together. "I'm so glad we ran into you. Let's have dinner together."

Jenna's eyes opened wide with panic. She shook her head quickly. "Oh, no, we were just about to leave."

Her mom waved the statement away with the flick of a wrist. "Nonsense, it looks like you just got fresh drinks delivered," she said as the waitress showed up with their Aperol spritzes.

Jenna grumbled inwardly, taking back everything good she'd said about fate. Of course things were going *too* smoothly. Of course it couldn't last. Fate had to throw something devastating in the way at the last second. It always did.

"I'll go tell the waitress we'll be four tonight," her mom said. "This is a lovely table. I'm sure they can pull two more chairs up." She tried to spot someone to help.

Joe, never one to wait on an employee for something he could do himself, pulled two chairs from an unoccupied table and set them up across from Connor.

"Dad, I don't think they want you to—"

"It's fine," her mom said with another flick of the wrist.

Jenna stared at Connor, her eyes still panicked. He only looked back at her with an equally helpless expression, then shook his head with wide eyes.

She stole a glance at Marcel. He was *finally* within reach. At a cozy, romantic table for two. All alone. And there was absolutely nothing she could do about it. She squeezed her eyes shut and forced herself to return to her seat at the corner table. She reluctantly scooted in beside Connor, trying to communicate her anguish to him without her parents knowing. He gave her a tight grin of sympathy, probably realizing he was as powerless as her in the situation. Pain developed in her throat, and she propped up her head on her closed fist as she felt the pressure of time working against her.

"So, what have you two been doing in the city the past couple days?" Joe asked.

"It is romantic, isn't it?" her mom interjected before Jenna could answer.

Thankfully, Connor spoke first, chatting away, giving her parents a rundown of the things they'd seen in the city. Jenna was grateful for him occupying their attention so she could tune out the conversation and keep her focus on Marcel. She angled her body in his direction, and her eyes darted back over to him. He leisurely ate his meal, picking up his glass of wine to take a sip. Then he wiped his mouth with a napkin, then took another small bite of food.

Her mom and dad gabbed away incessantly about the sightseeing they'd been doing. Jenna nodded along, acting as if she was listening with interest. She forced herself to keep her eyes directed at them, glancing behind them every so often to check on Marcel.

If only he would look up. If only he'd glance in her direction and meet her eye. If only she could smile at him, give him a chance to see her, like he had when they'd locked eyes on the street. Or at the flower market, before he'd hopped into the car. She yearned to be properly noticed by him. For him to come over and approach *her*. But with a faux boyfriend and two parents at her table, she knew it was impossible. Why was she always so close, yet so far away? He was just within reach, but unable to be grasped.

She let out a hard sigh of irritation then quickly noticed she'd done it out loud. She covered it up, pretending to have laughed at something Connor said. After an appropriate amount of time feigning interest in the conversation again, she let her eye wander back in Marcel's direction. She willed him to look up at her.

Instead, she felt her mother's narrowed eyes on her, as if they were burning through her skin.

Deena turned around in her chair to see what Jenna was looking at. "Something else got your interest?" she asked.

"No," Jenna said a little too quickly. "Just admiring the restaurant. It's beautiful." She swallowed, forcing herself to return her attention to the table, and to Connor in particular. She moved in closer to him, acting as if she adored him. It was becoming easier to do, she had to admit. They had grown more comfortable around each other, and it no longer felt like the elaborate show they'd performed at the wedding. Even so, this was the worst moment imaginable to have to keep up the act. She stared at Marcel, then quickly looked away.

Her mom pursed her lips, reading the menu in front of her. Jenna's attention slowly diverted back over her shoulder. This time, her dad turned around to see what she was looking at. Her mother's gaze soon followed, landing on Marcel, and she instantly turned around to give Jenna a pointed look. She let out a judgmental release of air and raised her eyebrows in warning as a tsking sound came from her throat.

Connor noticed and took Jenna by the hand to bring her back to reality—or to fake reality—as the waitress returned for their orders. Jenna asked for a salad, unwilling to commit any time to picking out something more creative. Connor wrapped his large hand around hers and gave it a squeeze of sympathy. She felt a tingle course through her body. Her hand fit so nicely in his, so warm and cozy. So safe. Like this little corner table. If only it were just the two of them still. If only the evening hadn't been hijacked by her parents. She shook her head, trying to regain control of her focus. Connor wasn't actually her boyfriend. Clearly the ruse was beginning to rub off on her a little if she felt as if their date had been crashed. She internally ridiculed the absurdity of her current mindset.

"You two are so romantic," her mom said, seeming to read her face. Deena picked up a butter knife and clinked the side of her empty wine glass.

Jenna stared, her eyebrows pinching together as her mom continued to quietly clink away, not saying a word. Jenna met Connor's eye. He frowned, letting go of her hand to stir his drink.

"What are you doing?" she finally asked her mom.

"You know, the tradition of clinking on a glass to get a bride and groom to kiss. We did it at your sister's wedding, remember?"

Jenna shook her head and squinted her eyes in confusion. "Mom, we're not at a wedding. Do you see a bride and groom anywhere?"

"Not yet." She gave a sly nudge to Jenna's dad and bobbed her head at him with wide eyes to encourage him to join in. He let out a chuckle and started to tap his knife against his glass too. "You know your mom and these traditions," he said with a slight roll of the eyes.

Jenna felt her stomach drop to the floor at the realization of what her mom wanted her to do. Her cheeks grew hot, and she placed a hand against one. "You mean us?" she asked in horror, motioning between her and Connor with a wagging index finger.

Her mom practically bounced in her seat, eyes shining while still clinking away. She wasn't going to stop, and people were beginning to turn their heads. Marcel didn't, though. He continued to eat his meal, unaware.

"Right here?" Jenna asked, her face now growing pale.

"What better place than Paris to kiss your boyfriend in the middle of a restaurant?"

"Mom, I don't think—"

Deena dropped the knife onto the table with a thud, startling them all. She threw a glance behind her, at Marcel, and folded her arms across her chest. "Well, Jenna, I don't think it's appropriate—"

A hand appeared under Jenna's chin. Before her mother could say anything else, Connor turned to Jenna, gently grabbed her face, and brought it closer. His lips parted slightly as he leaned in. Was he really going to ...

She pushed the hesitation from her mind, realizing it was too late to stop it. She closed her eyes and allowed her mouth to connect with his. Her firm lips instantly melted, tingling with excitement. No, it was more than a tingle. It was a full-blown electric spark. It felt like the first time she'd seen the Eiffel Tower, glittering at night and electrifying her entire soul. She breathed in the clean scent of his clothes and the faint aroma of Aperol on his breath as the kiss deepened. Her head spun with a thrilling dizziness, and he grazed a light hand against her cheek that matched the tenderness of his lips.

No. She pulled back, her heart pounding, eyes wide and her head light. She put a hand against his chest and pushed him away gently. "I think that's good," she said, disengaging with a nervous laugh. She reached for her drink and took a long sip.

Connor nodded, straightening in his seat. He gazed at her with unblinking blue eyes that glowed against the candlelight. Her mind reeled from the intense pleasure she'd felt from that kiss. She pulled back further and scooted away from him. She looked down at her lap and swallowed. Yes, there was undoubtedly a spark. But like the one that had damaged the Notre-Dame, this one had the potential for disaster as well.

Her mom smiled with approval. She held a hand to her heart and sighed. "So romantic. Don't you think, Joe?"

"Mm-hmm," her dad replied, putting on his reading glasses to peruse the wine list.

Jenna raised her head and stared at Connor, not quite realizing what had happened. He returned her gaze with an expression she couldn't easily read. His cheeks were pink. She gave him a slight smile of gratitude, thankful he'd saved her bacon in front of her mother—again. Still, she couldn't understand the heat behind that kiss. Where had it come from? Had he felt it too? Surely not. He was only doing her a favor. Saving her once again from the wrath of her mother's judgment. She didn't need to read too much into it.

Even so, she couldn't get her mind off the feeling that now swam in the pit of her stomach. It was like the one she'd had when he'd almost kissed her at the wedding. As if something wonderful was about to happen. Only this time, it *had* happened. She eyed him carefully, then looked away, too timid to meet his gaze. She wished she knew what was going through his head, but his face wasn't giving anything away as he resumed the small talk with her parents. Just then, he looked over at her with a wink. She let out a breath of relief. Yes. Good. It had only been part of the act. It hadn't been real.

She blinked the disbelief of the moment from her eyes and forced herself back to the true mission at hand. She turned her head and returned her focus to Marcel's table. Her eyebrows flew up. No. It couldn't be. He was gone.

The table had been cleared entirely, a waiter already getting it ready for the next party. How could she have taken her eyes off him for that long? How could she have let herself get distracted by that kiss? That pretend, meaningless kiss.

Wasn't it?

Jenna closed her eyes in pain, wondering how she could have been so stupid. Once again, she had let her true destiny slip through her fingers.

CHAPTER SEVENTEEN

Connor

Connor stepped out of the hotel the next morning, motivated and ready to take on the day. He took a brisk walk to the metro station and descended the stairs, waiting for the train that would take him to the part of the city he needed to go.

In an early morning text, he had told Jenna he planned to spend the day alone—that he had some personal stuff to catch up on. It was true. He did need to take care of those mundane tasks he usually completed when he was between trips: pay some bills, return phone calls. It was typical for a Tuesday, when he wasn't flying.

What he *didn't* mention to Jenna was the lead he'd gotten as they'd left the restaurant the night before. She'd been so excited to see Marcel there, only to be let down in the end—again. He didn't think he could stand to watch the optimism on her face give way to disappointment one more time. He would track down this one alone.

Besides, it was probably a good idea for them to have a little space from each other for a day. A cooling-off period. After that kiss last night he felt more confused than ever about what he was doing there. Sure, the only reason he had kissed her was to throw her mom off the scent of the fake relationship. It was a spontaneous, necessary move. A quick-thinking judgment call to save Jenna from having to explain why she was staring at another man.

Even so, he hadn't expected a fake kiss to feel so real. And he certainly hadn't expected it to complicate his feelings as much as it had. He couldn't help but wonder whether he was truly doing the right thing in helping her with this search for another man. Was he making everything more confusing by involving himself? Maybe he was proving to be a distraction more than anything else. He rubbed his temples as he considered a serious question: Was he simply doing, again, what he hated himself for doing in the first place—sticking his nose where it didn't belong?

And yet he'd made Jenna a promise, and he was determined to see it through. It was about time he tracked down this guy once and for all and then stepped back from the entire thing.

Connor boarded the train and found an empty seat. He leaned his head back and closed his eyes. His thoughts drifted to that night, six months ago—to that fateful conversation with Luke that set everything in motion. The heedless interference that was responsible for Jenna's heartbreak.

IT WAS A LATE-AUTUMN EVENING, and Connor had just returned from a long trip and was ready for bed. As he pulled his flight bag up the walkway to his front door, a figure caught his attention out of the corner of his eye. He glanced over to see Luke sitting on Jenna's front porch, the glow of the overhead light casting his shadow ominously against the ground. His elbows were on his knees, and his face was in his hands.

"Hey, Luke. You OK?" Connor yelled to him.

Luke didn't look up. He only shook his head to indicate that he wasn't.

Connor frowned and left his bag on the doorstep, stepping over the leaf-filled lawn to get to Jenna's porch. He pulled up a chair beside Luke and sat down. Although Connor had been friends with Luke for a couple of years, he had never known him to be particularly morose like this. He liked Luke. He was easy to talk to, fun to watch a game with, and Connor had had a blast at his bachelor party the previous weekend.

"What's going on?" Connor said. He mimicked Luke's body language, turned to look at him, and waited.

Luke dragged his hands through his blond, floppy hair, then viewed Connor with a pained expression. "I don't know what to do. The wedding is next week."

Connor felt a slight burn develop in his stomach. He had no idea what Luke would say next, but he already knew it had to be serious if it involved the wedding. "What do you mean?" He cleared his throat. "What's going on?" he asked again.

Luke opened his mouth, but nothing came out. He hung his head instead.

"Is everything OK with Jenna?" Connor asked.

"I think . . . well, it's not that I'm having second thoughts, exactly." Luke let out a groan. "Or maybe I am. I don't know."

Connor's eyes flew open. "Oh. I see," he said calmly, trying to hide his shock. He quickly realized this wasn't going to be a brief conversation. He was exhausted and ready to go to sleep, but he let out a long stream of air, taking the focus off himself and putting it back where it needed to be—on Luke. "Well, I think some last-minute jitters are normal," he said.

Luke remained quiet. His eyes held a glassy stare.

"Aren't they?" Connor asked.

Luke continued to stare into the darkness as if he wanted to be anywhere but there. "I don't know. I'm finding myself rethinking my entire future."

Connor rubbed an eyebrow. "Wow. Um, have you talked to Jenna about this?"

Luke shook his head.

"Maybe you need to . . ." He stopped himself. Connor had no idea *what* Luke needed to do. He did know that if anyone knew how to handle this situation, it would be Jenna. After all, she was a relationship therapist. Who better to handle whatever was going on in Luke's brain than her? On the other hand, what was she supposed to do once she held the knowledge that her fiancé was having doubts about marrying her next week? It wasn't exactly something she would forget once Luke came back to his senses.

Connor waited for him to say something else.

"Luke?"

His friend only shrugged, as if he couldn't be bothered to answer with any actual words.

Connor gave him a pointed glare. "Well, if you aren't entirely sure, then you probably shouldn't be getting married," he snapped, trying to startle Luke out of the grumbling attitude and into a response. He wasn't sure what had caused his sudden annoyance, especially when Luke was clearly struggling, but he couldn't figure out why he seemed so distraught, especially when he was about to get *married*. To a great girl. No, to an amazing girl. He had everything he could possibly want, right there at his fingertips. It seemed to Connor as if Luke didn't appreciate what a good thing he had.

Luke looked at him, his eyes wide. "Really?"

Connor stared back at him in disbelief. He scoffed. "Yeah. Really." He couldn't believe Luke was being so obtuse. He also couldn't believe he was having these thoughts at all. Especially now, when he and Jenna had been together for *years*. Connor rubbed the back of his neck, his frustration growing with his friend's attitude.

Luke was quiet as he looked out to the dark night sky. "You mean, cancel the wedding?"

Connor's jaw firmed. "Forever is a big commitment, Luke. And if you're not excited about getting married, then . . . maybe you're simply not ready for it." Sure, he may have been using a bit of reverse psychology, trying to get Luke to see what a ridiculous, immature ingrate he was being. He figured some tough love would go further than sympathy in this case. But it was also true. Jenna deserved better than this. She deserved someone who couldn't *wait* to marry her. Didn't every bride deserve that?

He knew Luke well enough to know that these doubts weren't going to stop him from marrying Jenna. They were simply poorly communicated, last-minute nerves coming out, and he just needed a jarring reminder of what he'd be losing if he indulged them.

Luke appeared to be lost in thought, as if his mind were

up there swirling around in the stars that glowed above their heads, a million miles away from Earth.

Finally, he responded. "You're right. Thanks, Connor."

CONNOR SHUDDERED as he relived it all in his mind. How could Luke have done it? Never in Connor's wildest dreams could he have imagined that Luke would break up with Jenna the very next day, with no explanation, other than that he was moving to Seattle for a job—without her. Surely Connor's harsh words would have opened Luke's eyes to realizing his love for Jenna. A love he was in jeopardy of taking for granted, and a bright future he was at risk of throwing away. At least that's what Connor had assumed would happen.

He'd heard the gossip that had poured out through some of their mutual friends in the days that followed the announcement of the canceled wedding. Connor had listened to it all, tight-lipped and racked with guilt. It was rumored that Luke had told Jenna that "forever is a big commitment," as if he'd only realized that fact recently. Connor's very words used in the most appalling way imaginable. His advice the justification behind it all. The rationale for Luke having broken Jenna's heart, leaving her completely devastated and utterly confused.

They had been careless words—flippant advice—given when Connor was exhausted from a long flight and not thinking clearly. He'd been kicking himself over it for the past six months. Agonizing over everything he'd said. And hadn't said.

Perhaps he should have told Luke it was simply a case of cold feet—nothing to worry about, and certainly no reason to call off a wedding. Better yet, he should have kept his mouth shut. Perhaps Luke and Jenna could have worked it out. Instead, it ended in the most unfair way imaginable to Jenna. And he had gotten pulled into it. Just as he had now, he seemed to always find a way to mess things up.

He knew she had no idea that he and Luke had ever spoken that night. She never knew about their conversation —the missing piece. He also knew that if she ever found out, she would never speak to him again. And he wouldn't blame her.

Connor's thoughts returned to the present. He couldn't stop now. He sat up straighter in his train seat. He was more determined than ever to track down Marcel. For Jenna's happiness. For his remittal. He turned his attention back to the mission at hand and reviewed in his mind the information he'd learned as they'd left the restaurant last night—the lead he was now determined to follow through.

AFTER DINNER, Connor had run back inside after they'd left the restaurant, leaving Jenna and her parents on the sidewalk, claiming he'd left something behind on the table. Instead, he'd hurried over to the maître d' and asked him for the full name of the man sitting at Marcel's table earlier. The man claimed ignorance and refused to accommodate Connor's next request—looking up his credit card transaction—dismissing him with a quick swat at the air. As he walked away, Connor stole a glance at the iPad that sat atop the hostess stand, showing the online reservations for that evening. He quickly scanned the list of names. Suddenly, he saw it: Marcel Marchand, table for one.

He hadn't wanted to say anything to Jenna about it

though. He needed to do a little more research first. He needed to find out who this Marcel Marchand *really* was.

After dinner, he'd spent the remainder of the evening alone in his hotel room searching the internet for *Marcel Marchand Paris*. He quickly found Marcel's name listed on a website for a photography business. A deep dive of the website, along with a social media account that went with it, verified it was indeed him—their Marcel. *Jenna's* Marcel. Unfortunately, Connor couldn't find much information about his personal life, but he did discover that his photography business was shooting an event at the Tuileries Garden the next day. And *that* was where the train was headed that morning.

Connor had no idea whether Marcel would be there or not, which is why he'd decided to leave Jenna out of it. That, and he needed to do some vetting first. Sure, he'd had a quick conversation with the man at the flower market, but he needed to know more about this guy before telling Jenna he'd found her dream man. He got out at the stop indicated on his map and climbed the stairs to the street. He rounded a corner and walked several blocks.

Acres of pristinely manicured gardens welcomed Connor, the awe-inspiring splendor of the Louvre looming impressively behind them. A grand, round basin of water radiated with the cool fluidity of a bubbling fountain. People sat in chairs surrounding it, watching the ducks wander about. Tourists leisurely strolled the walkways that weaved through the gardens, and couples picnicked on blankets spread over the lush green lawn.

He breathed in the scent of freshly cut grass and scanned the area, eyes peeled for something that resembled an event. A white tent, or chairs set up somewhere, maybe.

He only hoped he wasn't too early. He decided to grab a seat by the pond and wait for Marcel to show up. He stretched out his legs in front of him and leaned his head back. The sun warmed his face, and he closed his eyes, enjoying a light breeze as it blew past. He opened his eyes and stared off toward the Louvre. He thought about asking Jenna if she'd like to visit it with him before they left. He'd been before, and he'd always thought that once was enough. But looking at it now, he realized how much he wanted to share it with her.

His eye landed on a tall man bending over a row of daffodils, a large camera covering his face. Connor sat up straight in his seat. He narrowed his eyes and thought he recognized that head of black hair they'd been chasing for days. He stood up and headed towards the photographer with caution. The man was snapping away with his camera, but when he glanced up Connor caught a glimpse of his face. It was him.

Connor stepped over the grass carefully and cleared his throat. "Hi, um. Marcel, was it?" he said, trying to appear as nonchalant as he could manage while his heart sped up.

Marcel turned. He frowned, obviously trying to place Connor's face. "Yes?" he said, his forehead wrinkled.

"I'm Connor," he said. "We met the other day."

Marcel raised an eyebrow.

"At the flower market," Connor clarified.

Marcel gave a nervous chuckle. "Oh, yeah, nice to see you again," he said in his thick French accent. He picked up his camera and went back to snapping photos of the flowers, moving further away.

"So, um, I'm glad I ran into you again," Connor continued, following behind him.

"And why is that?" Marcel asked, not looking up.

Connor cleared his throat again. "Well, I have this friend."

Marcel raised his head and lowered his camera. He eyed Connor.

"And she would like to meet you," Connor said. He cringed at the awkward sound of his voice. "I was wondering if you'd like to have dinner with her tonight."

Marcel stared at him, probably trying to figure out if he was serious. "No, I don't think so," he finally said.

Connor clenched his jaw and drew in a breath through his nose. "It's just that she, my friend—"

"Your friend?" Marcel asked, studying Connor with a look of scrutiny.

Connor's eyes got big. "Oh, no, really, it *is* for my friend. I promise. In fact, she was at the flower market the other day. Remember?"

Marcel narrowed his eyes.

"Anyway, she wanted to meet you then, but—"

"That woman in the lavender dress?" Marcel dropped his camera, letting it fall around his neck by the strap. He observed Connor, his face tight.

"Mm-hmm."

A slight smile crept over Marcel's mouth. "She wants to meet me?"

"She does, yes."

"Ah," he said, with a lift of an eyebrow. "I remember her. She was beautiful."

Connor nodded in agreement.

Marcel looked as if he was considering it with a tilt of his head. "Well, I'm flattered, but . . . I don't know."

"Just a quick dinner. My treat."

Marcel considered him under a skeptical brow. "And

what is your relationship with this woman? That is not your girlfriend?"

"No, no I'm only a friend." He held up his hands, waving his palms in front of him.

Marcel inspected him with a curious glare. "And how is it that we happened to run into each other again? Have you been following me, Connor?"

"Of course not," he lied, with a casual scoff at the ridiculousness of the idea. He noticed his breathing had become shallow, and he tugged at the collar of his shirt. "I guess you and I hang out around the same places." He chewed the inside of his cheek and held his breath to see if the Frenchman would buy it. "We're both flower lovers."

Marcel crossed his arms with a tight expression.

"Look, I get it, this is kind of strange. But Jenna really wants to meet you. Attraction just works like that. Or at least that's what she tells me."

Marcel couldn't seem to stop the smile that was deepening on his face. "Ah, she was that attracted to me, huh?"

Connor rolled his eyes. He suddenly had an overwhelming urge to punch this guy in his perfect face, but he refrained. What was it about French men that made them so flirtatious? It was as if everything they said in that exotic accent of theirs was a dripping line of romantic poetry used to attract women. He pressed his lips together and nodded with a pasted-on grin. "Mm-hmm."

Marcel's eyes held a bit of intrigue.

"So, what do you say?" Connor asked. "Will you meet her?"

Marcel squinted at him, trying one last time to uncover any hidden motives.

Connor looked back at him with pleading eyes.

Marcel looked down at his watch. "I'll be finished here tonight at six o'clock," he said.

Connor balled up his fists in excitement. He could already imagine the look of delight on Jenna's face when she showed up to dinner to find her surprise date. Finally, it was all working out the way it was supposed to.

CHAPTER EIGHTEEN

Jenna

With Connor off doing his own thing for the day, Jenna decided to take up some sightseeing. She figured she may as well explore the city while she was there. She needed a day off from trying to track down Marcel. A day to reset. To think about everything. She couldn't help but wonder about the *real* reason Connor wanted to spend the day alone. Maybe he thought they'd been getting a bit too close lately, and maybe he was right. Or perhaps, he was spending the day with a girl—the one he'd been thrilled to talk to at the café the other day. She pushed the idea from her head, refusing to go down that road of twisted jealousy; however, she was wrought with confusion over that kiss at dinner the night before. It was probably a good thing, for both of them, to have a little time apart.

She and Connor had made plans to meet up later for dinner, so she'd satisfy her nosy curiosity then. For now, she had the day to herself. She walked along the streets of the 7th arrondissement, gazing at the app on her phone that showed her the city's intricate layout, dotted with red stars to identify landmarks.

She gazed up at the Eiffel Tower. In the afternoon light, its iron glistened with a rose-gold tint. The sun's glare reflected off the tower, making it look like a glittery piece of jewelry. It was funny how the same landmark could look so different, depending on the time of day. Depending on the different light that hit it. The bronzed, iron-latticed tower she gazed at was so unlike the bright, sparkling tower it became at night. But it was just as beautiful.

She made a quick decision to take a trip up and she hurried, her excitement to see it up close growing the nearer she came. She reached the base of the tower and felt a rush of energy, jogging to get underneath it. She stood in the center and threw back her head, then turned in a slow circle, gazing upward. Her arms spread out as she reveled in the expansive space of one of the world's most iconic structures. It was magnificent. She looked up, her eyes narrowing through the climbing steel that appeared to go all the way up to the sky. She pulled out her phone and tried to take a selfie in front of it, but quickly grew frustrated trying to get the tower in the background. She was entirely too close to get a proper shot.

She hopped in line to buy a ticket for a ride up in the elevator.

"To the top, or to the second-level observation deck?" the attendant asked when it was her turn.

"Oh, uh." Jenna shut her eyes, thinking about how high the tower climbed, and shuddered at the idea of being all the way up at the top. "Second level," she replied, acknowledging her slight fear of heights.

She joined the elevator queue with a crowd of people, and once in a car she gazed outside as she was eventually lifted higher over the city. She stepped out of the elevator and cast a glance around. Iron surrounded her and tourists shuffled about—taking pictures, sipping drinks in the café, and shopping for souvenirs in the gift shop. She walked over to the edge of the observation deck and clenched her teeth as her eye landed on Paris from above. She swallowed a nervous lump. This may be considered the *second* level, but she felt as if she was miles above the ground.

She forced herself to relax as she gazed at the city below; a sea of Parisian architecture sprawled across dozens of square miles. She could see the River Seine winding its way through the city and the bridges that connected one end to the other. She gazed at the stone pillars that made up the Arc de Triomphe. The glass pyramid of the Louvre shined in the distance, surrounded by its iconic palace walls. The cloudless sky gave way to a perfect ray of sunshine that sent a shimmer of radiance across the entire city.

"Wow," she said out loud.

A woman beside her turned in her direction. "Pretty amazing, huh?" she said in an American accent.

"It sure is," Jenna said, her eyes glued to the view.

"Your first time up here?"

"Yeah," Jenna said, with a quick glance and a polite smile.

The woman pointed ahead. "It gives you a whole new perspective on things, doesn't it? Seeing it from up here?"

"Yeah," Jenna said again, in barely a whisper, her eyes wide and staring out at the city.

"You look at all those people down there and it makes

you realize just how small we are in the grand scheme of things."

Jenna's thoughts jumped to Marcel. He was down there, somewhere. This woman was right. Jenna hadn't realized just how big this city really was, and how many people were out there running around it. What were the odds that she would find him—again?

"It's like finding a needle in a haystack," she said to herself.

"Excuse me?" the woman asked.

Jenna blinked and shook her head. She turned to the woman, who looked to be about her mother's age, petite, with short blonde hair and a green sweater. "Oh, I've been looking for someone, here in the city," she explained. "Seeing it from this perspective makes me realize how impossible it probably is that I'll ever find him."

"Ah. Looking for love?" the woman asked.

Jenna gave a shy smile and a slightly guilty nod.

The woman gave her a soft, understanding smile in return. "I'm Ellie," she said, throwing her backpack over one shoulder.

"Jenna," she replied, shaking the woman's hand.

Ellie raised her eyebrows and gazed out at the city. "On the other hand, look."

Jenna looked.

"See *how* many people are down there? You're bound to find one that's a good match."

Jenna let out a breath. "That's just it. I don't want to find one. I want to find *the* one, but sometimes I wonder if that idea is just a fantasy. A spell I seem to have been under since coming to this city."

Ellie laughed. "Paris can do that to you. But it's worth consideration, I suppose. You won't know if you don't try."

Jenna chuckled. "My friend, Connor, says the same thing." A wide smile spread across her face as she thought of him. She peered down below, feeling her cheeks grow warm. "He's down there somewhere too. He came to Paris with me."

Ellie watched her, as if she were paying close attention. "Well, what about this friend, Connor, who seems to make you smile like that? Any reason he isn't the one?"

Jenna waved her off. "Oh, no, Connor is just a friend. I've never looked at him in that way." *Until that kiss last night.* She buried the thought. "Besides, he's a friend of my ex, and it's all extremely messy."

Ellie frowned, as if she wasn't convinced.

"It's complicated, trust me. Besides, I've known Connor for years," Jenna continued. "If we were meant to be together, if he were *the one*, it would have happened by now. That's how fate works, right?"

Ellie scrunched up her nose. "Maybe. But sometimes you need to nudge it along a little too. Do things to encourage it. Put in some effort. Love doesn't simply fall into your lap, after all."

Jenna laughed at the absurd irony of being schooled on the very idea she had lectured a room full of people on only days ago. She knew that truth better than anyone else. Even so, she'd found herself examining everything through a different lens these days, even love. Maybe her sister *had* been right all along: When you know, you know. If that was the case, all that time Jenna had spent trying to make things work with Luke had just been— wrong?

Ellie continued, seeming to read Jenna's mind. "Sometimes all we need is a change in perspective to see the truth. Sometimes it's time to look at something differently, from a new vantage point, and your eyes will be opened in ways they weren't before."

Jenna swallowed. "You mean Connor?"

Ellie shrugged and gave her a kind smile.

Jenna was silent, thoughtful as she gazed at the tiny people below, scattering about like ants. She wondered where Connor was right now, what he was doing, *who* he was doing it with. She shook the thoughts from her head. What was wrong with her, anyway? She needed to be thinking about where Marcel was, not Connor. She couldn't get sidetracked now, and this conversation with Ellie only reinforced it. After all those coincidental sightings of Marcel, she had no doubt that fate was driving this entire experience. And yet maybe it was time to nudge it along a little too. Yes, she needed to stay focused and keep her eye on the goal. She was not going to let her feelings, as confusing as they may be, get in the way of who she was truly meant to be with. Fate had been clear as day with that dream. It was time for her to find Marcel once and for all.

JENNA HURRIED her steps as she made her way to the restaurant near their hotel where she'd planned to meet Connor for dinner. The night air was warm and breezy. She glanced down at her watch, realizing she was running late. After a day of sightseeing, a quick nap, and a long shower, Jenna couldn't wait to catch up with Connor again and come up with their next plan to track down Marcel.

She thought again about what Ellie had said, about how love didn't simply fall into your lap. She was absolutely right, and it was crucial that Jenna didn't lose focus on that. It made her realize it was time to ramp up her efforts.

She opened the door to the tiny bistro and was hit by a draft of warm air and freshly baked bread. She took in a long inhale and smiled.

"Bonjour," the hostess said.

"Bonjour. I'm meeting someone. He's probably already here."

"Your name?"

"Jenna Westbrook."

"Ah yes," she said. "He's right over here." The woman led Jenna around the corner to a small table for two near an open window.

Jenna gave a half glance at Connor, sitting there waiting for her. Then she did a double take. She froze, and her heart stopped. Her eyes grew big, and her jaw dropped to the floor. It wasn't Connor. Her mouth flew open as she stared at the man looking back at her. She was looking into the glistening green eyes of Marcel. He sat at the table and looked right at her with his gorgeous smile. *He* had been waiting for her.

It had happened. Love had fallen into her lap.

CHAPTER NINETEEN

Jenna

"Hi . . . hello . . . bonjour," Jenna stammered, unsure of what to do next. Her eyes darted frantically around the restaurant, unsure where to fix them. Was this really happening? She pinched the side of her leg to ensure she was truly awake.

Marcel stood from his chair and walked around the table to greet her. He leaned in, taking her by the elbows, and kissed her on one cheek, and then the other. "Jenna, I am Marcel, and it's lovely to meet you," he said in a solid, very attractive French accent.

She stared at him, her heart racing and her body growing warm. "But what . . . who . . . how?"

He smirked at her. "Your friend, Connor. He set this up."

Her eyes grew wide. "He did? But, how?"

He only shrugged.

She let out a nervous giggle, smoothing down her cotton dress, relieved she'd changed out of the jeans she'd been in all day. She raked through the ends of her hair nervously, then tossed them behind her shoulder.

He pulled out her chair for her. She sat down and wiped her sweaty palms against her napkin as she laid it in her lap and waited for him to sit down across from her. She couldn't believe it. They were actually on a date! She gazed at him, her lashes giving way to an involuntary flutter. She leaned forward in her seat, her eyes wide with excitement.

"Wine?" he asked, picking up the bottle.

Her head bobbed, and she let out another slight giggle as he poured some into her glass. *Calm down, Jenna, play it cool.* She cleared her throat. "Well, I'm not sure what Connor told you, but—"

Marcel held up his hand. "He told me that you were interested in meeting me and, I have to say, at first I was unsure." He poured some wine into his glass. "But I noticed you at the flower market too."

"You did?" Her eyes grew wide, and her heart raced. She wanted to ask if he remembered her crashing into him on the street also, but didn't, remembering how mad he'd been and not wanting to complicate things.

He nodded and smiled again, that gorgeous left eyebrow drooping ever so slightly, just as it had in her dream.

She snuck a slight lick of her lips. "So tell me about yourself," she said, then immediately cringed at the high-pitched tone of her voice. She sounded as if she was on a job interview more than a date. "I mean, where are you from?" she said with more ease.

"I'm from Paris," he said as if it was obvious.

"Oh. Have you lived here all your life?"

"Yes." He picked up his menu and looked it over.

She placed her hands gently on the table and stared at them, trying to conjure up her best first-date conversation starters.

"And you?" he finally asked.

"Oh, um, I'm from New Jersey."

He regarded her answer with a face of disgust. "Oh, I'm sorry."

She sniggered. "Why? It's lovely there."

"I've been." He frowned. "I guess we'll agree to disagree on that one."

Jenna felt a sting in her heart she couldn't ignore. She wasn't sure why her home state always got a bad rap. Sure, there were parts of New Jersey that were crowded, smelly, and a perpetual concrete construction zone. But that wasn't *her* Jersey. Jenna grew up in the most beautiful part of the Garden State, full of farmstands and horse pastures, and the most wonderful four seasons you could imagine. Sure, she lived in Newark now and, OK, maybe it wasn't the most *charming* city. But compared to Paris, what was? Even so, she adored everything about her state. The people, the food, the scenery. She hated when people dissed on it.

Jenna tried not to take offense and decided to change the subject. "So, what's good here?" she asked, turning her eyes to her menu.

"We must get the beef tartare for an appetizer," he said. "It's delicious."

"Oh, I'm a vegetarian."

He squinted at her underneath a furrowed brow, as if he didn't understand the word. Maybe he didn't. Although he spoke English, obviously it wasn't his first language.

"I don't eat meat," she said to clarify.

He continued to glare at her with the same confused look.

"So, what do you do for work, Marcel?" she asked, changing the subject again.

He observed her, clearly taken aback, as if she'd just asked him his deepest, darkest secret. Was that not a normal first-date question here in France? He snapped his fingers to get the attention of a passing waiter. The waiter approached and Marcel spoke to him in French. The waiter nodded and disappeared.

"I'm a photographer," he finally answered, slightly amused.

Jenna looked at him and nodded, urging him to continue.

"And you?" he asked with a casual shrug.

She was beginning to feel as if she were in that familiar awkward first-date ping-pong match. She'd been on her fair share of those, when each person would gently toss a question back and forth to one another, never settling into any meaningful conversation. She shook off the feeling. They were just getting started, they'd warm up to each other soon enough. This was her soul mate after all, she reminded herself.

"I'm a clinical therapist," she answered. "I own a practice in New Jersey specializing in couples counseling."

He shook his head and gave her that same confused look to indicate he didn't understand most of what she'd said. She let out a sigh of frustration, picked up her glass, and took a long sip of wine.

The waiter came over and set down a plate of raw meat between them. Jenna leaned back, her chin tucked into her neck. She breathed in the smell of uncooked flesh and felt her stomach turn. She covered her mouth with her hand.

"What is this?" she asked.

"The beef tartare," Marcel said.

Jenna pursed her lips.

Marcel caught sight of something just past her shoulder, and his eyes narrowed. "Excuse me for a moment," he said.

She forced a smile. "Sure."

He got up from the table and left.

She sat back in her seat and crossed her arms. Obviously, there was a language barrier that was going to make this harder than your typical first-date awkwardness. She scoffed. Really? As if this situation wasn't hard enough, her soul mate had to speak an entirely different language than she did? She shook her head in frustration over fate and its cruel sense of humor. Clearly this relationship was going to take more effort than she'd anticipated.

Even if love *had* fallen into her lap, it was still going to require some labor. She could make it work though. She *would* make it work. It was just like what she told her clients. She needed to commit herself to sticking it out, to seeing it through. After all, it was the only way to get to the happy ending.

CHAPTER TWENTY

Connor

Connor sat at his tiny table near the kitchen, tucked behind a half wall where he could observe from a safe distance. He clenched his fists as he watched it all unfold: Jenna coming into the restaurant, seeing Marcel for the first time; her eyes full of shock that quickly gave way to excitement.

He lowered his head and gnawed on his lip. Then he forced his eyes ahead. Jenna was on a date with a complete stranger. He needed to be nearby, in case Marcel turned out to be dangerous. What if he was a con artist or something? What if he was a jerk? As much as Connor had wanted to vet him in the gardens, getting Marcel to agree to the date had been harder than he'd imagined. He hadn't wanted to turn him off with any additional questions.

He narrowed his eyes as he watched Marcel use his smooth-talking French flirtation on Jenna. He winced as he watched him lean in to kiss her on the cheeks while he held her intimately by the elbows. *Slow down there, Casanova—* or whatever the French version of Casanova would be.

He focused on the sandwich in front of him and read some news on his phone, unwilling to put himself through the torture of watching Jenna flirt with another man. Why did it suddenly bother him so much anyway? He waved away the jealousy, glancing up every now and then to make sure nothing sketchy was going on. Marcel seemed fine so far, albeit a little arrogant. Everything about the man was loud and over the top. His laugh, his gestures, his facial expressions. It was as if he was playing some character in a movie—the overly polished, good-looking foreigner that everyone found charming because of his accent.

Connor rolled his eyes and shifted his attention to Jenna and immediately noticed her discomfort. Her back was to Connor, but he could tell her arms were folded across her chest protectively, and her shoulders seemed tense. She didn't seem to be talking much as Marcel used up most of the oxygen in the room. What was that on that plate in front of her—raw beef? Well, no wonder she looked like she wanted to be anywhere but there.

Connor rubbed his hands over his face. He probably should have given Marcel a heads up on a few things before the date to make it go more smoothly. After all, Connor wanted Jenna to have a good time, despite what his inner selfish desires were leading him to believe. He needed to tamp those down and remind himself of the reason he had set this thing up in the first place: He wanted her to be happy.

He leaned forward in his seat and waved his hands back and forth, his elbows close to his sides, trying to get Marcel's attention. Thankfully, he was out of Jenna's view, but he still didn't want her to notice. The last thing he needed was for her to see him there and think he was interfering in her date. Well, he was, but only with the best intentions, of course.

Marcel's chair faced Connor's table, but his eyes were glued to the menu. Connor continued to discreetly wave him down, until eventually he glanced up. Marcel raised his chin and gave Connor an odd look of confusion. He glared at him underneath a pinched brow. Connor quickly motioned for him to come over, holding a finger to his lips to communicate that he didn't want Jenna to know he was there.

Marcel awkwardly rose from his seat and said something to Jenna. She only nodded. He shuffled his way over to Connor and, mercifully, Jenna didn't turn around to watch where he went. Connor motioned for Marcel to sit. He leaned in close, his voice a hushed whisper. "How's it going?"

Marcel sat down beside him. "What are you doing here?" he asked, his lip curled and his eyes cold.

"I'm just staying nearby to make sure she's safe." He shot Marcel a look of warning.

Marcel frowned. "May I remind you that this was all your idea?"

"I know, I know," he said, waving him off, realizing he didn't have much time. "I should have thought of this sooner, but I probably should give you a few tips."

"Tips?" Marcel scoffed.

Connor gave a wry smile. It did sound ridiculous. As if *this* guy needed any tips on dating. He cleared his throat. "You know, like things to talk about with her. Her interests and such. I mean, I've set you up completely blind here."

Marcel gave him a quizzical look and let out a breath.

"OK, let's hear these tips of yours then," he said, throwing up his hands.

"Well, first, she doesn't eat meat, so get rid of whatever that is on your table."

Marcel rolled his eyes. "Anything else?"

Connor thought for a moment. He closed his eyes and recalled the things he knew about Jenna. "She loves cherry blossoms, especially the ones she's been seeing around Paris this week. You should talk about those."

"OK, I'll make sure to do that," Marcel said, pretending to make a mental note, but clearly dripping with sarcasm.

Connor ignored him, thinking more about Jenna. "She loves coffee, but always orders 'just a splash,' so that it doesn't get cold too quickly." Thinking of her holding up her pinched fingers made him laugh inwardly. "She likes to drink it slowly."

"A splash?"

"She loves anything pink, her laugh is contagious, and she always closes her eyes when she tastes something for the first time."

Marcel shook his head as if he was trying to process it all. "Is that all?"

"And her idea of a perfect moment is to watch the sun rise over the Seine."

"Anything else?"

"Yeah." He paused and took a breath. "She's a great girl. You're a lucky man, Marcel."

Marcel nodded and got up from the table to return to his date. He stopped and turned around with an uncharacteristic look of sincerity. "Thanks, Connor."

Connor raised a corner of his mouth. "No problem." As he watched Marcel go back to the table, he wondered again if he was doing the right thing for Jenna. Doubt was beginning to creep in about whether he was taking things too far. He had found Marcel for her, wasn't that enough? Why was he pushing them together, manipulating the situation so it would turn out the way she wanted it to?

He chewed his lip. Maybe he should simply let things happen naturally instead. Wasn't that the very idea of fate? He twirled a straw around his glass of water and wondered if the whole thing was a major overcompensation for his previous mistake. Sure, he'd messed things up for her once. But was pushing her to fall in love with this French guy the best response to that? On the other hand, nothing ever *really* happened on its own, did it? Wasn't a bit of human intervention always at play when it came to these things?

He glanced over at Jenna again. She turned her head as she watched Marcel return to their table. She smiled, and her entire face lit up with excitement. It was the same expression he'd caught glimpses of over the past couple of days. He'd do anything to see that joy return to her face again, the joy he'd taken away from her six months ago.

This wasn't simply the right thing to do; it was the *only* thing to do. He was giving her what she'd always wanted, what she deserved. It's what she would have had already, if it hadn't been for him.

CHAPTER TWENTY-ONE

Jenna

Marcel returned to the table with a look of apology. He sat down and leaned forward in his chair, immediately reaching for her hand.

The intimate gesture caught Jenna off guard. They didn't seem quite *there* yet. Even so, she forced a smile and placed her jittery hand into his. He gave it an intense squeeze. She watched him and fluttered her lashes the tiniest bit, just enough to show her romantic interest, but not enough to give away her true intentions. His green eyes sparkled against the glow of streetlights that shined from the other side of the window. It instantly brought her mind back to her dream, and she remembered why she was there in the first place. She took a deep, satisfied breath, and her face softened, the tension lifting from cheeks that had been forcing a smile. She had waited for this date for days now. Or maybe she had waited a lifetime. She stared at his drooping eyebrow, gorgeously lowered as he watched her. Her heart rate slowed in the peaceful knowledge that a connection was imminent. She leaned in closer and stared into his eyes with a weightless gaze. Into her future.

"So tell me your thoughts on my beautiful city so far," he said. "I hope you've noticed the cherry blossoms. They're especially lovely this time of year."

Her eyes shot open, and she felt a vibration in her chest. She sat up in her seat. "Yes! They certainly are. I keep noticing them everywhere I go. We get them back in New Jersey this time of year, only they haven't bloomed yet. But the ones here in Paris are simply breathtaking."

He wrinkled his nose, somewhat amused, letting go of her hand so he could pick up his drink. Leaning back in his seat, he swirled the wine around in his glass, staring at it intently. He hooked his other arm around the back of his chair.

"I love all the flowers here in Paris," she continued, trying to keep the momentum going on the still-fragile conversation.

"Yes, me too," he agreed. "In fact, I was photographing the Tuileries Gardens earlier today, and I got some great shots of the roses. The pink ones are my favorite." He examined her with a lift of his perfect cheekbones. "I'd love to show them to you sometime."

Jenna's stomach did a slight flip, and she felt her pulse quicken. She took in a deep breath and let it out slowly through her mouth, forcing herself to temper her excitement. She beamed. "I would love that."

"How long are you here in the city? Just visiting, I assume?"

"Yes, I came for my sister's wedding. Then I decided to

stay a few extra days afterwards to . . ." She stopped herself. " . . . to see the sights."

"And have you had a chance to see many of them yet?"

She took a sip of her wine, relieved to finally be settling into a comfortable position for the first time since she'd been there. She set down her glass and folded her relaxed hands on the table in front of her. "I went to the Eiffel Tower today," she said.

"Oh, well, that's good. Probably the most important thing to see here." He chuckled. "But you'll have to go up at night sometime too. It's a completely different experience in the dark. And there's a place up there where you can get un café. The best in the city. Do you like ah . . . coffee?"

She nodded with enthusiasm.

"Me too," he said, "but only when it's really hot. I like to take my time drinking it."

"Me too!" she screamed, perhaps a little too loud. She clapped a hand over her mouth. Her heart hammered, but she forced herself to overcome the impulse to announce that she was ready to marry this guy already. She forced her body to subdue its overly stimulated state. She compressed her lips, the excitement surging through her. "I mean, I like it that way too," she said.

"Really?" he asked, one eyebrow raised.

She nodded with enthusiasm. "Yeah."

He snapped his fingers again for the waiter and asked him to take away the beef tartare. The waiter set down a basket of freshly sliced baguette instead.

She let out a breath of relaxation and leaned closer to Marcel, gazing at his dimpled chin.

"Well, if you like coffee," he said, "I would love to take you out for one tomorrow morning if you're free. I can show you around."

She gave a wide-eyed nod, popping a piece of bread into her mouth. She chewed slowly.

"Maybe . . . we could even get up before dawn, catch the sunrise over the river. If you're up for an early morning date, that is."

She grasped the edge of the table, her eyes bulging; she could hear the blood swooshing in her ears. "A sunrise over the Seine?"

"Is there anything more perfect than that?" he asked.

She let out a laugh of disbelief, wondering how they could possibly have so much in common. But of course they did. They were soul mates. Jenna inhaled and exhaled slowly. She closed her eyes in gratitude. It was all happening. It was all really, finally, happening.

"Yes, Marcel. I would love that," she said.

CHAPTER TWENTY-TWO

Jenna

Jenna awoke before dawn the next morning, excited for a new day and all the possibilities that came with it. She sat on a bench overlooking the darkened sky that hung over the River Seine and waited for the sun, and for Marcel. Her light-pink jacket, the only one she'd brought on the trip, was pulled tightly around her body in the chilly morning air, her arms wrapped around herself, and her crossed leg bouncing.

She pulled out her phone and opened an email from her secretary, Blair, to confirm that her appointments had all successfully been scheduled for the following week. Now that she'd found Marcel, she could start thinking about her real life again. In fact, it was more imperative than ever that she did. She had plans to make.

Jenna knew she and Connor would need to leave Paris soon. She would need to get back to work, and Connor would need to resume his flying schedule once the investigation cleared him. That left her with little time to firm things up with Marcel and figure out what their future together was going to look like. What *would* happen between them now that they had found each other? She hadn't spent as much time thinking about that part of things as she should have, her attention having been so focused on tracking him down. Now that she had though, it was time to get practical about the logistics of it all.

She closed her eyes with a soft smile as she watched it all unfold in her imagination. He would come visit her often in New Jersey, even if he did seem to loathe the place. She rolled her eyes at the reminder of his comment and made a mental note to show him the best parts of the state on his first visit. He'd come around on its charm. She'd certainly visit him and was thrilled by the idea of that. What better place than Paris to allow a budding romance to grow into a full-fledged love? They would exchange flirty texts and probably talk on the phone daily. Oh, and there would definitely be love letters. Then, soon, one of them would move so they could be together—forever.

She chewed on her lip, somewhat in disbelief that these thoughts were coming from her mind. It just went to show that everyone had wild fantasies buried deep in their psyche somewhere. She still couldn't believe that one dream had pulled them all out of her.

She didn't want to get *too* far ahead of herself, though. After all, Marcel didn't even realize they were destined for each other yet. She needed to let him figure that out on his own. She'd keep the fact that their future was secured to herself, for now. She shivered, forcing herself to wake from her daydream of the future. She needed to slow down and not make any rash decisions. She'd found him, and that was the hard part. The rest would take care of itself in time.

She glanced up from her phone to see Marcel approaching. He smiled at her with those piercing green eyes, his perfect hair frozen in place and a skinny scarf wrapped around his neck. Walking along the cobblestoned streets of Paris, he looked like a dashing model in an upscale travel magazine. The fantasy of Europe, for people pining to see the world, certainly included men who looked like him. The sight of him in the flesh made her heart flutter with excitement, just as it had the first time she'd laid eyes on him on the busy street. Just as it had in her dream. It was confirmation that she was on the right path. The path that had been laid *for* her, and that she simply needed to continue to follow.

Marcel sat down on the bench and put his arm around her. He pulled her in close to keep her warm. She breathed in the rich, smoky scent of his cologne. It was like a heavy incense that clung to his clothes. He crossed one leg over the other, his leather ankle boot dangling over his knee. He leaned back and let out a breath, the mist rising before him. She gently leaned her head against his shoulder.

Jenna gazed out on the river with wistful eyes as the sun slowly painted the sky above the horizon. The orange and pink filter of dawn's artistic haze glistened over the water. She sat motionless, in awe, staring as if it were the first time she'd ever seen a sunrise. It was just as beautiful, just as captivating, as the first time she'd seen it over the river. Well, almost. It was pretty hard to beat a first impression when it came to something like that.

"Wow," she said in a whisper. The sunlight gleamed off the water, and she felt that familiar glimmer in her heart. A pull to something beyond her comprehension. The start of something special. A brand-new relationship, just in its infancy. The dawning of a new day.

She glanced up at Marcel. His eye was firmly fixed on his lap where his phone sat, opened to his email.

"Marcel, are you looking at that?" She nudged his arm then pointed ahead.

He pulled in his arm with an abrupt movement, so he could tap the screen of his phone with urgency. "One second, I have a quick message to send."

She turned her gaze back to the glowing sky, the sun's radiant light now fully illuminating the scenery around them. "Wow," she said again, louder this time, and chuckled to herself. She remembered what Connor had said about how often she used that word.

"Ooh la la," she said. Then let out a snicker.

"What's funny?" Marcel asked, not looking up from his phone.

She laughed. "My French." The memory of the afternoon on the Champs-Élysées came pouring back, and she couldn't help but recall the amused look on Connor's face at her attempts to learn the language, all in an effort to converse with Marcel. The whole idea seemed ridiculous now, and she pressed her lips together as she tried unsuccessfully to tamp down her giggles. "Sacrebleu!" she said, falling against Marcel's shoulder as her laughter escaped.

He glanced up, his lips forming a tight line. "I don't understand."

"Connor and I," she said, wiping away a tear of amusement. "We tried having a conversation in French. Let's just say we still have a long way to go before we're fluent." She sniggered.

Marcel stared at her.

"He said I sound like a Mid-Atlantic Pepé Le Pew," she said, as she doubled over in laughter, reliving the afternoon in her mind.

He gave her a tight grin.

"Never mind," she said, waving a hand. "I guess you had to be there." She sat up and quickly composed herself. She blew out her cheeks, then slowly released the air through her mouth as she tapped her palms against her thighs, shifting her focus back to the seriousness of the relationship beside her and the beauty that unfolded before her.

The sun was now glittering brightly in the sky, but Marcel didn't seem to notice the spectacle in front of them at all. It probably looked like any morning in Paris to him. Jenna wasn't sure how anyone could ever get used to this view, no matter how many times they'd seen it. She wondered what it would be like, someday in the future, when the two of them were old and gray, sitting on a bench like this one. Would she still feel the magic of Paris once she'd been there so many times? Maybe it was inevitable that after so many years seeing the same thing, day in and day out, people eventually grew immune to the beauty of what was right in front of them. The entire idea made her think of her clients; for many, that was exactly the case.

"Un café?" he asked, abruptly putting his phone in his pocket.

She weaved her fingers through her hair, reluctantly pulling herself up off the bench, the magic of the moment over far too soon.

Marcel walked slightly ahead as he led her down the city streets. Like during the early walk with Connor from the Ritz, she realized dawn was her favorite time of day in Paris. The street noise was still muted, leaving room for the sound of birdsong chirping through the air. She could hear the rustle of the leaves in the soft wind and the very first boat horns of the morning along the river. The sidewalks were nearly empty, the bustling life of Parisian cafés just getting underway.

A cool gust blew, and the intense scent of Marcel's cologne filled the air. It seemed to be growing stronger somehow, and Jenna felt a slight headache coming on. The fragrance was obviously European, and most likely extremely expensive. It was so different from the faint smell of fresh soap she'd grown used to smelling on Connor. That clean yet masculine spice she had slept like a rock next to at the Ritz for hours. She shook the thought from her head. Why was she thinking about the way Connor *smelled* right now?

They continued along the sidewalks. Marcel pointed out different landmarks and talked about the history of each. She listened halfheartedly, relaxed and happy, simply enjoying the fact that she was finally with the man she was meant for. It was quite a feeling, no matter how weird the circumstances were that got her there. She wondered if he'd ever had a serendipitous dream about *her*. Maybe there was something familiar about her face that caught *his* eye. The idea made her shiver with excitement. Or perhaps it was the cold.

They approached a café, another delightful Parisian charmer, and Jenna suggested an indoor table where it would be warmer.

"I'd prefer to sit outside," Marcel said, already grabbing a table that faced the city street.

Jenna gave a willing nod through a pained smile and pulled her jacket tighter as they sat. She picked up the menu to peruse the pastry offerings. She never got sick of the sweet, carb-loaded delicacies of France and couldn't help but notice that, even after several days eating like this, she felt great. Her clothes weren't fitting any tighter, her energy wasn't lagging. Parisian food had to be healthier, compared to the food she was used to eating at home where everything was chock full of additives and chemicals.

"Should we share a chocolate croissant?" she suggested.

Marcel fiddled around for something in his coat pocket. She eyed the soft wool of his heavy jacket and couldn't help but wonder if he was going to offer it to her, the way Connor surely would have by now. She rubbed her arms over the light nylon of her trench coat to drop a hint.

"I'm not very hungry," he said.

"Oh, well, maybe I'll eat one myself then," she said with a playful smile.

He frowned.

She bounced her heels against the ground beneath the table, her hands pressed together between her knees for warmth. "Connor and I ordered the most delicious chocolate croissants from a café the other day." She sniffed, her nose beginning to run from the chilled air. "Although we didn't get around to finishing them." She closed her eyes and smiled, reliving the excitement of having spotted Marcel just before getting the chance to fully enjoy their food. Her body instantly warmed as she thought of that afternoon in the sun.

As relieved as she was to be in Marcel's presence, she had to admit the chase had been kind of fun. Perhaps more fun than she was having now? She pushed the ludicrous idea from her mind. She thought again about her clients and the common mistakes she saw with them daily. The thrill of the chase, fading once the target was caught, allowing room to take it all for granted if one wasn't careful. She needed to be mindful not to do that now.

Marcel peered at her sideways. "You and Connor seem to be very close, no?"

Her face reddened. "Oh, no, not really." She tugged at her earlobe. "We live next door to each other back home. He came to Paris so that . . ." She paused. "He could study flowers," she finished, remembering his rouse from the market. She stopped herself from saying more.

Marcel studied her through narrowed eyes, waiting for her to continue.

"Well, what exactly did he tell you?" she asked, the pitch of her voice rising. Her heart began to hammer in her chest. She wondered if Marcel knew about her failed relationship; the fiancé who took off. She desperately hoped Connor hadn't told him anything about it. It certainly didn't make her look like the catch she wanted him to believe she was.

"He said the same thing. Neighbors, friends, nothing more," he answered. "I was just making sure," he said, as he pulled a pack of cigarettes from his shirt pocket. He set them on the table and retrieved the book of matches he'd been fishing around his jacket pockets for. He pulled one out between pinched fingers and lit it. The tip of the cigarette burned a fiery orange, turning to ash as he inhaled the smoke and held it in his lungs.

Jenna's eyes grew big. "You smoke?"

He laughed, the smoke trailing out. "I'm French."

She chuckled too, although more nervously than before. She wondered if she should tell him that she couldn't stand the smell of cigarette smoke. That she thought it a disgusting habit. Of course she shouldn't. There would be no reason to do that. She didn't want to be one of those annoying Americans who looked down on other countries' habits with disdain. She supposed that smoking was as much a part of European culture as gambling by the sea was a part of New Jersey's. Like jug handles or not being allowed to pump your own gas. They were all things outsiders could look down upon with judgment, but that she found endearing and homelike. She was in *his* city after all, and she needed to respect their ways. Cigarette smoke was commonplace here—part of the unique fragrant landscape of the city, only much less charming than the other scents. The wind blew, and the smoke drifted into her face. She waved it away with her hand.

"So tell me more about your photography business."

"Well, I photograph weddings, family portraits, anything really." He looked at his watch. "In fact, I have an appointment this afternoon, so I won't be able to spend the entire day with you."

"No, of course not," she said, suddenly feeling like a nuisance. She tucked her hair behind her ears. "I have a lot I need to do today too." She quickly reached into her purse and pulled out her phone as if to check her busy schedule. She swiped a finger along it, staring at the emails she'd already responded to. "Oh, my," she said in fake surprise. "It looks like I need to touch base with my secretary back home. She had to reschedule all my client appointments for next week and they appear to be piling up." She glanced up at him discreetly, then focused back on her screen. "It's tough to take a vacation when you own your own practice," she continued, hoping he'd be impressed, or at the very least interested in her professional life.

He ran a hand through the top of his hair and gazed around the café, showing no further interest.

A waiter approached and Jenna put her phone away. She ordered a splash of coffee and timidly added a chocolate croissant at the last second. She wished Connor was there. He would not only encourage her excessive French eating, but join in, going along with it all. He would probably be laughing right now about the ungodly amount of carbs and sugar they had consumed—while also ordering more with a mischievous grin.

She shook her head and forced herself to stop thinking about Connor. She was with *Marcel*. The man of her dreams. Sure, she wished he was a little more fun. Perhaps a little more romantic. A little more . . . something. She couldn't quite put her finger on it, but something was still missing—the *je ne sais quoi*, perhaps. But it would come with time. Wouldn't it?

She rubbed the sleeves of her jacket for warmth and blew a puff of air out of the side of her mouth. She kicked herself for her sudden lack of enthusiasm. After all this, how could she suddenly feel so ungrateful? Maybe it was just that her brain hadn't sorted out everything yet. The truth was, she still hadn't decided how she felt about Marcel. Maybe she was putting too much pressure on herself for there to be instant chemistry. Maybe it didn't *need* to be instant when she already knew they were meant to be together.

"I have been invited to an event tonight," Marcel said, interrupting her thoughts.

"Oh?"

"Some friends are having an engagement party on a péniche."

"A what?"

"A rooftop bar, on the Seine."

Her eyes grew wide. "*On* the Seine? You mean, on top of a boat?"

He smirked. "Would you like to be my date?"

Jenna hesitated, although she had no idea why. She bit her lip and crossed her arms in front of her stomach. She couldn't ignore the feeling that her gut wanted to decline the invitation, although she couldn't possibly comprehend why. *Jenna, say yes. Of course you want to go.* Her time in Paris was running short. They needed to ignite this spark already.

Even so, she remained quiet, unable to say the word out loud. *Yes. Say it, Jenna. Oui.* Why was she not jumping at this opportunity? She had just spent the past three days searching all over Paris for this man. Now she had him, and he wanted to take her on the most romantic Parisian date imaginable, and she *wasn't sure* if she wanted to go? Jenna couldn't believe the insanity of her own thoughts.

"I'll need to check on a few things first," she mumbled, wincing in awkward pain. What was going on with her? Maybe she was subconsciously playing hard to get. Not a bad idea, making him work for her a little since she'd pursued him up to this point. Still, it made no sense. Time was running out. Besides, what would Connor think to hear she'd turned down a date with Marcel after all he'd done to get her to this point?

Marcel flicked an ash. "Well, let me know. The party starts at nine."

Jenna sat back in her chair and watched with narrowed eyes as he inhaled a mouthful of smoke and blew it out in a billowy cloud of fumes. She pulled her arms tighter in front of her and crammed her lips together.

This was her future husband?

CHAPTER TWENTY-THREE

Jenna

Jenna shuffled back to the hotel alone, lost in a deep sea of confusion. So maybe things with Marcel weren't as fall-into-your-lap, love-at-first-sight romantic as she had hoped. But with some work, she was confident she could uncover the characteristics that made him her intended mate. It was kismet after all, right? Surely the relationship was brimming with potential, with possibilities—all simply hidden beneath the surface, waiting for her to draw it out. She only wished he seemed as eager as she was to uncover it.

In her dream, it had been unmistakable love. There were absolutely zero doubts in her subconscious mind that she had found what she'd been looking for. The feeling she had while in that altered state of bliss—*that* was what told her she needed to keep going with this. The reminder of that feeling made her glow from within. It was her motivation to keep going down this path. She only needed her conscious mind to get on the same page.

Even so, as much as she wanted to, she couldn't ignore her lack of enthusiasm for their potential date that evening. Maybe she was simply being lazy, refusing to do the hard stuff. Maybe a quiet dinner with Connor sounded more appealing than anything else simply because she was assured of having a great time with him, as opposed to putting in the effort to get to know someone new. Yes, that was probably all it was. She forced herself to remember what she told her clients constantly: Relationships take work. She needed to push beyond the instinctive desire to play it safe. She needed to suppress her emotional response —her gut response—and remember that love was an action, *not* a feeling.

Jenna breezed past the restaurant on the corner beside their hotel, the one where she'd met Marcel last night. She stopped suddenly, her eyes widening in recognition, then reversed her steps slowly. Turning her head, she stared through the window at the figure that had caught her eye. It was Connor, looking happy and relaxed. And across from him was a woman. A drop-dead gorgeous, blonde, tanned, supermodel-looking woman. Jenna scurried out of the way where she could get a better look at them without being detected. She placed herself behind a leafy tree and glared through the window.

Connor gazed at the woman with his chin resting on top of his hands. The woman tossed her silky blonde hair behind one shoulder and let out a laugh, her perfect white smile gleaming. Connor leaned in closer and said something that made her laugh again.

Jenna firmed her jaw and narrowed her eyes. As she watched the two of them, an overwhelming jealousy burned deep in the pit of her stomach. That must be the woman who had called him when they were at the café the other day. Jenna supposed she lived in Paris, and she and Connor got together whenever he was in town.

Connor picked up a bottle of sparkling water and poured it into the woman's glass. She smiled with appreciation, then brought the glass to her full, rosebud lips.

Jenna's shoulders slumped forward, and she lowered her head, feeling as though she'd been kicked in the stomach. She felt the air deflate from her lungs. She wasn't sure why seeing them together had taken her so off guard. Of course she hadn't expected Connor to be single. A handsome pilot like him, traveling the world? He probably had a beautiful woman in every city to choose from, all dying for a meal with those gorgeous blue eyes whenever he was in town. Still, it would have been nice if he'd mentioned it to her, instead of her finding out like that. It wasn't like he owed her anything, but they were friends, weren't they?

She resented the sharp pang of envy she felt deep in her soul. She chewed on the inside of her cheek, internally berating herself for feeling that way. For the confusion she'd created in her own mind. Maybe her mom was right. Maybe relationships didn't work out for her because she couldn't figure out what she wanted. Maybe she was the victim of her complicated emotions, constantly creating chaos in her love life, and spilling it over to her professional life as well.

Maybe it *was* all her fault that Luke had left. Perhaps it had been another example of her not appreciating what was right in front of her. *Had* she appreciated Luke enough when she had him? She didn't know. She didn't know anything, except that Connor was with that woman, and she hated it. She couldn't help but wonder what it meant that she wished more than anything that *she* was the one in there, laughing with him.

She forced herself to push aside her ridiculous feelings and be reasonable. She needed to get a firm hold on her emotions. To stop letting her shifting moods get in the way of her happiness. She was glad Connor had found this woman, despite what the quiver in her chin was telling her. She wanted him to be happy. If anything, it only solidified the want in her heart to have that kind of relationship herself.

She wasn't going to sabotage her chance at happiness again. She had Marcel—the one she'd been seeking, the one she'd been *wanting*. And now that she had him, she refused to make the same mistakes she had with Luke. She wouldn't let this one slip away. It was time she kept her attention where it needed to be and finally went after what she wanted with level-headed focus, keeping her eye, sensibly, on the prize.

She reminded herself that nothing aside from endurance and grit could get someone to the destination they desired. And she was running out of time to get to hers. Things needed to come together, and quickly.

She pulled out her phone and immediately sent a text message.

> Marcel, I would love to be your date tonight.

CHAPTER TWENTY-FOUR

Connor

Connor sipped on his sparkling water; his attention was focused on Amy as she told a hilarious story about a passenger from her flight the day before. He burst out in laughter, appreciating the momentary diversion from obsessing over Jenna and Marcel and what they were up to. It was nice to catch up with his sister, especially in Paris. He hadn't seen her since they'd both had a layover in Chicago a couple of months ago.

"So how long are you here?" he asked. He scooped a spoonful of French onion soup and sipped the warm broth, the melted cheese stringing behind it.

"Only for the day." She peered at her watch. "I fly the red-eye out tonight."

Amy flew for a different airline than Connor and was based out of JFK as opposed to Newark. They lived close enough that they could see each other at home, but it was funny how most of their get togethers happened when they were on the road. Connor was thrilled when he'd gotten the call from her the other day, and even more so that their schedules aligned to allow for a quick meetup in Paris.

As much as he wanted to talk about the investigation with her, he knew he couldn't. It was considered confidential at this point, and he wasn't willing to do anything to jeopardize his chances for a complete exoneration.

"How's David?" he asked instead.

"He's good," she said, chewing on a piece of ice. "He's going to join me out here next month for a long layover. A little bonus honeymoon."

Connor smiled. "I still can't believe you're married now. All grown up and settled down."

"I know, the time goes fast, huh? So how are *you*?" Amy asked. She tore a piece of croissant from her sandwich and held it between her fingers, the buttery flakes peeling off. "Anyone special in your life these days?" she asked with a lift of the eyebrows. She popped the croissant in her mouth and wiped her hands on a napkin.

He rubbed his forehead and let out a breath. "I don't know."

"What's going on, little brother?"

He leaned forward and grabbed a piece of bread from the basket. He turned it over in his hands, then ripped off a piece and chewed it slowly while Amy waited. He blew out a puff of air then ran his hands through his hair. "OK, here goes," he said.

He inhaled deeply, then released everything onto his sister. He wasn't sure if it was the weight of the entire week crashing down on him, or the lingering effects of jet lag, or the pressure of the holding pattern he'd been in. But something in him suddenly combusted, compelling him to give Amy all the details in an emotion-fueled earful.

He told her about the wedding; the fake relationship; about Jenna's dream of Marcel. He even told her about everything that'd happened with Luke. He had no idea how he could so easily confess everything to his sister when he'd spent the better part of a week keeping it all covered up from Jenna. It was almost as if his true feelings had been itching to get out, and they finally found the source they'd needed. It was as if saying it all out loud grounded the emotions that had been flying around his head for days. Just like the feeling of finally putting down a 300,000-pound aircraft onto the runway after a long flight. That final phase, once the aircraft wheels touched down and he felt the weight come off his shoulders in relief at having brought in the plane safely. It was then, though, that he needed to ease back on the controls, to apply the brakes, to maintain directional control. He reminded himself to do that now.

"Whoa," Amy said once he'd finished, her eyes wide. "Connor, it sounds like you're in love with this woman."

He scoffed.

"You need to tell her how you feel, before she falls for this Marcel guy."

He held his forehead in his palm. "Amy, it's not that simple. If she knew the truth about what I did, she would never talk to me again." He stirred his soup, watching the glob of white cheese slowly swirl into a creamy bisque. "Besides, she has her sights firmly set on this guy, and there's nothing I can do to change her mind. When someone believes they're destined for someone, how are you to convince them otherwise?"

Amy was thoughtful. "Well, maybe you can't. But you

should at least tell her everything you told me. And then let her decide for herself."

"Decide what?"

"Her future. It sounds like that wasn't something this Luke guy ever gave her the chance to do. Right? So put it out there—how you feel about her. Let her have some say in it. Let *her* decide how to move forward, and who to do it with, having all the information."

Amy was right. Luke had never given Jenna the chance to be a part of the decision over their relationship. And Connor had only encouraged it when he'd given him that stupid advice. He'd thought his words would have reminded Luke of what was at stake. That Luke would have come to his senses, and Jenna would have never even known about his second thoughts. But it had been wrong for him to get involved, and with what he now knew about Jenna, it hadn't been necessary. Life was all about handling tough decisions. You couldn't avoid them, and you certainly couldn't make them for other people. Jenna was fully capable of figuring things out on her own. Of making decisions that were best for her. If only she could have known everything back then. If only he could tell her everything now. If only it wasn't as complicated as it had all become.

"What about the thing with Luke though?" he asked. "How will she ever forgive me?"

Amy gave him a pointed look. "Connor, do you really think Luke broke up with her because of what *you* said? Was Luke really that fickle that he decided to leave his fiancée a week before the wedding because of your advice?"

He shrugged.

"Well, it doesn't add up to me," Amy said.

Connor was thoughtful, his eyes glued to the table.

"Connor, listen to me."

He raised his head in obedience, staring at Amy's focused gaze.

"This guy was going to bolt anyway, and he used your advice to justify it to himself."

Amy always did have a way of cutting through all the nonsense to get straight to the truth.

"How else would he have already had a job lined up in another city? No, he used your words to convince himself he was doing the right thing, instead of having the tough, honest conversation he actually needed to have with his fiancée. And here you are, doing the same thing."

She was right. For the first time it occurred to him just how self-centered his thinking had been all this time. He'd been so focused on getting his conscious scrubbed clean that he hadn't considered what it must feel like for Jenna. To have that missing piece of the puzzle still floating around out there. Sometimes the unanswered questions took a harder toll on someone than learning the truth, as hard as it was.

He needed to explain it to Jenna. He needed to give her all the details of what had happened that night so she could get the closure she so desperately wanted. There was always something at play behind the scenes, a contributing factor. And as much as he didn't want to admit it to her, it had been him.

More importantly, he needed to tell Jenna how he felt about her and let her decide her destiny. The only problem was, he didn't *know* how he felt about her, exactly. Despite what Amy had said, he couldn't possibly be in love with Jenna, could he?

Connor hugged his sister goodbye so she could head back to her hotel and prepare for her next flight. He walked back to his hotel, thoughts fixated on what he needed to say to Jenna. Surely she'd be spending the evening with Marcel, giving Connor a much-needed chance to figure out how to be honest with her without driving her away. He was almost out of time to do it.

Before heading to his floor, he stopped by Jenna's room to drop off the box he'd picked up earlier. He left it propped up beside the door, knocked lightly, then scurried off.

When he got back to the room, he plopped onto the bed and stared at the TV for nearly an hour, mindlessly scrolling through the channels. He finally flipped off the screen and pulled out his iPad to check his email for any updates. He rubbed his temple as he thought about the flight, confident he'd done everything right that day. Still, doubt lingered in the shadows. There had to be *some* explanation, and he knew the airline wouldn't rest until it had been uncovered.

A knock sounded on the door and he got up from the bed to answer it. His mouth dropped open before he could stop it, and he leaned against the doorway, sucking in a breath. His head suddenly felt light and feverish. Jenna stood in front of him in the dress. He was relieved to see he'd gotten the size right. In fact, it couldn't possibly fit her any better.

"Wow," he said, unable to keep from smiling at her. "Ooh la la," he corrected, with a playful twinkle.

She stared at him, a wide smile on her face. "Connor, I can't believe you bought me the je-ne-sais-quoi dress."

He lowered his head shyly. "Well, there was just something about it."

She ran a hand along the rose-colored satin fabric and smiled. She threw her arms around him for a hug then quickly pulled back and did an enthusiastic twirl. "Do you think it's too much for a boat party?"

He shook his head, a bead of sweat forming on his brow. "You look incredible."

A slight blush crept over her cheeks. "Thanks," she said, her head bowing.

"Well, it looks like you have a big night ahead of you," he said.

She peered at the floor. "I suppose you probably do too?" She raised her head slightly, peeking at him from underneath her dark lashes.

He pursed his lips. "Something like that."

"Connor, before I go . . ." She raised her head and directly met his gaze. "I wanted to come by and tell you . . ." She closed her eyes and drew in a long breath. "I just wanted to say—"

"Yes?" He stared into her brown eyes, which were gleaming with sincerity. He waited for her to tell him what he longed to hear, although he wasn't exactly sure what that would be. Anything at all that may give him that faint glimmer of hope he needed to be able to tell her all the things he wanted to. To know there was even the slightest opening for forgiveness, for redemption. For a chance at a fresh start.

When coming in to land a plane, if something went wrong, the worst thing a pilot could do was force the landing. Instead, they needed to go around and try again. Start over and take another shot at it. He only wished he knew how to adjust his approach for this situation. Instead, he felt stalled, like an aircraft having lost its power, unable to do anything but glide where the wind took it.

She cleared her throat. "I just want to say thank you again for everything. For finding Marcel. For being here in Paris with me. For the incredible few days we've had here."

He nodded, swallowing the painful lump in his throat.

"I'm glad it all worked out." He wanted to say more. So much more.

But before he could, she gave him a faint smile, then turned to leave.

"Jenna?" His ribs grew tight, and his breathing quickened.

She turned around. "Yes?"

He stared at her, his mouth clenched shut and his body frozen. This was it. This was the moment to finally tell her the truth, to give her all the facts so she could have some say in her fate.

He gazed at her pink lips, which were puckered as if in deep thought, as if she knew what he was about to say. But how could she, when *he* didn't even know what that was? He wanted to tell her about what had happened with Luke. He wanted so badly to tell her the truth about everything that had caused her heartbreak. More than anything, he wanted to tell her about his feelings for her. But how could he, when he couldn't even articulate them to himself?

He studied her face. He couldn't deny the fact there had been a brightness in her eyes again, ever since she'd laid eyes on Marcel. They shined now with possibility, with hope for an exciting future. He couldn't bring himself to do it. Not when she'd found that happiness again, and that light was coming back in her life. He wouldn't take that feeling from her again. It was time he got over his selfish need for forgiveness and considered only her well-being. He wouldn't complicate things further by throwing this at her, just as she was about to get everything she'd hoped for.

"Nothing," he said. "I hope you have a great time tonight."

"Thanks," she said and lowered her head. She peeked up with one more half smile then turned to leave.

CHAPTER TWENTY-FIVE

Jenna

"Bonjour, ma belle." Marcel greeted Jenna with that signature kiss on both cheeks, and she instantly felt her heart speed up with excitement. She nervously smoothed her hair, which was pulled back in a neatly styled ponytail. He was dressed in a slick navy-blue suit, the buttons of his shirt unfastened at the top, showing off the upper portion of his tanned, hairless chest.

The night air was cool, but pleasant. She inhaled a generous whiff of his cologne and felt an intense quiver of nerves in her stomach. Marcel scanned her up and down and let out a whistle. She grinned, realizing she'd never felt more beautiful in a dress before.

"Marcel, this is amazing," she said as he led her up the ramp to the boat. She grabbed his arm to steady herself on the incline. The long boat was moored to a dock, the Eiffel Tower behind them aglow with a soft luminescence. It looked like a tall, glistening wine glass, filled with golden sauvignon blanc. The lights gleamed with a bright stillness. She longed for them to sparkle again. For the wine to transform to champagne, effervescing with millions of tiny bubbles.

After five days in Paris, she knew the Eiffel Tower only put on its impressive, sparkling display once per hour. She just needed to wait; it would happen. It was sort of like her relationship with Marcel. Maybe it didn't start with an instant shimmer, but with a little patience, it would happen eventually.

It made her think of how the waiters always asked if they wanted their water still or sparkling. "Sparkling, of course," she had said the first time she was asked. Who wouldn't want a little extra something in their most basic drink? In the days that followed, though, she began to realize that sometimes what you needed was some still, thirst-quenching water. Refreshing and calming to the soul.

Marcel offered his arm to lead her up a short flight of stairs to the second level of the boat, and she took it eagerly, her pink jacket draped over her arm. Jenna's eyes filled with anticipation as they entered the party and were greeted by an elaborate tabletop display. A waterfall of champagne cascaded down a massive tower of glasses, falling to a river of collected wine that trickled through a garden of colorful flowers. A fountain in the center of a party, buzzing with energy; vitalizing and exciting, it summed up the feel of the evening perfectly. The centerpiece was surrounded by lush greenery and the glow of dancing candlelight. Jenna reached out to touch one of the flowers, a soft petal falling into her fingers. She held it to her nose and breathed in the sweet scent of lily, combined with a hint of alcohol.

They approached the bar where they each ordered one

of the enormous signature cocktails, complete with a trop-ical flower floating on top.

"This place is great," Jenna yelled over the thump of European techno music.

"What?" Marcel said, cupping his hand around his ear.

"I said, this place is great."

He shook his head, unable to hear, and they reached for their drinks. Jenna took a sip of the bright-blue liquid and made a face. Marcel led her to the back of the boat, pulling her along through a sea of dancing, sweaty bodies, where they could hear each other better. They snagged a tiny table as soon as another couple got up.

Marcel immediately pulled out his phone to take a picture of the two of them. He scooted his chair closer to hers and pulled her in close for a selfie, leaning his head gently against hers. She put on her prettiest smile, the ideal romantic backdrop of the most beautiful parts of Paris perfectly displayed behind them. He snapped the photo, then took another one, this time giving her an affectionate kiss on the cheek. She beamed beside him.

Jenna let out a calm release of breath and cast an eye over the entire scene. There was romance in the air, to be sure, and it hadn't come a moment too soon. She gazed at the tower and felt her shoulders relax, relieved she'd talked herself into coming tonight. There was no place she'd rather be, and she squealed internally with anticipation. It was all coming together.

Marcel recognized someone from across the bar and waved with excitement.

"Who's that?" Jenna asked.

"A client. I should probably go say hello." He observed the crowds of people standing around, eyeing their table.

She knew what he was thinking: If they got up, this table would be gone in a second.

"Go ahead," she said with the wave of a hand. "I'll stay here and hold the table."

"Are you sure?" he asked. "It will only take a minute." He was already up and out of his chair, his eyes scanning the crowd.

She swallowed through the dull pain that had formed in the back of her throat. They'd been taking a romantic photo one second and he was bouncing off to be a social butterfly the next? She turned her lips into a forced smile, convincing herself it was all fine. So what if he was social? That wasn't a bad thing, and they had the entire night ahead to get to know each other better.

"Of course." She shooed him away. "Go. I'm going to enjoy this view. Don't worry about me."

He studied her expression.

"Really, I couldn't be happier," she said, at that point *wanting* him to go so she didn't feel like a ball and chain, already, on their third date.

"OK." He exhaled in relief and hurried off through the crowds.

She leaned back in her chair and inhaled deeply, gazing at the sight of Paris all lit up, the lights reflecting off the river. She stirred her drink with the tiny cocktail straw, then took another sip. She winced at the sourness and puckered her lips, having no idea what she was drinking, but knowing it was definitely not to her taste. She longed for a glass of that sweet champagne she and Connor had drunk at the wedding the other night. Now that had certainly been her taste. Or the light, refreshing wine they'd enjoyed with their picnic lunch. She smiled, remembering the grape landing in her glass with a splash.

The view, on the other hand, was breathtaking. Connor would absolutely love to see the city from this angle. They'd taken several walks along the river during the day, but they hadn't had the chance to see it up close at night. Maybe she'd bring him tomorrow night to show him. If they were still there. On second thought, she supposed he would probably want to bring that girl instead. Maybe he *had* brought her here before. Jenna felt that annoying pang of jealousy return at the thought of that beautiful blonde getting to experience the magic of Paris with Connor. She wrinkled her nose and forced herself to push him from her mind. She needed to keep her focus solely on Marcel. There was a lot riding on this date tonight. Her entire future in fact. It was no time to get distracted.

She draped her jacket over the back of her chair in an effort to save the table and left her cocktail behind. She knew she shouldn't leave her drink unattended at a bar, but she had no plans to continue drinking it anyway. Standing up, she walked to the edge and leaned against the railing, gazing out at the water. She let out a breath of frustration, before inwardly laughing at the irony of standing there, alone, on the most romantic date her imagination could have conjured up.

Jenna pulled out her phone to check the time and thought about where Connor and that girl might be having dinner. What if they had gone to that adorable pastel place to have macarons for dessert? A dull pain washed over her heart; she couldn't stomach the idea of that. She smiled with longing as she thought about Connor tasting those desserts, his intense attention focused on identifying the flavors. She could imagine that same look of concentration on his face when flying a plane.

She quickly scrolled through a few recent photos to pass

the time. They were all of Connor, surrounded by the many charming scenes of Paris. She closed her phone and threw it back in her purse. She stared down at the black water instead and watched a wave ripple across the surface, shaking all thoughts of Connor from her head, reminding herself that she wasn't giving up on Marcel just because the attraction wasn't instant and the chemistry wasn't easy. *Jenna, this is what you tell your clients all the time: Don't be looking for greener grass.* She owed it to herself to give it more time; to let an attraction fully develop. Like the Eiffel Tower, you couldn't count on the sparkle to appear at every moment. But when it did—she remembered from the night of her sister's wedding—it took your breath away.

Marcel eventually returned with a look of apology and another blue drink for Jenna as a peace offering. She gave him a faint smile in return as she took it and pretended to be pleased. She breathed in the smoke-filled air and tapped a hand along the railing in beat to the music.

Glancing over at their table, Jenna noticed it had been taken, her jacket tossed on the ground and her drink shoved aside. She hurried over to grab the jacket and shook it out. She put it on, feeling the chill from the breeze that swept over the river.

Noticing her shiver, Marcel came behind and wrapped his arms around her. She instantly shuddered, although she didn't think it was from the cold air. She could feel his warm breath against her neck, and she felt a wince-like shiver run down the length of her arm. She flinched, lifting her shoulders to her ears.

Turning around, she faced him so she could gaze into his green eyes instead—the ones from her dream. She smiled shyly, knowing he was about to kiss her. She straightened and lifted her chin. This was it—the moment for their first real connection. That long-awaited spark. With the Eiffel Tower glowing behind them, and the Seine beside them, she couldn't think of a more perfect intimate moment. This was where it would all begin.

Marcel leaned in closer, and she closed her eyes with excited anticipation. She leaned forward and raised her face to his, puckering her lips ever so slightly in invitation. His lips met hers, and he pulled her in close to his body. She could taste the faint hint of cigarettes, and his lips were firm. She didn't move, her eyes closed, and her mouth frozen against his. She pressed further into his lips with hers, hoping to awaken something between them. Nothing stirred at all. Nothing sparkled, nothing glowed. It almost felt as if the City of Light had suddenly lost all its electricity. No brightness, no shimmer. There was no flicker or gleam. It was like a glass of tap water, void of any effervescence whatsoever.

She pulled back and opened her eyes, her mind reeling with a sudden uneasiness over what it meant. OK, so it was a lackluster kiss. So what? Was it even a realistic notion—to feel a spark? Maybe that whole idea was simply invented by hopeless romantics while in those temporary stages of lust. It seemed the entire concept of *feeling a spark* was based on a fleeting emotion, a momentary psychological state.

Her thoughts went back to the other night—when Connor had kissed her. The current that had surged through her entire body then had felt like a million twinkling pin pricks. As if her skin was glowing with flashing lights. Perhaps, it was the only time she'd ever truly felt that. Had it even been real?

She couldn't even remember now if she'd ever felt it with Luke. Maybe in the beginning, when the experiences were new. But she could hardly remember any passion between them. It all seemed like a lifetime ago; as if the final months of their relationship had been overshadowed by wedding planning and logistics. Trying to make everything work. Trying to make *them* work. Perhaps that had been the case much longer than she'd realized. Maybe it had *always* felt like work.

Well, she wasn't going to let that happen again. Jenna was unsure of so much at the moment, but she was suddenly hit with an awareness that gave her full confidence: She wasn't going to force something that wasn't right. With a disappointed release of breath, Jenna rolled back her shoulders as she admitted something to herself. *Marcel* wasn't right, and she couldn't ignore her gut any longer.

She held her hands to her stomach and took in a deep breath. Then, she released it all, letting go of a dream that would never become reality. The vision for her future, once again, shattered in front of her. She shook her head in slow disbelief at what she was about to say.

"Marcel, I'm so sorry."

He looked at her underneath a quizzical brow. "About what?"

"I don't think this is going to work out between us."

"Oh," he said simply, folding his arms and bowing his head. He appeared somewhat disappointed, but not terribly surprised.

"I'm sorry," she repeated. "But I don't think we're the match I thought we were."

He let out a laugh. "The kiss was that bad, huh?"

She winced in embarrassment at the awkwardness of the moment, over the complete disbelief at what she was doing. How could she be so sure about this? It was as if her heart was doing all the talking for her, without even consulting her brain.

"It wasn't the kiss, Marcel," she said, trying to let him down as gently as possible. After all, she had pulled him along on this entire charade, and she couldn't help but feel bad for her sudden change of heart. "You see, I had this preconceived notion in my mind that we were meant to be." She let out a murmur of annoyance over the entire situation. "It's hard for me to explain. Heck, I can't even fully understand it myself." She threw up her hands.

He gave a curt nod, as if she had made sense, or perhaps not caring if she did. "Well, it was worth a try," he said simply.

"Yeah, I guess." She stared ahead into the river, unable to quite grasp that after all that searching, she was going to walk away. From *him*. She shook her head trying to make some sense of it in her mind. But she couldn't. It didn't make any sense.

Why had she even had that dream in the first place? How could fate be so cruel to her—to lead her on this chase only to have her end up with the wrong guy? Even so, there was no doubt in her mind: He was the wrong guy. As much as she hated to admit it, she simply didn't connect with him. There was nothing there. How could fate have gotten it so wrong? Especially with all the things they had in common. How he had seemed to *know* her from that first date. The cherry blossoms. The way they liked their coffee. The sunrise over the Seine.

A question suddenly occurred to her.

"Marcel, where did you get the idea to take me to watch the sunrise this morning?"

He ducked his head. "Connor may have mentioned

something about it. He caught up with me at the restaurant last night and gave me some tips."

Her eyebrows drew together. "Connor?"

Marcel held up his hands in defense. "Just to give us some things to talk about on our date."

Her face slackened and she closed her eyes in complete understanding.

"Jenna, I think Connor wants you to be happy," Marcel said. "I can tell he cares about you."

Jenna squeezed her eyelids tighter and pressed her lips together. She nodded, fighting back the tears of confusion, while also unable to contain her smile. It had been Connor. Of course it had. The idea made her stomach flutter with joy but also quake with fear. She needed to confront her growing feelings for Connor. She couldn't deny them any longer.

Was it possible the dream had gotten it all wrong? Was there any explanation of what she had seen where Connor was, in fact, the one for her? She couldn't think of one, however hard she tried. The dream had been crystal clear. And no matter how much she didn't want it to be true, *Marcel* had been the one in it.

"Marcel, when I bumped into you on the street that day—"

"So that *had* been you. I thought so," he said. "I apologize for my anger, but I had just bought a slice of cake from my favorite bakery, and it got destroyed."

Her eyes flew open. *The cake.* Those two little words that started the whole thing. It wasn't a sign. It wasn't proof. It had only been . . . cake?

Jenna closed her eyes and rubbed her forehead to process the massive disappointment life had just handed her. She leaned in to give Marcel a hug goodbye and thanked him for everything. Then she left him to head back to the hotel to figure out what was going on in her heart.

She needed to have an intense therapy session with herself, to sort out her feelings. She had no idea what to say to Connor about anything. Maybe she should avoid him, at least until she'd had time to figure out some things. Because, despite her years of experience helping others work through their feelings, she'd never been more confused about her own in her entire life.

CHAPTER TWENTY-SIX

Connor

Connor's aimless steps drifted along the bank of the darkened Seine, his head down and his shoulders slumped. His emotions were swirling around with an angsty energy, his thoughts focused solely on Jenna and his intensifying feelings for her. After all he'd done to get to this point, he couldn't comprehend why he felt so sickened by the whole idea of her ending up with Marcel. It was the one thing he thought would bring him the peace he so desperately wanted.

Sure, maybe he'd always harbored a slight crush on her, but it was never something he thought too much about. But it wasn't as if he was truly in love with Jenna, as Amy had suggested. Was he? Maybe he was simply being jealous, just as he'd felt when Jenna and Luke had first begun to date, although he hadn't realized it until now.

Sure, at times he'd wondered what would have

happened if he'd had the guts to ask her out before Luke had. But that had simply been a curious, hypothetical question. A competitive instinct, more than anything else. Right?

Connor shook his head, clearing the cobwebs of confusion from his brain. He gazed at the river. The bright glow of the city danced across the polished black surface. Like an airport runway in the dark of night, the gleam of perfectly placed lights to guide the way; to make the path clear, that couldn't be seen before. He focused his eyes as they brightened with the realization that he could no longer fool himself. Amy had been right. Of course he was in love with Jenna. What was not to love? She was fun, and driven, and insightful. Her eyes danced when she was excited, and her lips puckered when she was thoughtful. Her very presence could warm his soul with one radiant smile. With one simple brush of the hand.

He looked up and his eye landed on a group of people having a party on top of a boat. Young couples danced to the pulsing lights and loud music. The action-packed enchantment of Paris nightlife. His gaze landed on a couple standing alone at the back of the boat. He instantly felt the breath rush from his lungs as he recognized Jenna's pink jacket. She and Marcel stood at the railing together, gazing out at the water. Marcel stood behind her, his arms wrapped around her waist.

Connor tightened his jaw. He clenched a fist by his side, his knuckles cracking as a heat of anger flushed through his body. He held his breath as he watched Jenna slowly turn around. Marcel leaned in, and Connor's heart pounded. They kissed—their bodies close, their mouths pressed together, the Eiffel Tower aglow behind them. His and Jenna's Eiffel Tower. He looked away as fast as he could, holding an arm across his stomach as he bent over, hit with a wave of nausea.

He couldn't put himself through any more of this torture. He needed to simply shut off his feelings for Jenna. It was the only thing he could do. It didn't matter that he was in love with her. Not at this point. He needed to push aside his jealousy and instead consider nothing but *her* feelings. Her happiness. She had finally got what she'd wanted, what she'd been waiting for. What she deserved. He had done what he needed to do for her. It was time to take himself out of this situation.

He couldn't possibly mess up everything in her life again, just when it was all within her reach. It was about time he stopped standing in the way of her happiness. In fact, it was time he left Paris and let her have her happy ending, without him.

He shuffled away from the river, his chin buried in his chest. He took a deep inhale and released it. Then he looked up and threw one last glance at the river, throwing any thoughts of Jenna and Marcel with it. It was over. He cast an eye around the city view, then stuffed his hands in his pockets and let out a long exhale of resignation. He knew at that moment that he'd never look at Paris the same way again.

He pulled out his phone to see a new email had appeared in his inbox. It was from the fleet captain.

The investigation is complete. Expect a phone call shortly.

He thought again about the sudden loss in altitude that day and the human factors that were undoubtedly behind it in some capacity—and what had been uncovered as the true culprit of the incident. He closed his eyes and ran a shaking hand through his hair. His entire career flashed before his eyes as he was reminded again of the fleeting nature of life. Nothing lasted forever.

He closed his email and shook his head. He opened the airline employee app and booked a seat on the late-night flight home then headed back to the hotel to pack his things.

CHAPTER TWENTY-SEVEN

Jenna

Jenna left the party and took a cab back to the hotel. There was so much she needed to work out in her brain. Her gut was clear though, as much as she didn't want to admit it. She had feelings for Connor, and she needed to figure out what they meant.

She rushed through the hotel entrance into the lobby, her high-heeled feet aching, when she was stopped by a familiar voice.

"Jenna."

She froze and turned to see her mom stand up from a chair, an impatient scowl painted across her face.

"Mom, what are you doing here?" she asked, discomfort creeping up through her toes.

"What exactly is going on with you?" her mother asked.

Jenna swallowed. "Mom, this isn't the best time." She turned her back to her, unwilling to engage. The last thing she needed was her mom's voice in her head with everything she was trying to work out. She started to walk away, desperate to get up to her room where she could be alone to think.

"What do you think you're doing?"

The words sliced Jenna in the back. She stopped and turned around, looking into her mother's narrowed eyes.

"What do you mean?" Jenna said.

"I just got a call from your sister." Deena slowly walked closer, anger in her expression. "She said her wedding photographer posted a picture of you on his social media account."

"So?" Jenna had assumed plenty of pictures had been taken of her at the wedding. Why did her mom care that the photos were being posted? And why was it *her* fault that they were?

"It was taken tonight. It's of the two of you together, on a romantic date." She held up her phone to show Jenna the picture Marcel had taken of the two of them, looking cozy and romantic. He was kissing her on the cheek, and she beamed with happiness beside him.

Jenna grabbed the phone from her mom and narrowed her eyes. She studied the picture, trying to catch her brain up, to understand why it was in her mother's hand. She shook her head, not connecting the dots. "What do you mean, her wedding photographer?"

"Jenna, are you already two-timing your new boyfriend?" her mother asked pointedly.

Jenna's brow was furrowed with confusion. "Marcel? He was Lauren's wedding photographer?"

Deena stared at her through suspicious eyes. "Yes, Jenna. And the question I have for *you*, is why the two of you seem to be an item?"

Jenna let out a gasp as everything clicked in her head. She threw a hand over her mouth and her eyes popped as a memory from the night of her sister's wedding barreled into her mind. That moment out on the terrace, when Connor had almost kissed her. They'd been interrupted by a photographer's flash as he took a picture of the cake. She could remember it all so vividly now, though she hadn't seen the guy's face at the time. But maybe she *had* glanced at it, it just hadn't registered in her consciousness. She inhaled sharply. "The cake," he had said to her that night as he tried to angle his way in to get the shot.

She quickly reviewed everything she'd learned in her years of psychology classes about dreams. About the pieces of information from the day that make it into your subconscious and how they get there. Dreams were made of bits of data stored in unknown places throughout your brain. A random face. A distant memory. All coming together.

That was all Marcel was? This entire time? He had only been a random face she'd seen that night?

He had been there, during that magical moment. In that instant when she felt her entire body sparkle like the tower. When she'd felt that something wonderful was about to happen. When Connor had been about to kiss her! *That* was why Marcel's face had made its way into her dream? Her subconscious must have made note of his features, mixed it with the romance of the moment, and her mind had played out her deepest desires in her dream. With the wrong face!

And those two simple words. *The cake.*

"Jenna, I'm not sure *what* your problem is with commitment," her mom continued, "but I guess this would explain what happened with Luke. Was your head turned by

Connor while you were still with Luke? And that's why he called off the wedding?"

Jenna rubbed her forehead. "Mom, that's not what happened."

Deena threw up her hands. "I noticed you doing it the other night at dinner—staring at the man over at the next table. Was that the photographer? This Marcel guy? All while you have this perfectly nice boyfriend who seems to adore you sitting right next to you. Jenna, what is the matter with you?"

Jenna shook her head, desperate to explain, but suddenly unable to form any words.

"You can never be happy with what you have, can you?" her mom continued. "And you're the one who makes a living counseling people about this very topic. How do you suppose you have any leg to stand on with your clients when you are entirely lost yourself?"

"You have it all wrong," a firm voice interjected.

Jenna and Deena both whipped their heads around.

"The breakup wasn't Jenna's fault at all," Connor said. "It was mine."

CHAPTER TWENTY-EIGHT

Connor

"Connor, what are you talking about?" Jenna studied him, confusion burning in her eyes. She rubbed an eyebrow.

He walked closer to her. Connor dropped his hands to his side and stuck out his chest, ready to face it all. He was unwilling to hold in the truth any longer. He couldn't let Jenna take the blow from her mother like this. He couldn't let her take it from herself any longer either.

He looked Jenna squarely in the eye and said what he should have told her a long time ago. "I told Luke that he should call off the wedding. That he shouldn't get married."

Jenna's entire body flinched as she absorbed his words. Her mouth fell open and she stumbled backwards. She blinked rapidly. "What?" she backed further away from him slowly, her eyes wide with panic. "Connor. Tell me that's not true." She held a hand to her stomach and bent over as if in pain.

"I've been wanting to tell you for so long, but I couldn't. That's why I've been so adamant about helping you find Marcel. It was my way of making up for what I'd done."

Her gaze was still, a hurt look beneath the surface of her eyes. She held her shaking palms up to her cheeks. "But why would you do that, Connor?" she asked, her voice growing rough. "Why would you sabotage my relationship like that?"

He shook his head. "I didn't want to. I mean, it's not what I meant to . . . Jenna, Luke was having second thoughts. And I . . ." His lips tightened as he tried to find the right words to say next. He studied her eyes that were riddled with betrayal and lowered his head. "He asked for my advice, and—"

Jenna's face was a bright shade of scarlet, her jaw clenched tightly. "Your advice," she said through gritted teeth. She breathed in shakily and squeezed her eyes shut as she exhaled. She opened her eyes and glared at him. "This whole time—the missing piece I could never figure out, the part that didn't add up. It's been *you*."

"Jenna, let me explain."

"Explain what?" she snapped. "That you were the one responsible for my heartbreak? I've agonized over the *why* behind this breakup for months. How many times over the past few days alone did you see me struggle with understanding it? You knew all along. And you *never* told me this?"

"Jenna, I'm—"

"No, Connor, I don't want to hear another word from you," she said with a cold stare. "Just leave. Leave me alone. You've done enough damage already."

She turned on her heel to face her mother, who stared at her with her mouth wide open in disbelief.

Her mom reached for her hand. "Jenna, I had no idea—"

Jenna snatched her hand away. "Connor's not my boyfriend, Mom. He never was." She glared at Connor. "He's just an illusion. And I'm done chasing things that aren't real."

Connor flinched, feeling the dagger slice straight into his heart. He bent over at the waist, the wind knocked out of his lungs. He wanted to say something, but no words would come out. What could he possibly say?

Jenna sharply turned her back to them both and ran for the door. She took off into the dark night, her hurried steps frantic to get away from him.

He stared after her with dead eyes as all the blood drained from his face. He held a hand against his throat as he swallowed the pain. The one thing he'd been trying to avoid over the past few days, or perhaps the past six months, had finally happened—he had lost Jenna for good.

CHAPTER TWENTY-NINE

Jenna

Jenna got away from Connor and her mother as fast as she could. She raced through the lobby and hopped straight into a cab outside, fighting the deluge of tears that threatened to overpower her. She was unsure where she was even going. She was completely directionless, confused. Just as she'd been over these past six months. She gazed ahead, and her eye landed on the brightened Eiffel Tower. She spoke to the driver and they headed toward it.

When she got out of the cab, she scurried along the sidewalk in her high heels and satin dress. She arrived at the base and immediately got in line to buy a ticket to the top. At the late evening hour the line was much shorter than before, and she got up to the window before she had time to talk herself out of it.

"To the summit," she said, the anger burning inside overriding any fear of heights that dwelled in her mind. She had no idea what had compelled her to go up, but something else was leading her. She'd surrendered control and was riding the wave of complete despair.

She squeezed her eyes shut as she rode the elevator to the top, fighting the fury that was bubbling up stronger inside with each passing minute. How could Connor, of all people, betray her like that? How could he have kept something so important from her? Especially when she'd been analyzing every step she'd made, wondering if it had all been her fault. She covered her face with her hands, stricken with the absolute injustice of it all. How could anyone truly be destined for each other? Especially when the flawed human condition ultimately destroyed everything that was inherently good—even love.

JENNA STEPPED off the elevator at the very top of the tower and walked to the edge with timid steps. Her stomach tightened. She glanced over the railing, catching her first glimpse of the city below and felt slightly dizzy. Closing her eyes, she steadied herself, pressing her hands against the sides of her head. She summoned every ounce of courage she could and forced the feeling to pass. She quickly ran through a few mindfulness exercises she used from time to time on her clients. *Tolerate the fear, don't avoid it.* She focused her breathing and visualized a place of calm.

She inched her way closer to the railing, then stepped up and grasped it tightly. She gazed out over the city and felt the breath rush out of her at the sight of the vast blanket of darkness dotted with thousands of glowing bursts of tiny lights. She felt as if she were all the way up in heaven, gazing down at a sky full of stars beneath her.

"Wow," she said, her fear instantly vanishing before her as a sense of wonder overtook all her other senses.

From there, the city looked entirely different to how it had from the second level. She was zoomed out further than she'd ever been to anything in her whole life, a vantage point she'd never even considered. For the first time, she was able to see it all: the entire city.

Her thoughts jumped to Luke, and her mind scrolled over the advice Connor had given him—the advice that had ruined everything. She thought back to the day Luke had broken up with her. In some ways, she'd known it was coming. As shocked as she'd claimed to be at the time, there was also something about it that had seemed inevitable, and she realized this was the first time she'd ever admitted that to herself. She'd been so focused on her bitterness, on her broken heart, that she hadn't given herself the opportunity to consider the idea that, on some level, the breakup had felt . . . right.

She felt the return of that familiar feeling of despair, just as she had when Luke had called off the wedding. She thought about what her mom used to tell her when she was a child, scared in a difficult situation: The darker the night, the brighter the stars. Sometimes it took a complete blackout in order to see a flash of light. And sometimes it took a dark day, a cold shadow, a long winter, to finally see the sun. Just as quickly as the despair had come on, it also vanished, clearing the way for something else. Something better for her.

She took in a deep, steadying breath and felt a switch flip somewhere inside her brain. And her heart. Yes, she could see things up here that she'd never been able to see before. The truth.

A calm washed over her body as she closed her eyes in

silent reflection of the entire relationship. Luke had one foot out the door for months before the wedding. She realized it now. And it wasn't only him; she'd had her doubts too. She remembered the thoughts that would often creep into her head at night, right before falling asleep. The little voice that told her that Luke wasn't right for her. The one that reminded her that he never laughed at her jokes. That she rarely laughed at his. The one that whispered warnings that they were headed down different paths. She remembered the way he'd roll his eyes whenever she'd wanted to stay in and have a quiet evening alone together, instead of going out with their friends. She recalled the lack of interest he'd taken in the mundane details of her day, and she'd been no better at caring about his.

Even so, she'd pushed those thoughts from her mind, so focused on fighting for their relationship. On pushing through to the other side, the way she always urged her clients to. She had refused to let those subconscious doubts creep into her awareness at all. Her life's work was devoted to helping couples work through their problems. To stay together. To persevere through the struggle. It was clear to her now, though, that she simply hadn't wanted to admit defeat. In the process, she'd ignored her instincts and continued to fight for something that she knew, on the most basic level, was wrong.

Something about standing nearly a thousand feet above Paris made her able to see things in her heart from an entirely different perspective. She was looking at things through a new lens—the eyes of real love. Everything she'd ever thought she knew about love, about romance; about dreams and destiny. It all suddenly looked so different.

Gazing over the city, she could finally see the full

picture. Luke leaving her wasn't Connor's fault at all. And it wasn't hers either. Really, it wasn't even Luke's.

She had been blinded before, by so many things. Dreams were random, sure. But they also showed us our most honest desires, our underlying fears and ambitions. Our deeply rooted insecurities and our strongest wants. Maybe they needed to be listened to more than people realized. Maybe our gut reactions needed to be considered more than we knew. Maybe we needed to be open and accepting to our emotions telling us something we don't fully understand.

Destiny, by its very nature, wasn't something that could be changed or controlled. But that didn't mean we were capable of understanding it completely either. Sometimes we simply couldn't see the forest through the trees in our mind, despite the diplomas on our wall or the experience under our belt. Sometimes we needed to surrender to the plan, trust in the process and realize our interpretations of things could be very, very wrong.

After all, everyone's looking at things through a limited perspective, all the time. Even when we think the universe is telling us something, it may be leading us somewhere else entirely. Even if it's not what we wanted or planned. Luke leaving her. The cancellation of her dream wedding. Connor coming to Paris with her. Marcel not being the one. All those things—those seemingly chaotic, random events— were all leading her to this one moment of perfect clarity. Yes, there in the City of Light, she was finally seeing it for herself.

All the missing pieces were falling into place. She thought about the emotions she'd felt since being in Paris. The night on the terrace with Connor. The sunrise over the

Seine. The blossoming hints of spring that were all around her, drifting throughout the Parisian air. It was all—hope.

She thought about the counseling she'd done over the years, and how her perspective had gradually shifted since Luke left, until she no longer recognized her methods anymore. She had forgotten that the heart of being a therapist was getting into people's psyches. The things they didn't say out loud, but that held all their real, authentic feelings. How had she gotten so far away from that? It was almost as if after years of being in a tired, hard relationship, she'd reconsidered those ideas altogether. Until, eventually, she had become wrong about one pivotal thing: She'd thought it was sheer willpower that could bring about a happy ending in a relationship. That if two individuals—a couple—were determined enough, it would all work out.

But in all the talk of missing pieces, she had been missing a very important one herself: Real love had a little something extra. Something you couldn't always put into words. Sometimes it was instant, and sometimes it wasn't. But the emotional high of a new romance was just as important to a great love story as the ending. Because those were the feelings that inspired us to dive in, to take a risk. Those were the emotions that came from our innermost soul. Our gut. Our heart. And when life gets real, and we wonder if we've fallen out of love, that's when it gets even better. Because that's when we develop the best kind of love—the kind that remains patient, enduring, forgiving. Rooted. Even when our emotions would have us run away in anger, like hers had.

Jenna pulled out her phone and did a quick calculation to see what time it was back home. Still early enough to make a phone call, she dialed the number for the Fowlers at their house, desperate for one of them to answer. Nobody did.

She composed a long text instead, to send to both of their cell numbers, her fingers flying with raw emotion.

Hi guys. Please don't give up yet. I think I know what can help with our sessions, and I understand things I didn't before. Things that can truly help you. You see, in our time together, we've focused so much on actionable items. Reading assignments and exercises. I think I found the missing piece though. The most important piece— the way you feel about each other. The emotional response you used to have with each other, and probably still do. We need to find a way to let it bloom again. Perhaps it's time for a re-birth of the magic.

She sent the text and closed her eyes in hopeful anticipation. The response was immediate from Heather Fowler.

Wow, Jenna. I like the sound of that.

Another response soon followed from Paul Fowler.

We've been reconsidering the split. We'd like to give it another try.

Jenna let out a breath of relief and put away her phone with a peaceful smile. She gazed out on the city and surveyed all the tiny specks of humanity below. All those people. All those relationships.

Maybe it was impossible to love someone perfectly, but you *could* have a perfect love. It was the kind of love she saw between Paul and Heather Fowler. It was the kind of love her sister had with her new husband. It had both the bubbling effervescence of a club soda, and the calming peace of still waters. It was ignited with a spark. And it also endured through the hardships. It was in the little things, such as knowing how they liked their coffee. It was in the big things, such as standing up for them when they needed someone to. It was wanting the best for them, including their happiness, and putting that above your own comfort. And, sometimes, it meant making mistakes. And forgiving mistakes. It was the kind of love she had for Connor.

She inhaled sharply. Yes, she was undoubtedly in love with Connor. She needed to find him. She needed to tell him.

The night was nearly over, and daylight would be coming soon. It was time for her to finally wake up from her slumber.

CHAPTER THIRTY

Jenna

Jenna entered the hotel, her heart racing with excitement, and darted up the stairs to the third floor to get to Connor's room. Her mind reeled with the possibilities in front of her. She had no idea how he would react to the bombshell of emotion she was about to unload on him. She had no idea how he felt about her. About anything. All she knew was that she needed to tell him that she loved him. It was time she finally put her heart in front of her brain and let it do its part. After all, it was just as important.

She reached the top of the stairs and rounded the corner, out of breath. The door to Connor's door was propped open. She slowed her steps, a tightness forming in her stomach. She was about to declare her love for someone in a way she'd never done before. Not in the communicating words way, as she had with Luke plenty of times over the years, but in the pouring out of her soul, her innermost *feel-*

ings. The truth. The idea made her sick to her stomach—it was both thrilling, but also utterly terrifying—like walking out onto the summit of the Eiffel Tower.

The hotel corridor was quiet, except for the faint sounds of movement coming from inside Connor's room. She froze, panic flowing through her at the realization that the beautiful blonde could be with him. She pushed through the discomfort. *Tolerate the fear, don't avoid it.* She needed to do this and couldn't let anything stop her now. She was so close. It was all just within reach.

She approached the partially opened door and peeked inside. Her eyes narrowed in confusion at what she was seeing. No. It couldn't be. The bed had been stripped of its sheets, and a housekeeper was vacuuming the carpets. Jenna yanked open the door fully and stepped inside the room. She cast a glance around. Connor's luggage was gone. Everything was gone. She hurried into the bathroom, but nothing remained aside from his clean, comforting smell. Her eyes popped with panic. She stared at the empty room, realizing what it meant.

Connor had left Paris.

JENNA RETURNED TO HER ROOM, her eyes unblinking, in a daze of confusion and sadness. She held the keycard to the door and pushed it open as it beeped. She stepped in and her high heel landed on a white piece of paper, folded in half, that had been slid under the door. She bent down to pick it up and stared at it, crouched on the floor. Her hand covered her mouth as she read.

Dear Jenna,

I'm so sorry for everything. Over the past few days here in Paris, I have discovered so many things. But the most important thing I've discovered is my feelings for you, as much as I've tried to resist them. Maybe the way we feel about someone, and they us, is a lot like sleep. It can't be manipulated. It's not something that can be forced. There are things we can do to help nurture it, or stifle it, but at the end of the day it's going to happen in its own way, when you finally surrender to it. It's time I stop standing in the way of the happiness you've always deserved. It's time for me to leave and face the music that awaits me at home.

Connor

Face the music? Was Connor in some sort of trouble? The investigation. Jenna closed her eyes, devastated. How could she have been so selfish? She had been so focused on herself the entire time, she'd never once thought about Connor and how this experience had made him feel. He went along with all her crazy ideas, found Marcel for her, and all this time he'd been struggling with his guilt. And for something that had never been his fault in the first place. And who knew what he'd been dealing with in his job?

She held a hand to her chest, as she stood up too fast, quickly growing dizzy. She steadied herself and placed a palm against her head and sat down on the edge of her bed. Her chest caved in with heaviness, and she bent over, the tears that formed but wouldn't flow out stinging her eyes.

She was too late. She'd finally figured out exactly what she wanted, what she was truly meant for. *Who* she was meant for. And she had missed it all. She had let her true love slip through her fingers.

Jenna felt numb as she fell backwards, crashing onto her bed. A lightheadedness overwhelmed her, and she slipped out of consciousness in a crushing cloud of despair.

CHAPTER THIRTY-ONE

Jenna

Jenna stood in front of the Eiffel Tower on a star-filled night in a pink satin dress. The soft grass brushed against the sides of her high-heeled feet. As she wandered towards the tower, her shoes melted away slowly, gradually, with every stride until she was completely barefoot. She strolled through a patch of flowers, the delicate petals cushioning each step she took. She gazed up at the cherry blossoms. Even in the darkened night, she could see the flowering white flora waving softly in the breeze. So delicate, so fleeting. Like a dream. It was a dream.

She walked closer to the tower, drawn by something she couldn't explain, but something she had been longing for her entire life and could never quite catch. She looked up. There, in front of the tower, stood a handsome stranger. No, it wasn't a stranger at all. It was Marcel.

Tall, with jet-black hair. He smiled at her, his green eyes

glistening from the light that radiated behind him. Why was it Marcel? She noticed the small dimple in his chin. The feeling was familiar, as if all her dreams were about to come true.

No, it shouldn't be him. This wasn't right. Her confusion strengthened. She walked closer to him, drawn like a directionless moth to a fading flame.

Suddenly, Marcel grabbed a large camera that had been hanging around his neck. He held it up, placing the lens to his eye. The click of a shutter stopped her in her tracks. He snapped a picture, the bright flash of a bulb startling her into motionlessness. She squinted in the light and blinked a few times.

"Marcel?" she asked, confused, blinking the light out of her field of vision. "What are you doing here?"

He moved to the side, stepping out of the way. He held out his free arm to show her the way to go; to let her pass. She paused, giving her eyes a moment to adjust, until she could see clearly again. She continued to walk, still drawn by the same unexplainable force, although growing stronger. It felt more real, more lucid. She walked past Marcel without a turn of the head. Where was she going now? What was she being drawn to?

She walked closer towards the Eiffel Tower. Her feet stopped, and she shifted her gaze upward. She gasped, and a wide smile crept over her face. There he was. She instantly recognized the back of the sandy-brown head that slowly turned around to face her. He looked at her, his bright-blue eyes twinkling. He beamed with delight as if he'd been waiting his entire life for her and dropped to one knee. Her stomach fluttered and a shiver of excitement coursed through her entire body. She ran to him, her heart soaring and her body floating as she realized she'd found what she'd been longing for this whole time.

JENNA WOKE up with a start before the entire scene played out, her eyes wide with excitement. She sat up straight in bed, heart pounding with adrenaline. The man of her dreams. It was him—Connor. It had always been him.

She took a few breaths to calm her racing heart. Of course. It all made sense. She simply couldn't see it before. Marcel had been standing in the way the whole time. Her perspective had been off. Her field of vision had been obstructed by her misconceptions. Her fragmented understanding. Her confused beliefs.

Perhaps it always had. Maybe something or someone *like* Marcel had always stood in the way of her seeing the truth all along; a distraction, a misguided turn, a wrong path. She'd been too close to Marcel in her initial dream, which didn't allow her to see the big picture. It was like when she'd tried to take the selfie with the Eiffel Tower, unable to get it all in due to being too close. But now, she was able to see everything, the missing pieces having fallen into place. And it was Connor all along. *He* was her happily ever after.

She needed to get to the airport before his flight left. She needed to tell him everything. She needed to track down the *real* man of her dreams.

CHAPTER THIRTY-TWO

Jenna

Jenna sprinted outside, into the cool night air. She ran to the curb and flagged down a cab. "To the airport please, and quickly. S'il vous plaît!" she pleaded through the open window.

The driver threw a glance out the windshield and threw up his shoulders to indicate that he couldn't do anything about the heavy traffic that clogged the street in front of them. She got in anyway and shut the door as he inched away from the curb, pushing the nose of the cab into the crowded streets full of cars and pedestrians.

She wiped a bead of sweat from her brow and bit down on her lower lip. "What's going on tonight?" she asked. "Why is it so crowded this late?"

The driver replied in French, Jenna unable to make out anything he said other than the words *le concert*.

She glanced out the window and scrubbed her hands

over her face, hoping she would make it to the airport before Connor left. She had no idea where he was even headed next. For all she knew, he would be off flying the world, thinking Jenna blamed him for everything. Thinking she never wanted to see him again. She couldn't stomach the thought of what that would mean. Everything they'd shared over the past few days, their magical Parisian spark, would be dead before the heat could consume them at all. Before they could even begin building the foundation of a relationship. The destruction having come before the beauty was ever enjoyed.

She stared at her lap, her fists clenched tightly beside her as the cab made minuscule progress, inching its way down the busy street. Connor could already be gone. Surely he'd be gone by the time she finally reached the airport, if she ever got there. She glanced at her watch and shook her head with overwhelming sadness. She squeezed her eyes shut and swallowed the lump in her throat.

The car came to a complete stop. She looked up to see a row of barriers set up, blocking off the road ahead, and a policeman re-directing traffic. The driver shook his head and turned around to her in the back seat with a resigned shrug. She let out a slow breath of defeat. It was over. She had missed him. She lowered her face into her hands and finally let the tears pour that had been needing to come out for so long.

An entire one hundred and eighty days' worth of emotions spilled out of her at that moment. In the days after Luke had broken up with her, she could never seem to cry the way she'd expected herself to do. The way she felt, surely, she must be able to do to remain mentally healthy. It had always bothered her that she'd never had a proper pouring out of all the emotions surrounding her heartbreak, instead doing the harder thing—analyzing what had gone wrong. Or perhaps it had been the easier thing. But now she was making up for lost time. Her back shook as she sobbed into her hands, the release lightening the load she'd been carrying on her shoulders for far too long.

The driver handed back a box of tissues and she grabbed one out of it as she continued to weep. After several minutes of crying, she dried her eyes, then leaned back in her seat. She smiled, the peace of finally surrendering to her emotions lifting all the tension from her body. She felt cleansed somehow, the scarred remains of her broken heart washed away like a bubbling fountain of refreshment; an afternoon thunderstorm, clearing out the dead leaves, making way for new life with its renewing showers. She smiled softly, thinking about springtime in Paris.

She took in a long, cleansing breath and felt her attitude recalibrate and her heart reset. It was out of her hands. Even if she never got to tell Connor how she felt, nothing could take away the week they had spent together in the City of Light. It had been the most incredible few days of her life. She held a palm to her heart and took another slow, measured breath. She raised her chin and stared out the window, observing the Parisian streets of a mid-week evening, bustling with activity. A light mist of rain was beginning to fall, blurring everything it touched. It really was the most romantic city in the world; she had no doubt in her mind. Couples walked hand in hand along the street, and concertgoers shuffled along with excitement.

Her eye suddenly landed on a man who looked familiar.

She sat up straight, and her eyes opened wide as her gaze settled firmly on him. She followed him with her stare, her eyes narrowing. The gait of his walk, the shape of his head, the way his profile popped against the glistening lights of the dark, dampened city street.

She beamed, and her heart burst with anticipation. She threw back her head and let out a howl of delighted laughter at the serendipity of it all. Yes, she knew that man. It was the man of her dreams. The real one, this time. And she wasn't going to let him go.

She sat up straighter with a new resolve. "Stop!" she yelled to the driver, which was unnecessary since they weren't moving.

She pulled open the door and hopped out of the cab. The crowds were thick, and the sidewalks were packed. She pushed her way through, weaving in and out with urgency.

"Wait!" she called to the back of his head, knowing he couldn't possibly hear her. "Wait!" she yelled again, her shoes slipping against the wet pavement.

The rain fell harder. She ran through the streets, wondering if she had imagined him entirely. Was he actually there? Was any of this real, or was it all some romantic fantasy?

No, this was definitely real. There was one thing she was certain of: She was not dreaming this time.

She lost him in the crowd and had no idea which way he'd gone. She panted, the breath rushing in and out of her as she examined her surroundings. She looked up and saw the Eiffel Tower aglow with light off in the distance. She was drawn in its direction and ran towards it, almost stumbling as she slipped along the wet ground. She stopped, regaining her balance. She'd never make it. It was so far away.

She slowed her steps and dropped her chin to her chest, unable to keep moving in her heels. She shuffled along, eventually stepping off the crowded sidewalk into the grass to escape the press of people. Bending over to catch her breath, she felt the soft blades of grass brush against the sides of her high-heeled feet. They ached, so she reached down and pulled off her shoes. She held her heels in one hand and took a few more steps, feeling the water rush between her toes. Looking down, she noticed she'd stepped right into a patch of flowers with a trickle of rainwater running through the soil. She gazed up into a beautiful cherry blossom tree as the white flora waved softly in the breeze above her head.

She kept walking, slowly, instantly knowing she was on the right path. Adrenaline shot through her as she rolled back her shoulders and sped up, her heart racing along with her barefooted steps. She felt so alive, so awake, so aware of every sensation. She wasn't dreaming, far from it; her mind was the clearest it had ever been. She picked up the bottom of her dress as she hurried, not exactly sure where she was headed, only knowing she couldn't wait to get there.

She pushed away all her subconscious fears and distractions, tossed away all the regret, disappointment, and hurt. She threw it all out and focused on what was right in front of her. Her eyes were wide with excitement as she ran, out of breath, until she reached the park that overlooked the tower in the distance.

Suddenly, she saw the familiar sight of the back of a sandy-brown-haired head. She placed a hand on her stomach, holding her breath in anticipation. He turned around slowly, raised his head, and met her gaze. His eyes widened as a beaming smile lit up his face. As if he'd been waiting for her his entire life.

She ran to him, panting. "Connor, I'm so glad I found you." She reached up to touch his face, to make sure he was real. The rain fell softly over his head, trickling down his cheeks. She ran a finger along his chin, gazing into his eyes. So close, and now able to reach it too. She released a lungful of air and felt a weight lift from her shoulders.

"Jenna! I've been looking for you everywhere. You weren't in your room, and you left your phone behind."

She shook her head. "But I thought you'd left."

"I was about to." His eyes were wild with anticipation. "But then I was at the airport waiting to board and I got a phone call."

She stared at him, her eyes wide.

"It was weather."

"What?"

"A gust of wind. A freak occurrence that couldn't have been foreseen or avoided. It was outside of any human's control. My flying schedule resumes next week."

"The investigation?"

"Yeah, it's a long story," he said. "But it all boils down to this: Some things are bigger than us. There are forces that are beyond our control, and even our own understanding."

She smiled. "Fate."

He nodded, eyes dancing. "A gust of wind. A vivid dream. A wild-goose chase. It all led us here."

She smiled softly.

"Jenna, I'm so sorry I didn't tell you about Luke."

She reached for his hand. "It wasn't you, Connor. It was *never* you. Luke and I had our own issues, and it had nothing to do with anything you said to him. I know that now, with all my heart."

"You do?"

She nodded.

He gave her hand a squeeze, and her eyes closed in pleasure at the feeling, like her first taste of a Parisian cappuccino. The rain intensified, and the drops poured over them both. She wiped the water from her face, clearing her vision. She blinked a few times, studying him. He was certainly no illusion.

"Connor, I gained some badly needed perspective on this trip."

He pulled off his jacket and placed it around her shoulders. Then wiped a wet piece of hair out of her face and tucked it behind her ears. "So did I. In fact, I saw my sister today, and she said—"

Jenna held up a hand, her eyelashes fluttering away the rain. "Your sister? You mean, the woman at the café?" She swallowed. "The blonde woman?"

"Yeah, that's Amy," he said. "She was in town for the day." He peered at her with a look of amusement. "Why? You saw us?"

She let out a laugh of intense relief. "Yeah." She pressed a palm against her cheek in embarrassment. "I may have gotten the wrong idea."

He gave her a flirty lift of an eyebrow. "Oh, yeah?"

Her face grew warmer, and she looked away, waving it off with her hand.

"Well, what about you and Marcel?" Connor blurted out. "You two seemed pretty cozy at that party."

"Why? You saw us?" she teased. Then she shook her head. "That was never going to work out." She sighed, looking into his eyes with a soft smile.

He smiled back. "Well, my sister made me realize I need to give you a say in things. So I'll tell you the truth and it's up to you to decide what to do with it." He swallowed hard and stood up straighter. "So here goes . . ." He gazed down at her and stared directly into her eyes. "Jenna, I love you."

She closed her eyes as bliss coursed through her. She

understood the power behind those words in a way she never had before. Yes, they were emotional. Yes, they were romantic. But they were also honest. True. Strong.

"Connor, I love you too," she said with complete sincerity, her eyes twinkling.

His smile glowed back at her. "I'm just glad we've both finally woken up."

"Me too." She beamed.

Connor pulled her in close, his lips moving towards hers. She watched him with a smile of wonder and a heart full of hope. The rain fell over them, washing away the past. Opening the future for growth. And for vitality.

A wet cherry blossom petal fell against her cheek, and she let out a long breath of relief. Winter was over, and spring had finally come. His lips met hers, and she melted into him, the shadowy freeze in her heart now gone, replaced by the awakening light of a new beginning.

One year later

Jenna stepped out of the car and smoothed down her dress. She was there—Paris. She gazed at the Eiffel Tower in front of her, standing right where he'd asked her to meet him. She wore the pink satin dress, the one that had that little something extra. It was her boyfriend's favorite after all, and she couldn't imagine wearing anything else for their romantic evening in Paris to celebrate one year of dating. One year of being in love.

The spring night was aglow, a sky full of stars clearly visible, despite the glowing sparkle of the city lights. A breeze blew past, sweeping the hair back from her face. She closed her eyes and enjoyed the serenity of the moment. She studied the tower and beamed. Her chest expanded and she felt a tingle of breathless excitement. She'd seen this sight before. She'd seen it from a grassy park. From a river boat's rooftop. From underneath the base itself, and all the way to the very top. No matter what vantage point she'd observed it from though, the glow of the tower at night still took her breath away.

The darker the night, the brighter the stars, as her mother always said. She smiled, thinking about her mom and the progress the two of them had made over the past year in their therapy sessions. Understanding each other's perspectives, in new ways. In fact, she now held a new appreciation for her mom's fondness of all things traditional. Every one of her seemingly silly rituals had a meaning and a well-intentioned thought behind it. An orange in a Christmas stocking—spoiling her with sweet abundance; a piece of wedding cake under a pillow—opening her heart to new possibilities; a butter knife against a wine glass—encouraging the romance she truly pined for. It was all her way of showing Jenna how much she longed for her happiness. And now, in Paris again, Jenna held the knowledge firmly in her heart that her mother loved her. After all, she had provided the scaffolding in her life, offering her support until Jenna was finally able to do it on her own. Love, fully.

Her thoughts returned to the moment in front of her. Jenna continued to walk slowly toward the Eiffel Tower. The soft grass brushed against the sides of her high-heeled feet as she wandered towards it, and she kicked off her shoes, wanting to feel every bit of the experience with all her senses. She strolled right through a patch of flowers before she even realized it. The delicate petals cushioned each step, and she closed her eyes, drawing in a long breath, savoring the moment. She gazed up at the cherry blossoms. Even in the darkened night, she could see the flowering white flora waving softly in the breeze. So delicate, so fleeting. Like a dream. But she was no longer dreaming.

She thought about the Fowlers and the new light they'd

discovered in their relationship over the past year. Stronger than ever, they were still seeing Jenna regularly to keep their relationship solid. Like nature, it would ebb and flow, blossoming at times, but also unable to avoid exposure to the harsh elements of winter. But through it all, the roots remained.

Sometimes a new perspective was all it took to see the truth. It was why Jenna's client base had nearly doubled over the past year. Sure, she'd put in a lot of work to get there. It was hard finding new clients and managing a growing schedule. It wasn't only about the work. She'd also put her heart into her business and she knew she always would. After all, it was equally important.

She continued towards the tower, drawn by something she couldn't explain, but something she'd been longing for her entire life. She looked up. There, in front of the gleaming tower, stood a handsome man with jet-black hair and green eyes. He had a dimple in his chin. When he smiled at her, his left eyebrow dropped a bit lower than his right. For someone she hadn't seen in a year, she recognized every detail of his face, and knew she'd never forget it.

A bright flash popped in her face. She let out a laugh of delight, appreciating the additional touch her ever-thoughtful boyfriend had added—having hired Marcel to photograph the evening. Of course, it would only be fitting. No, it was more than that—it was serendipitous. Marcel had been a part of their story, as much as Paris had been. As much as Luke had been. It had all led them to this moment in time. This very real moment, when she was undoubtedly awake.

She felt the thrill of intense anticipation all the way down to the pit of her stomach.

The feeling was oddly familiar, but also something she'd

never felt before with this much clarity, as if all her dreams were about to come true.

She walked past Marcel and his clicking camera, her eye clearly focused on who she knew would be waiting for her. She approached him and smiled, her eyes dancing with excitement. The top of his sandy-brown hair blew in the breeze. He beamed with delight as if he'd waited his entire life for her.

The next thing she knew, he was down on one knee. He looked up at her, holding an open ring box with a gleaming diamond engagement ring inside. She stared at the ring, her mouth wide. She felt as if she was at the top of the tower, a simultaneous wave of exhilaration and awe causing her head to spin. Then she gazed into his blue eyes as he asked the question, the one she had hoped he would. She nodded as tears of joy slid down her cheeks. She wiped them away. Her face felt as if it was glowing like morning dew upon freshly cut grass. She swallowed and took a deep breath, finally able to say out loud the words she'd wanted to say for so long.

"Yes, Connor."

He stood and they embraced as they entered a new phase of their relationship, and she knew the truth: Their love was real. It was enduring. It wasn't perfect, because they weren't perfect. A year of choosing him, a year of working things out together. A year of solving problems, of staying committed. And a lifetime to go.

Their love was an action. But it was also a feeling. And that feeling was still magical.

Connor pulled her close and she inhaled his cool, clean scent. She felt the brush of his delicate touch upon her skin. Like a cherry blossom, beautiful and soft. Coming and going. Like emotions. But something you could count on to bloom every year. Forever. To give us hope, to stir up our innermost feelings—the ones that contribute to a perfect love.

His lips lowered to meet hers and she melted into him as an electric current surged through her entire body. Like sparkling water. Like a glass of champagne. Like glittering gold. With impeccable timing, the lights of the Eiffel Tower shimmered behind them. She may have woken up, but Jenna knew that her heart would always remain in a dream.

ACKNOWLEDGMENTS

This book would not have been possible if not for the efforts and support of so many people.

First, I am forever grateful for the team of professionals at Harpeth Road Press, especially Jenny Hale, whose passion for publishing has been an inspiration to me. Thank you, Jenny, for your confidence in my stories and for helping me grow as an author.

I'd also like to thank the talented editors who worked so hard to help strengthen this book—Charlotte Fry, Abigail Fenton, Lara Simpson, Lauren Finger, and Charlotte Hayes-Clemens. I have learned so much from your valuable insight. Thank you for helping me develop this story and for your eagle-eyed attention to detail. You all make me a better writer. A special thanks to Sarah Hansen, for your creative talent in designing this gorgeous cover.

A heartfelt thank you to my entire family, especially my parents and sister for your constant encouragement. To my three wonderful daughters, I adore you. Thank you for your creative input and for always being my first readers. You make this writing adventure so much fun. To my husband, thank you for supporting my dreams in every way, and for inspiring this story by taking me on a romantic anniversary trip to Paris.

Finally, my deepest appreciation goes to all the readers who picked up my novel. I appreciate your support more than you know.

A LETTER FROM CAROLINE STOWE

Hello!

Thank you for picking up my novel, *Dreaming of Paris*. I hope this story surrounds you with the charm and beauty of the most romantic city in the world and leaves you feeling uplifted.

If you'd like to know when my next book is out, you can sign up for new Harpeth Road release alerts for my novels here:

www.harpethroad.com/caroline-stowe-newsletter-signup

I won't share your information with anyone else, and I'll only email you when I have news or when new books are released.

If you enjoyed *Dreaming of Paris*, I'd be so grateful if you'd write a review online. Feedback from readers helps persuade others to pick up my book for the first time. It's one of the biggest gifts you could give me.

With love,

Caroline